Love is
a time of enchantment:
in it all days are fair and all fields
green. Youth is blest by it,
old age made benign:
the eyes of love see
roses blooming in December,
and sunshine through rain. Verily
is the time of true-love
a time of enchantment — and
Oh! how eager is woman
to be bewitched!

THE PAINTED FACE

To track down a mystery so old seemed impossible at first. But fashionable artist Nicholas Carradine had become obsessed with the death or disappearance of his young half-sister Odette, twenty years before. And so he approached the famed Inspector Lintott, who agreed to take the case. Their search brought them to Paris, where the Inspector turned up some shockers for Carradine. For he had uncovered a trail of adultery and incest . . . and the incredible secret which could free — or destroy — Nicholas.

Books by Jean Stubbs
Published by The House of Ulverscroft:

KIT'S HILL
THE IRONMASTER
THE VIVIAN INHERITANCE
THE NORTHERN CORRESPONDENT
THE LASTING SPRING
LIKE WE USED TO BE
SUMMER SECRETS
KELLY PARK

JEAN STUBBS

THE PAINTED FACE

Complete and Unabridged

ULVERSCROFT
Leicester

First published in Great Britain

First Large Print Edition
published 1996

British Library CIP Data

Stubbs, Jean *1926–*
The painted face.—Large print ed.—
Ulverscroft large print series: romance
1. English fiction—20th century
2. Large type books
I. Title
823.9'14 [F]

ISBN 0–7089–3640–7

Published by
F. A. Thorpe (Publishing) Ltd.
Anstey, Leicestershire
Set by Words & Graphics Ltd.
Anstey, Leicestershire
Printed and bound in Great Britain by
T. J. Press (Padstow) Ltd., Padstow, Cornwall

This book is printed on acid-free paper

To my brother Jake, whose affection
for the French is as deep as my own,
but whose knowledge of them is so
much greater. With my love, and my
thanks for sharing Paris.

Acknowledgements

As always, I thank the Borough Librarian of Merton, Mr. E. J. Adsett, F.L.A., and Miss Lynn Evans and her staff at Wimbledon Park Branch Library, whose ability to unearth positive truffles for my background research must be unequaled. And to my artist friend of many years, Miss Sonia Robinson, a special thank you for lending me a boxful of art books and giving me a headful of information.

J.S.

'Who has not painted himself a face?'

Georges Roualt, French painter
1871 – 1958

Awakening

HE could not sleep: walking the house, candlestick in hand, seeking comfort from possessions. Mounting the stalls, solitary and without answer, Carradine would have welcomed the shadow on the wall, were it not his own.

Behind him lay the good living of cellar and kitchen, the gracious living of drawing-room and dining-room, the hushed living of bedrooms, the inner living of his studio. The gas globes on the wall were unlit, the dark was friendless. Up and up, into the attic, where all that was safe and comprehensible had been folded and put away. Into the past, where a childhood was locked in trunks, shielded by sheets of tissue, secured by moth-balls and lavender sachets against corruption.

The skirt of his dressing gown dipped in twenty years of dust. The candle flame vaulted the familiar into the grotesque.

1

His boyhood rocking horse became a rippling stallion on the beams, the trunks were hunchbacks full of secrets, the empty birdcage a distorted prison.

No time here, measuring his thirty-three years and pronouncing them void No woman to torment him, except she who had spoiled all others for him and was now dead. No unfulfilled canvases to make a mock of promise.

He set down his candlestick on a parcel of old books, unlocked and flung open the lid of one brassbound coffer at random, wiping his hands on a handkerchief before shaking out her morning gown.

Many summers ago Gabrielle had worn this at breakfast: a delicate affair of sprigged muslin which enhanced her arms and bosom. He heard her voice, courting even as it chided. Saw her mouth pouting or incisive; pretty hands hovering over china cups; black curls caught up by a ribbon. As he crushed the muslin to his face a ghost of her scent reached him. Gabrielle, his stepmother. A brief reign, miraculously given and unmercifully taken away. Gabrielle, whose image had been palely reflected in the stream of his temporary love affairs, ending tonight with the trauma of Evelyn Harrison.

★ ★ ★

There are more ways of killing than by taking life. Nicholas Carradine, artist and gentleman, watched the cab bear off his victim and experienced guilt and relief. Hands in pockets, shoulders hunched against the January rain of 1902, he took the steps at a run and slammed and bolted the front door behind him.

His housekeeper, turning down the gaslight at the end of the hall, observed him quietly.

"Will you be wanting anything more, sir?" Mrs. Tilling asked.

Carradine was leaning against the door, eyes closed, palms flat against the panels, reliving that disastrous and unorthodox hour in the drawing-room with Miss Harrison. Now he straightened up, answered the question she had not asked.

"I didn't invite her to come here, Tilley. She really should not have come."

Carefully noncommittal, Mrs. Tilling replied, "No, sir."

He had to explain, to excuse himself. "I mean, Tilley, to arrive unannounced, at this hour of night, and alone!"

"Quite so, sir."

He paced the hall, thinking. She waited, hands clasped over the comfortable stomach of her black silk gown. Carradine was reviving.

"Miss Harrison is an utterly charming and high-spirited young lady, Tilley. But then, London is full of charming and high-spirited young ladies — and their mamas, of course. You don't suppose, do you, that Mrs. Harrison thought of this little escapade to force my hand? No, certainly not." Seeing her expression change from patience to shock. "Certainly not, Tilley."

He had lost her sympathy and sought to regain it.

"The entire situation was a tragic misunderstanding on Miss Harrison's part, you see, Tilley. No question of an unofficial engagement or anything of that sort. Good Lord, if a man can't pay a few compliments, dance a few waltzes, present a few nosegays . . . "

His hazel eyes courted her: a direct appeal to her maternal instinct. Out of long practice she resisted.

"On my honor, Tilley" — hand on breast, mocking, beseeching — "I never met Miss Harrison except under conditions of absolute propriety."

"Oh, that I believe, sir."

"And I'm truly regretful that she misunderstood me, Tilley."

"I'm sure you are, sir. It's caused you a deal of embarrassment," she said tartly.

He put one long hand on her sleeve, humbled. "I know you're cross with me, Tilley."

"It's not my place to judge, sir."

"Oh, don't be stuffy, Tilley. You know you're the only person who can tell me the truth."

"If it's the truth you're wanting, sir. Yes."

Carradine's mobile face was wary, but he smiled nevertheless. "Come on, Tilley. Straight from the shoulder. You've jawed me ever since I was a little chap."

"Yes, sir," said Mrs. Tilling resolutely,

5

"and that's the problem, if you don't mind me saying so. You're no different now from what you were then, except in appearance. And still talking yourself out of scrapes. And you talk very nicely, and I'm sure you're very sorry. Only, then it was broken china, and now it's broken hearts."

He lifted his head slowly. "I don't mean to hurt anybody, Tilley."

"No, sir. You don't mean anything. But remember, Mr. Nicholas, that we're judged by what we do, and what you do seems to go wrong."

He turned away, subdued. "God bless you, Tilley. Sleep well."

She nodded, switched the skirt of her gown into one capable hand, and used the other to help herself upstairs by means of the banister rail.

"But I'm not a scoundrel, Tilley, am I?" he called after her.

She paused, sighing. What a child he was! "No, sir. You're just downright unreliable, if that satisfies you. Now I'm not going round the mulberry bush with you for half the night, sir, if you'll excuse me. I have to get up early in the morning. And just talking never got anybody anywhere."

★ ★ ★

Through the femininity of Gabrielle's morning gown he conjured up demons. Evelyn too had been blessed with a profusion of black curls, a pointed cat's-face, a high vein of coquetry. While she played him dexterously he remained fascinated. When hope silenced, when love softened her, he had known it was time to withdraw. And in that ruthless and gentlemanly withdrawal she had, most unexpectedly and dreadfully, challenged him.

Had Gabrielle ever wept and begged as Evelyn did? Had she ever abandoned herself before a man, as Evelyn had? He could not believe it. Gabrielle's fragrance was as elusive and enigmatic as herself. Her power made a nonsense of death. He could imagine her in no state except that of imperious possession. Evelyn had lost twice over: first by loving him, then by revealing herself as an anguished, discarded girl. Onto the gasping truths,

7

the threadbare proofs of his attachments, he had poured the oil of flattery. He might as well have tried to stop the sea from flowing.

"I couldn't have imagined your interest, Nicholas. I swear I did not. You said I was the dearest, sweetest companion a man could wish for — "

"So you are, my dear girl. Far too good for me."

"You kissed me once, in the conservatory. Mama would kill me if she knew. How could I allow you, unless I believed — "

"A momentary impulse on my part, and absolutely pure in its intention, I assure you. A homage to your beauty — "

"But I allowed you to kiss me! No one has ever kissed me before. I feel so wicked, so low. I feel like one of those low women — "

"Nonsense, my dear girl. I never for an instant ceased to honor and respect you. You are not compromised. Neither of us is compromised. No one shall ever know — "

"But I wanted you to kiss me."

Oh God in heaven! The final revelation of a virgin heart.

"My dear Evelyn, you always were an awful tease. Confess now! You don't mean a word of this." Clasping her fingers which were wet with smearing her eyes, her cheeks, of tears. "I wager that you and Mary Pedding have set this up between you to make a fool of me! You know perfectly well that you look even prettier when you cry." The stained face of defeat staring at him, incredulous. "I shall never forget those months of friendship. Here's your cloak. The joke's over and you've won hands down, indeed you have. And now you really must go before your parents find you missing. My housekeeper is the soul of discretion and won't breathe a word about this escapade of yours. No, not another syllable. I adore you too devoutly to scold you."

Then at last she comprehended the hardness of his intent beneath the raillery. She summoned up a little dignity, allowed him to escort her in silence to the cab, and at the window had the proverbial last word in a vehement whisper.

"Mama did warn me. I should have listened to her. You may excuse yourself

9

and pretend to yourself as much as you please, but you won't alter the truth. The truth is that you are heartless and purposeless and unworthy of any decent person's affection or respect. Live with that knowledge if you can."

★ ★ ★

"Blast all women!" Carradine shouted to the rafters, and envied his father who had been worthy of love, and crowned by Gabrielle's youth and beauty in his middle years.

The dark attic, the small steady flame. The love such as he yearned for and had never attained. His father's maturity, Gabrielle's pretty condescension, their child Odette. And he, as a child, secure in all three of them, happy as he had never been since. They had left him forever, these beloved ghosts.

Odette.

"I was thinking, madame, that the little boy might be jealous, being the only one for such a long time. But he's as pleased as Punch with his new sister."

Jealous? Of this image of Gabrielle

which could be possessed and protected as he could not protect her? Jealous of this demanding, adoring puppet? And he, Nicholas, suddenly the authoritative brother, suddenly somebody important, all his posturings admired and grown giant-sized in the child's eyes.

Among Odette's wrapped dolls and toys he entered another Gethsemane. A hoard of exercise books, written and illustrated with a flourish by Nicholas Carradine, aged ten, for her personal pleasure. The rough cleverness of the drawings, their originality, the dash with which he had applied nursery crayons and watercolors, attested him.

"I was good," he said aloud, and then to his absent visitor, "I was good. You can see for yourself. It's all here."

"But promise is not fulfillment," the memory replied.

★ ★ ★

The sound of cab wheels at midnight had alerted Carradine. Surely Evelyn had not returned? Cautiously he lifted one corner of the drawing-room curtain, afraid of what he might see. But it was, praise be, a man whom he revered above most others and doubly welcome because unexpected. Carradine ran down the stairs and unbolted the front door, alight with pleasure.

"I had no intention of disturbing you, my dear fellow, at such an hour," said the visitor, "but I saw your light. I called this afternoon, but you were out."

"So Tilley told me, sir. But better that you should look around my studio without my hovering hopefully at your back. I hadn't hoped to see you and hear your opinion so soon. Allow me to offer you some refreshment. I have brandy and cigars upstairs."

"No, no, thank you, my dear boy. No brandy. I've had enough already, Lord knows. My doctor would have a fit if he knew how much. No, no, not upstairs either. We can be comfortable enough in your hall for a few minutes. I climbed to your studio this morning, and my heart isn't what it was."

The flesh was fragile, but the spirit and vigor were not. Suddenly light, Carradine clasped the old man's hand and shook it

12

warmly. Ushered him to a chair, trying to read his expression.

"You saw the paintings, of course? You have come to humble me?" Believing no such thing. "You have glanced rapidly and expertly at my work and decided to consign it to the flames?"

The old man looked at him shrewdly. "Don't gallop so," he advised. "You will gallop, Carradine."

"I know, I know. It's a fearful fault of mine. Tell me, have I retrogressed?"

"You know perfectly well you have not."

"Then have I improved, broken new ground?"

His visitor pursed a pendulous underlip. "Nor that either."

Diminished, Carradine reached for his silver case and took out a cheroot. His hand shook slightly, but he continued to smile.

"Neither better nor worse, you say, sir? What then? How? New styles, new subjects, new attitudes, and no difference?"

"Not the least in the world, my dear fellow. But don't take my word for it.

There are other art critics. My opinion is a solitary one."

"You know the regard in which it is held, by me and by others. Tell me honestly what you think."

"If honesty is what you want."

Shades of Tilley!

"Come, sir. Straight from the shoulder."

Shades of himself!

"You have a perfect genius for staying in the same place."

He observed Carradine's dark frown, the impatient lift of his shoulders. "Your technique is excellent to the point of facility. As it should be, considering the quality of your former teachers and your own application. You handle your paint in a delightful manner. You have a profoundly pleasing sense of color. So far, so good. But you turn this very facility to disadvantage, by mimicking any fashion that catches your fancy at the time.

"This afternoon, in your studio, I saw a fair selection of post-Degas, a couple of lesser-Manets, half-a-dozen near-Whistlers, and even the odd Fauvist. Keep well away from them, my dear fellow. They are painting from depths of which you know nothing at all. And the question I asked myself, as I searched in vain among this dazzling display, was — what has become of Nicholas Carradine, whose paintings these are supposed to be?"

"He is here, sir," said Carradine with some arrogance.

"I do not see him."

"Perhaps because you are not prepared to find him."

"Why should I have to? He should reveal himself. In my humble opinion, you are playing at being an artist. Playing skillfully and prettily, but playing. To put your position in society's terms, you are having a love affair with art instead of a marriage. A love affair is a glorious thing — haven't I known that, by Jove — but it passes. The Lady Art, if so we may call her, insists upon connubial dedication until death do you part. You can fool a real-life charmer, Carradine, but you can't fool this lady, because she simply won't have it."

Carradine's face was a study of black temper.

The old man, garrulous now in his obsessions, continued. "You can't court her and leave her. You might break your heart, but you'll never break hers. You can't deceive her, however subtly. She doesn't care, you see. She has so many faithful suitors. She demands all of you, all the experience and knowledge you have gained in life, and then she might smile on you. Oh, she's fickle, Carradine. Fickle and difficult, and quite irresistible. Give me a hand out of this chair, will you, my dear chap? I must be going."

Tapping his opera hat smartly into place, he added with unconscious cruelty, "But the public will love them, and I'll lay a bet you sell every one."

Carradine dared not accept this personal revelation on top of the other. Pride and pique must be set aside. "How do I begin again?" he asked abruptly.

His visitor pondered. "Perhaps you should ask yourself the question I asked my pupils. *What is it I am trying to express? Who and what am I?*"

Carradine gave a short laugh. "They seem simple enough questions."

His visitor surveyed him long and

coolly. "They require the utmost honesty and endeavor of thought, and take a lifetime to answer. You must commit yourself, Carradine, for better or worse."

"To art?" Smiling, frowning.

"And to life. Above all to life. One can live without painting, but one cannot paint without living."

"You spoke of marriage," Carradine said sharply, "but marriage is a lottery."

"Life is a lottery. Pay up and take your chance if you desire a prize. You may not get it even then. You will never have it unless you pay with yourself first."

* * *

He had not been able to sleep. The phantoms of Gabrielle and Odette, of his father, could not answer him. He lifted his candlestick and prepared to leave. The parcel of books stayed him: wrapped in brown paper, tied with cord, sealed in wax, as though someone had said, *This is done.*

He felt in the pockets of his dressing gown and found a stick of charcoal, a safety pin, a penknife, a lady's

17

handkerchief — he could not remember which lady.

Protected from fading, the blue leather gleamed, the gold monogram GLC, Gabrielle Lasserre Carradine, glittered. The seven volumes were locked, but the locks were toys, easily pried open. He riffled the pages of the top volume, as white and fresh now as twenty years ago, and read the final words.

Gabrielle's foreign hand, Gabrielle's staccato French phrases.

The child died as I live, by fire.

His father had told him, that terrible spring of 1882, that Odette had died peacefully of a fever in Paris. Afterward Gabrielle had lain in her bed upstairs, hands lax on the coverlet, deep in shock.

The child died as I live, by fire.

Gabrielle's empty face, her languorous body, going through the motions of living. Death, twenty months later.

She wouldn't fight it, you see, Nick. She couldn't fight. Just the two of us now, my boy. Just the two of us.

He glanced here and there, picking up scraps of information among the expressions of grief, of self-blame, of

18

terror and incredulity. And suddenly the discrepancies between what he had been told and what was written possessed him. To a stranger, the reason was simple and humane. Odette Carradine, six years old, had perished dreadfully in a train accident on the Continent. They had spared the boy's feelings with a charitable lie.

But he was no stranger, and the questions that arose and could not be answered breached this old safe citadel on every side. Breached it, and demanded rebuilding, demanded explanation. His visitor's calamitous assessment sank, to await resurrection. This came uppermost, with an urgency that rocked him on his heels. As he flung down the volume the draft extinguished his candle flame.

For a long time he crouched in the dark, head in hands, and the attic became a furnace from which a child tried in vain to escape. Then, as her wraith shriveled at last, he felt his way out and down the stairs. He did not know how to begin, or where to go, but he intended to find out.

Part One

CHILDISH THINGS

'What are you doing here,
you Fool of the imagination?'

Georges Roualt

1

"**A** GENTLEMAN to see you, John," said Bessie Lintott, shy of such a presence in her home.

She was uncertain whether to let the gentleman see her husband in the parlor, without his coat, or to leave the gentleman standing in the cold passage, where the framed photograph of Queen Victoria was draped in black. A year's national mourning being proper, and the twelvemonth period not quite up, Her Late Majesty stared resolutely between small crêpe curtains.

Ex-Inspector Lintott looked at the grandchild sleeping against his shoulder, at the warm, untidy room, and made his choice.

"Well, fetch the gentleman in, my love. I daresay he's seen a family setting by the fire of a winter evening afore now."

"Will you kindly step this way, sir, if you please? Hoping you'll excuse us, but this is our youngest granddaughter.

23

Stopping with us a bit, on account of her mamma being poorly. Won't you take a seat, sir?"

Smoothing her black Sunday gown, shaking the patchwork cushion on the chair. Trying in vain to banish the cheese and pickled onions from the table, with one despairing glance.

Neither man noticed nor cared about these domestic preoccupations, measuring each other behind expressions of courteous interest. Lintott's plain countenance was bland, his eyes sharp, over the child's head. He sat comfortably in his striped shirt sleeves, minus his collar. His arms were both shield and fortress for the dark-headed little girl. The fingers of her right hand clutched a portion of his shirt, the left thumb was thrust in her mouth for comfort.

"Which she shouldn't," said Mrs. Lintott, disturbed by this too, "but I'm feared of waking her up by taking it out. She frets for her mamma, sir, you see. Not but what we aren't loving kindness itself — "

"Hush awhile, Bessie," said Lintott quietly. "Nobody's bothered but you, my dear. Now, sir, will you take a glass of my good lady's damson wine?" Having nothing grander to offer, though he would have staked it against the finest vintage in the world. "Or is your business urgent, and would you rather state it straight out?"

The gentleman had finished his survey of Lintott and smiled suddenly.

"They told me you were a forthright man, Inspector," he observed, "and I see they are not mistaken. I beg you to pardon this intrusion into your home and at such an hour. I live alone and am inclined selfishly to judge others by myself, to forget the pleasures and demands of the family hearth. I have dined and wined already, I thank you, if Mrs. Lintott will excuse me the delights of her hospitality." He turned toward her and bowed slightly.

"Should I take your hat and cloak, sir?" she asked, flustered.

"You are more than kind, madam." Relieved of encumbrance, he switched aside his coattails and lowered himself into the proffered chair, speaking to Lintott. "My name is Nicholas Carradine.

My business is personal, and important to me, but by no means urgent. It will take some little time to relate, if you can spare me half an hour or so."

Bessie's face changed. She stood in no less awe of this fine personage, but he had become familiar to her. "Excuse me, sir, but are you the gentleman as painted *Miss Lucy*?"

"I am indeed, madam, though I have painted other things."

"Oh, sir, if I haven't this minute got a copy of it, pasted into an album. Cut out of the *Harmsworth Magazine*."

"You honor me, madam. Miss Lucy was the daughter of a friend of mine. An exquisite creature of five years. She must now be close to fifteen."

"You're one ahead of me, Bessie," said Lintott. "I didn't know as the gentleman was an artist. Top marks, my dear."

Flushed with triumph, Bessie addressed herself to the parlor. "I'll just clear off the supper things, John. You'll be wanting to speak private. I shan't disturb you."

"What about six penn'orth of copper here?" Lintott asked, nodding at the child.

26

"She's well away by now, John. If you'll lift her careful, I'll put her to bed."

The little girl was transferred to Mrs. Lintott, who surveyed her with pride.

"We think our Mary here is quite a credit to us, sir. We're on the plain side as a family. But she reminds me of your Miss Lucy. Fancy you painting her all that time ago, and still a favorite by all accounts, or the picture wouldn't have been in the magazine, would it, sir?"

"It was a popular choice of subject, certainly. How old is Mary, Mrs. Lintott?"

"Going on six, sir."

Carradine bent over the small face, pink with sleep and stained with trouble, and smoothed aside a curl as deftly as Bessie could have done. He observed the straight nose and short upper lip, the arched brows and thick lashes.

"A future beauty," he remarked charmingly, "and quite a likeness, as you say. You must indeed be proud of her." The charm vanished. "But take great care of her. Life is often a savage business, and these little creatures need all the protection we can give."

Disquieted, Bessie pulled the shawl closer round Mary. The Inspector registered obsession in Carradine's tone.

"You needn't fear, sir," he answered stoutly. "I'd be surprised if you knew as much about savagery as I do, after forty years in the Force. We'll watch out for our Mary all right. Bessie!"

His tone hastened her from the room, and he reached for his jacket and concentrated on his visitor.

Carradine seemed remarkably respectable for an artist. Clean-shaven, splendidly tailored, good manners, and apparently an income to match. His unruly hair, curling into the nape of his neck, had been well brushed. The eyes were most curious, reflecting each change of mood. Mild enough when he chattered about nothing, narrowing and lightening as he spoke about Mary, remote over the picture Bessie had praised. Lintott supposed you called them 'hazel,' and sometimes the brown and sometimes the green came foremost. Lean and jumpy sort of chap too. Interesting.

Lintott, filling his pipe, watching Carradine over the bowl, said, "I haven't a cigar to offer you, but Bessie don't mind smoke in the parlor if you've one of your own. Shall we get down to the matter in hand?"

Carradine produced his silver case and selected a cheroot. He said, "The affair may seem trivial to you, Inspector."

"You'd best let me be the judge of that, sir. You said that they had told you I was forthright. Who are they, sir?"

"Scotland Yard. I went there in the first place, not knowing whom to ask. They said it was not in their province and suggested a private detective, Chief Inspector Mill . . . Milne . . . Miller — I have no memory for names, I fear."

"I know who you mean. We've done each other a deal of favors in the past. Yes, what did he say?"

"That you had recently retired but might be interested enough to help me. He said he knew of no one better, no one as good. For professional consultation, of course," Carradine added, lest Lintott should think otherwise. "You may name your own fee. I shall not question it."

Lintott raised a hand to check his guest. "Facts first, if you please. I don't need pinning down with a handful of sovereigns afore I hear what it's all about. Carry on, sir."

"It concerns the death of my half-sister Odette. She was killed in a train accident in France — my late stepmother was French — but the circumstances are singularly mysterious."

"When was this, sir?"

"Oh, twenty years ago. She was six years old."

Lintott shook out the match. "You took your time reporting it, sir," he said dryly. "I'm not surprised the Yard weren't interested."

"I only discovered the matter a couple of days ago. I've lost no time since, I assure you."

I believe that, thought Lintott. "What's mysterious about the accident, sir? Briefly."

Incoherent with his jumble of half-digested facts and overruling sense of disaster, Carradine talked nervously. As he gesticulated, a lock of hair fell across his forehead, his wrists shot from the immaculate cuffs, his air of cool elegance disintegrated. Lintott listened carefully.

"First of all, Inspector, my father told

me that Odette died of a fever. But she was burned to death in a railway carriage, on the way to the Swiss border — ”

“How old were you at the time?” Lintott interrupted.

“Thirteen. I was away at school — ”

“Just so. And your little sister was killed — ”

“Burned. Burned to death, Inspector.”

The child died by fire.

“ — was killed tragically. So they wanted to spare you the worst shock. Number two, sir?”

“The nurse, Berthe Lecoq, had been my stepmother’s nurse and then her personal maid, so you can imagine the devotion between them. She was sent back to her village within a week of the accident. My stepmother said she couldn’t bear to have her near. And yet Berthe had supported and helped her through those first terrible days — ”

“Just a minute, sir. Just one minute. The nurse was in this carriage, I take it?”

“Odette would hardly be traveling alone.”

“Then the nurse might also have been badly burned, certainly badly shocked.

31

They sent her home to recuperate. A well-earned rest, a bit of a pension like enough. She did what she could for your stepmother and retired."

"But under a cloud of reproach, Inspector? Reproach for what? And why was Gabrielle not with the nurse and child? This train was on its way to Switzerland. Why would they be going so far, and without Gabrielle?"

Carradine pushed the lock of hair back into place, knotted his lean hands, and drew breath.

"Didn't the train stop anywhere on the way?"

Carradine paused. "I don't know, actually." Nonplused.

Lintotte nodded. "Well, it might have been a stopping train, and the nurse and the little girl could have been taking a day out. If your stepmother was French she probably had a lot of French friends fairly near."

Carradine looked at him reproachfully.

"You're making absolute nonsense of this case, Inspector."

"Not at all, sir. I'm just trying to find what case exists."

"How can I explain?" Carradine asked, more of himself than of Lintott. His intensity had softened. "How can I describe what we all were, so that even you can see that my father's lying to me was incomprehensible? So that you can see the circumstances themselves were impossible, that this could not have happened as Gabrielle said. You have heard of perfect happiness, Inspector?"

"Heard? Yes, sir. Never seen it."

"I tell you this then — that we were perfectly happy. I swear it."

Unconvinced but fascinated, for even this brief retirement had hung heavily upon him, Lintott said, "Why don't you light up that cheroot of yours, sir, and make yourself comfortable. Bessie'll be busy with a dozen and one things, and the night's young enough. You tell me about this perfect happiness of yours."

"You don't want facts, Inspector?"

"I'll pick 'em out as we go along, sir. Talk away. Tell me about your — stepmother and your father. Your own mother died, I take it?"

Released, Carradine launched into narrative.

33

"When I was born. I must have had a nurse of some sort, but I don't remember. Curiously enough, I don't remember anything before Gabrielle came. She was only a girl. My father was in his middle forties, a wine merchant — "

"Carradine's Superior Wines?" Lintott cocked his head.

"That was, and is, the family business — though I earn enough money with my painting to pay my tailor. My father met Gabrielle in the course of his business. The match was an idyllic one. I adored her, as my father did. She was everything a mother could have been to me. When Odette was born I felt no jealousy — only that the child was an extension of Gabrielle. They were the passion and preoccupation of my boyhood. I have never been as happy since, except briefly in my work, as I was in those few years together. There was only one slight shadow" — but a shadow was on his own face as he spoke. "Gabrielle never really settled in London. She was a born Parisienne and made frequent trips to Paris, which my father fully comprehended. Though he must have missed her." This he added in a lower tone, as though comprehending the sacrifice for the first time. "He was indulgence itself where she was concerned."

"Roots can pull," Lintott suggested kindly.

"Of course. In the early years I accompanied her, and Berthe, and the baby Odette. When I went to school she took them abroad without me. Though she was devoted to my father and to me, she worshiped her child. They were never separated — at least, not for such an expedition as a railway journey. Her family were well connected but poor in comparison to the sort of circles in which they moved. When you say she had French friends elsewhere, I cannot deny it out of hand, but I would question it. The Lasserres were centered in Paris. I was never personally introduced or taken to anyone who did not live in Paris. Once Gabrielle was home, there she stayed, moving no more than a carriage ride away. That child was watched and protected and cared for twenty-four hours a day. When she died they feared for

Gabrielle's life. She was prostrated with grief for months. My father went to the length of removing all evidence of the child from the house. Clothes, toys, books, portraits, were banished to the attic. Less than two years later Gabrielle caught a cold, which turned to pneumonia. She died early in 1884, and then we were alone."

"And how did you get on with your father?" Lintott asked.

"We loved and respected each other but had little in common. They had taken the heart out of our happiness. My father initiated me into the wine trade when I left school, and I did my best to please him, but I am no wine merchant. I later inherited his entire estate and found myself a young man of means. His solicitor looked after my affairs and appointed an excellent manager to the business. I then attended the Slade School, where I was fortunate enough to study under the great Alphonse Legros."

"You must have done pretty well too," said Lintott, considering, "if Bessie has heard of you. She's no expert, if you get my meaning."

Carradine smiled, but it was a public smile counteracted by a private frown. "Mrs. Lintott has been most complimentary, and a discourse on the fine arts would hardly interest you, Inspector, but *Miss Lucy* was a very early picture. To return to our own matter, I wish you to find out all you can about this train accident."

Lintott sucked his pipe stem, contemplated the brilliance of those hazel eyes, the intensity of that cultured voice. He removed his pipe. "Why?" he asked flatly.

Carradine sat back, as dumbfounded by himself as by the Inspector. "The circumstances," he replied sharply. "I wish to elucidate the circumstances."

Trying to make his fancy sound like fact, thought Lintott.

"To what purpose, sir? Your father's dead. Your stepmother's dead. The child's dead. The nurse is retired, probably dead too. Why?"

And suddenly Carradine knew why. "Because the dead mean more to me than the living. They are my opiate. With them I can love without passion. I can work without pain. And I have been told, and know it to be truth, that living is both pain and passion."

Embarrassed, Carradine lifted his hands and let them drop. "I beg your pardon for disturbing your domestic peace."

He rose slowly and looked around for his hat and cloak. He stubbed the partly smoked cheroot in a small ashtray, which was inscribed *A Present from Brighton.* His smile was pure good manners, his frustration was real.

"Half a minute, sir," said Lintott. "Just one more thing. You might come across things as you'd rather not find out. Have a few illusions shattered. That always hurts, sir. Sometimes they're illusions as folk can't live without."

"If one is in prison," said Carradine deliberately, "and fairly desperate, one doesn't count the cost of jumping from a high wall to escape."

"And what'll you do when you leave here?" inquired Lintott, puffing away like a philosophical steam engine.

"Do? I shall find someone else, Inspector. Find a fellow fool who will be foolish enough to follow a wild goose with me. I have nothing to rely upon but intuition, and I have always found it traveled further and truer than rationalization. You are asking me for facts and reasons. I have none. That this is not good enough for you, I understand. It is more than good enough for me. Has Mrs. Lintott taken my things into the hall, perhaps?"

"Wait a minute, sir," said Lintott, amused, protesting. "What a sudden sort of character you are! Why, you don't know what you're about. Haring off as though the clues was laid like a paper trail!"

He was as vehement, as passionate now, as Carradine. Galvanized from his comfortable chair, passing one strong hand over his thin gray hair, gesticulating with the other, eyes keen. An old hunting dog with the prospect of a new hunt.

"I've taken on cases as was only a smell in my nostrils. Cases as Scotland Yard would say, 'Give it to Lintott. He'll ferret it out if there's something to ferret'. Because I'm patient, sir" — he balled his hand into a stout fist — "and I'm obstinate, sir. I won't be told." He shook his head. "Like you, sir. Like you. Well, sit you down again. Bessie'll fetch us a pot o' tea. Bessie!"

Carradine smiled wryly. "Do you always offer tea after a confession, Inspector?"

"Only to the hard cases, sir," Lintott replied. "You're not married, I take it?"

"Considered an undesirable bachelor, I'm afraid. I broke off — I say this with remorse — two engagements, to two admirable young ladies. My housekeeper has frequently given me her opinion, which is unfavorable."

"Well, well. Better a broken engagement than an unhappy wedded life. I was fortunate. Thank you, my love" — as Bessie appeared with a tray on which her best china was tastefully arranged. "You might as well go to bed, my dear. Mr. Carradine and me will be a while yet."

Observing her husband's hunched shoulders and lowered head, she said maternally, "So you're off again, are you, John?"

Sheepishly he replied, "You know me, my love, when I get a sight of something. I don't quite figure it yet, but I daresay I shall."

Carradine jumped up and held out his hand to her. "Thank you for lending him to me this evening, Mrs. Lintott. I understand that your time together is precious."

"Lending?" said Bessie, not so fluttered by his attentions as to lose her common sense. "I don't lend him, sir. He's his own man. Always has been, always will be. Good night to you, sir."

They were silent for a little while over the teacups. Lintott fingered his muttonchop whiskers, which grew more luxuriantly than the hair on his head.

"Now, sir," he said decisively, "where did you find out this information? Were there other diaries? Did you read them? No? Well, we can come to that later. What about your father's papers? His diaries, if he kept them? No? I see. You just read the one diary that set you off?" He pondered, stirring sugar round and round in his cup. "Did you notice the date of the train accident?"

Relieved not to be found wanting in this area as well, Carradine produced a notebook in which a very few facts were recorded.

"This never would have been a Scotland Yard matter anyway," said Lintott two minutes later, taking off the spectacles he had donned for the purpose of reading. "We'd have to go to the proper source for information, which is the police department in Paris. Their system is different from ours, I believe, though I never had the opportunity to find out. But they'll be bound to have records, as we have. I'd have to go there, and I can't speak the lingo, so I shouldn't know how to ask a blinking question. Could you spare the time, sir?"

"My time is my own, Inspector."

"We'd have to look to a number of details afore we started. I haven't a passport, for one thing. Tickets and times and places where we stop — that'd be your business. You do speak the language more than the odd parlay-voo, don't you?"

"I am bilingual. Gabrielle taught me. And I have a studio in Paris. We could work from there."

"Now, you'd find police work on the tedious side, sir, I'm warning you. You'd have to ask a mort of questions for me and translate every blessed word. We'd have to get details of the crash and the people involved, notices of the inquest, and the general newspaper reports," Lintott said.

"You can rely on me absolutely in that direction, Inspector."

"Good. Because once I start I don't let go, you see. So, to speak plain, I wouldn't want you letting me down halfway. I'm asking you," said Lintott seriously, "not to break any engagements with *me*. Do you get my meaning, sir?"

This was the third time in three days that Carradine had been brought to reckoning, and he registered the fact.

"You have my word, Inspector, on my honor. Will you take the case?"

Lintott stared hard and long into the mobile face and found resolution.

"I'll take the case," he said and assumed command.

2

THE crossing was rough, but Carradine and Lintott preferred to underline their seamanship by standing on deck. Lintott was secretly delighted by his resilience. He had faced the fact that his stomach might betray him, but apparently it was as long-suffering as his legs and accepted this latest excursion into the unknown with a stoicism worthy of its owner.

He held hard to the ship's rail, felt the spray on his face, tasted salt on his lips, and savored both salt and venture. Below deck, the ladies sought sympathy, cologne, and basins. Children prostrate and children rampant added further complications. One small hoyden, escaping from the clutches of her nanny, ran straight into Carradine's arms and was secured immediately.

"Oh, thank you, sir," cried the nurse, harassed by her charge and the pitch and roll of the ship. "Now come along with me, Miss Flora, and no more nonsense! else the bogeyman'll get you."

"No he won't, Nanny," the child retaliated from the safety of her rescuer's arms. "There's no such person."

"So there!" And she stuck out her tongue, but so swiftly that it was not noticed.

Stout and perplexed, the woman said pleadingly, "Come along, like a good girl now."

"Shan't!"

"But there's Master George and Miss Susan sick as cats, and your poor mamma and the baby to see to."

Lintott and Carradine smiled at each other in sympathy, and at the small, obstinate face.

"Madam," said Carradine, "Miss Flora will be quite safe with us, as you have other duties. This gentleman is an inspector from Scotland Yard, and if you care to show your mistress my card I'm sure she will have no objection. The sea is an enemy to delicate constitutions, but there is no danger, I assure you. This young lady may be better equipped to escape the ravages of sea-sickness on deck."

The nanny took his card between wet fingers, noted the address with respect, and said, "Well, sir, if you're sure. We're in such a pickle down below."

"Allow me, ma'am, to escort you," said Lintott and staggered chivalrously over the sliding planks.

Carradine smiled into the washed rose of the child's face and wrapped his greatcoat about her.

"Have you crossed the Channel before, Miss Flora?"

"Twice a year, sir," she shouted, hair and bonnet strings slapping. "My papa works far away, in a very hot place. So we come to England and then go back again. Mama and the children are always sick, but I never am, and when I grow up I shall be a sailor."

"Young ladies can't be sailors, Miss Flora."

"Then I shall marry a captain and travel with him all over the world," she said with a touch of hauteur, "but I don't know your name, sir."

"I beg your pardon, madam. Permit me

46

to introduce myself. Nicholas Carradine, at your service. The suddenness of the encounter," he added, with the same seductive courtesy he would have shown to a beautiful woman, "robbed me of the respect due to every member of your fair sex."

She clasped her wet cheeks, shut her eyes, and laughed with pleasure.

"May a humble servant ask how many years you have graced this wicked world?" he continued, at home in a world of his own making.

"Ten. But should a gentleman ask a lady's age, sir?" she countered, coquetting.

"Only if he is her devoted slave, madam, and she gracious enough to answer."

She laughed again, enchanted and enchanting.

"Now turn about, Miss Flora. You are safely wrapped, and I shan't allow you to be washed overboard. If you love the sea you should observe it in all its aspects. This is a boisterous and brave one. Let us enjoy it together."

So Lintott found them: Flora pointing, Carradine nodding, both of them shaking off the sudden swells of salt water with shouts of rapturous reproach. As the voyage progressed the weather became kinder, the noise lessened. Later the three of them sat in chairs, and Flora fell asleep, sated. Lintott even ventured to light a pipe and drew on it with considerable satisfaction.

"Now I've always thought I had a way with children, sir, being fond of them. But you can beat me hands down, though you are a bachelor gentleman."

Carradine brought out his silver case and joined Lintott in a convivial smoke.

"The first time we met, Inspector, you were holding a sleeping child, and I liked what I saw. We are both devoted to these little folk, but in different ways. You are an adult with them, a kindly, understanding, protective adult. But when I speak to a child I become a child, and yet a child with adult knowledge."

Lintott stared ahead of him, eyes half closed, and sucked his pipe reflectively.

"Little Miss Flora here, at ten years old, is already dreaming of womanhood. So I court her, but in a way she comprehends. She knows very well that I am not the man who will eventually win her, that the courtship is mere play. But it pleases her, and it pleases me, to play it so."

"I've no talent in that direction," Lintott admitted, but without regret. "My good wife tells me I came into the world fully grown, with a pair of policeman's boots on." He chuckled. "I take it that you have a different way with different ages, sir? And different again with boys, of course."

"Very different, Inspector. I treat boys as young men, for I believe them to be manly little fellows in humiliating disguise. I felt as passionately when I was seven years old as I now do for any woman who captures my heart. I'm not speaking of the flesh, which is another matter, but of the emotions. When I observe parents frequently mocking at, or sentimentalizing over, a boy's genuine feelings, I resent their attitude as much as he must. He may be no more than four feet tall and imprisoned in a sailor suit, but at center he is a hero. He would scale walls, fight battles, cut through dark forests, if he could. Indeed, he dreams of doing so — and is returned to his marbles instead."

Interested, Lintott asked, "So how do you speak to one of those lovelorn young chaps then, sir?"

"Of everything but the lady concerned, and he would understand and respect my delicacy." Then, mindful of his present companion, who might be compared to a child in a strange place, he added, "Inspector Lintott, if you look ahead of you you will see the shoreline of one of the most fascinating countries in the world. Look well, for the first sight is always the best — though France seems undoubtedly out of sorts at the moment."

This could have been anywhere, yet Lintott experienced a constriction of the throat that astonished him. At my age too, he thought. I ought to be ashamed of myself. One country's much like another except for the lingo.

But he was impelled to lurch to the rail and stare ahead of him as the ship approached the coast, needing to cherish this alone. And, though Carradine seemed occupied with Flora, he too stood by that rail in spirit and shared the tumult of an elderly man who had never expected to see anything new again. Almost, he comprehended the words that Lintott said shyly under his breath — "Lah bell France!" — and then, briskly over his shoulder, "Very misty, sir. Can't hardly see a thing."

★ ★ ★

Unused to being in such a subordinate position, the Inspector was for the moment passed from person to person, and place to place, like some awkward parcel. Carradine, in his second element, became the complete cosmopolitan. His fluency whisked them through Customs, opened the doors of cabs and trains, set food and drink before them, and hurtled them toward Paris. His demeanor, his tipping — neither under- nor overdone — his air of consequence, commanded excellent service. Still, he never forgot he was Lintott's one link with familiarity and acted as interpreter of all about them to the point of exhaustion.

51

I'll find my feet in a bit, Lintott thought as Carradine at last rested his head against the antimacassar, lulled by the rushing dark and drumming wheels. It's like being inside of a new case instead of outside of it. You don't quite know where you are, but you will, given time. This is a fine how-de-do though. If I lost him I'd be in a right old mess. I wonder what Bessie's doing without me?

He saw that Carradine slept and observed him closely. His animation gone, the man seemed wholly vulnerable.

Ah, well, Lintott thought, each man to his own patch. If we were walking St. Giles together I'd have to look out for him . . . Look at him now and what would you say he was? A gentleman that's suffered a hard knock. An odd customer. But tell him so and he don't contradict you. Tell him, even, that he's on the eccentric side — he agrees with you. Now how can somebody know himself that well and not be able to alter it? Take me, for instance. Bessie says to me, "John Joseph Lintott, you're a regular growler. Get your teeth into a bone and you don't let go." And there's more than one bone buried here if I know anything.

Carradine's eyes opened, softened at the sight of Lintott sitting foursquare on the edge of his seat, hands knotted in determination.

"All right, Inspector. Don't worry, we have plenty of time. This is Paris. I'll find a porter."

"I'm not the worrying sort, sir."

Holding tight to his Gladstone bag, pulling up the collar of his Inverness cape, Lintott followed his companion into noise and brilliance. Carradine ordered the cabbie to drive slowly so that the city might be seen in passing.

"Being an honest Londoner, you may disagree with me, Inspector. But in my opinion London is a glorious and lovable jumble. Paris is a work of art. I believe it was Emerson who said that England built London for its own use, but France built Paris for the world."

"Very laid out," said Lintott, faithful to his metropolis. "A mite on the deliberate side, sir."

"All art is deliberate."

"I thought as art was inspiration, sir."

"So do a great many people, until they come to lay paint on canvas. Then they find it's hard and skilled work like any other."

Lintott was seeking to counteract an excitement that embarrassed him.

"There's a lot of money about, and that's a fact, sir."

"The French, like ourselves, pay lip service to God and raise an altar to Baal. You can buy anything here, if you have the means to pay for it, Inspector."

"Money can't buy what matters," Lintott replied earnestly, though he had never been in a position to prove it.

"Few would believe you. This is a very practical nation, with practical deities. Gold, food, and lovemaking. They consider it wiser to enjoy their treasures on earth rather than postpone them in hope of something more nebulous."

"I'm surprised you think such a lot of them if that's the case, sir," said Lintott, secure in his own morality.

"Ah, but they do it with such style, you see," said Carradine and smiled sideways at his companion.

54

Lintott breathed on the cab window and rubbed it with his sleeve, the better to view the ungodly.

★ ★ ★

A night's sleep found them both refreshed. Over a breakfast that seemed lamentably light, Lintott surveyed Carradine's Paris studio with pleasant astonishment. Its simple furniture, its easel and dais and tubes of paint and mingled smells of oil and turpentine, produced an effect of lively untidiness but not of squalor.

"I thought artists liked a regular muddle, sir."

"Our backgrounds exert more influence than perhaps we comprehend, Inspector. My father was an orderly man. I was reared in an orderly household. A little dust and derangement do not trouble me, but I detest chaos."

"You don't find it inspiring, sir?"

"Not in the least. You seem preoccupied with inspiration, Inspector." Amused. "But inspiration is of the moment. It doesn't live at my elbow, and its occasional visitations demand an unconscionable amount of hard work."

"Our professions seem to have more in common than I thought, then," Lintott observed. "A mort of plodding and sometimes never a thank you at the end of it."

"That too," said Carradine.

He had temporarily forgotten the hollow at his center and viewed the canvases with ironic desperation, as one views guests one has invited but does not really care to entertain.

"Shall we begin?" Carradine asked, leaving the canvases.

Lintott was relieved to discover that the artist chose to dress like a gentleman even in Paris. Apart from a black velour hat with a wide brim and bright band, his attire seemed sober enough. The Inspector had visualized himself walking around the city accompanied by a French beret and a flowing smock.

The language was beyond Lintott, but he amazed himself by translating tones, gestures, and expressions.

No sharper, and a lot less comfortable, than your British bobby, he reflected. Oh, they were smart to the point of foppery.

Waxed mustaches, jaunty caps. (I'd have that one up for wearing it at that angle!) Polished and brushed. But bowing and grinning and flinging their arms in the air like a lot of chorus girls. No, give me a solid bobby any day. No flying off the handle.

He watched Carradine impress them. They began with routine courtesy, inclining their heads reverently at Lintott — round whom Nicholas wove a brief legend — and then placed files at his disposal.

"A pity," said Carradine, "that the case is twenty years old, or we could have taken advantage of France's unofficial detective force — the concierges, the caretakers. They see everything and forget nothing. Quite invaluable."

Lintott clicked his tongue at this loss and took out his notebook and pencil.

"Fire away, sir. Every word, if you please. I'll do the sifting later."

* * *

On this last day of May 1882, a dawn express bound for the Swiss border was already fifteen minutes behind schedule.

The driver, a reliable and punctual man, decided to make up lost time on the long run between stations. Visibility was deceptive in the morning mist, but both driver and fireman knew the line so well that they swore they could ride it blindfold. Perhaps familiarity coupled to professional pride confused them, or perhaps it was the haze, but they misread the distant signal as clear and speeded on. Ahead of them were two freight trains: one at a standstill on the line, the other being shunted in a leisurely fashion onto the sidings. The wooden carriages, lit by gas, jammed together on impact, reared up, heeled over. The ruptured gas pipes spouted into flame. Under the bridge, in a welter of steam, the shunting train and the express locked in a terrible embrace.

That, at least, was the story assembled by witnesses and reasonable conclusions. The train had been crowded, so the injured were many. But the list of the dead was surprisingly short — driver, fireman, and the seven passengers in the first coach, which had been gutted. These were all identified by friends or relatives. Among them was the name Odette Carradine, aged six, resident of London, England.

"The train crammed from end to side," Lintott mused. "Seven passengers and eight seats. So the nurse escaped, probably badly burned, as I said. Still, give me the names and particulars of those that passed on, sir. Then newspaper reports next. All the information we can get on the accident and inquest."

"And every word to be translated and written down? Very well, Inspector."

"I did say as police work was tedious, sir," said Lintott with a twinkle of apology.

He watched a number of notes change hands. "You pay for the privilege here, sir, I take it?" he said dryly.

"A contribution to one of their charities, Inspector."

"H'm. Charity begins at home, I reckon. I daresay they think so too."

"We shall make a good Frenchman of you yet."

Lintott's snort of disgust was distinctly audible.

All afternoon Carradine tracked down

59

and translated old news. All afternoon Lintott wrote, and licked the point of his pencil, and wrote again. Once or twice he raised his eyebrows but made no comment until they had ransacked the past and sought out a steamy café.

Then he said, "The nurse was never in the carriage, sir, after all."

Gabrielle Carradine had made news by her absence at the inquest, which was attended by her husband and Berthe Lecoq. It was explained, and sympathetically accepted, that the bereaved mother could make no further emotional effort. Berthe testified on her behalf that the child had been traveling, care of the guard, to friends who would meet her in Switzerland.

The body was so badly burned that Odette was identified by means of a gold bracelet.

"Hadn't you better have a drop of something strong with that?" Lintott asked, indicating Carradine's untouched cup of coffee.

Carradine shook his head. He was punishing himself for something in which he had taken no part.

"Mind you," Lintott continued, treading carefully, "it ain't unknown to send a child care of a guard. Label pinned to her coat. Kind folk in the carriage as'd keep an eye on her and entertain her and themselves. Delivered safe and sound at the other end. Friends waiting on the platform. My elder son lives in Brighton, and he's sent a little 'un that way. Not so young certainly, and not so far, but then maybe customs are different over here."

The explanation appeared to be unsatisfactory, and they finished their coffee in silence.

"If you have no objection," said Carradine, swathing himself in his cloak once more, "I should like to make one last visit, a purely sentimental gesture. I suppose you could call it a fact. My father, Gabrielle, and Odette lie buried in a fashionable cemetery not far from here."

"Certainly, sir," Lintott replied as sympathetically as he could, and added something about paying last respects.

Abruptly Carradine rose and paid the bill. He was subdued now. He sat in the cab, chin sunk into his collar, hands thrust in pockets, brooding.

Lintott, used to marble angels, effusive verses, dearly beloveds, and fresh flowers every Sunday, now stood among the wealthy dead. This forest of miniature temples proved too much for him. Bowler hat held reverently to his chest, he followed Carradine's swinging cape down narrow avenues, past gleaming black slabs engraved in letters of gold, past open marble books and framed portraits, mourning statues, plaques and busts, china urns filled with china flowers. All the paraphernalia bestowed by the living upon those who had no further use for them.

A small chapel stood higher than the rest, in the middle of the cemetery, surmounted by an ornate cross. Above the wrought-iron gates glittered the name *Famille Lasserre*.

"My stepmother's family," said Carradine and inserted a key in the padlock.

Lintott had feared the sweet stink of corruption, but only stale air oppressed him. The chapel was the size of his Richmond parlor, gloomily lit by four stained-glass windows depicting four saints. At the far end a marble slab served as an altar, bearing an urn full of faded artificial flowers, two bronze candlesticks turning green and a plaster Madonna holding her Child. From the domed ceiling hung a heavy bronze candelabra, also green. Round the walls pedestals were placed a few feet apart, each holding a Lasserre bust. A tableful of framed photographs displayed lesser members of the family. Before the altar, two mildewed velvet prayer chairs knelt in vain.

Lintott thought of the country churchyard where he and Bessie would lie at last, and thanked God for it.

"Obscene, don't you think?" Carradine remarked dispassionately.

"That's coming it a bit strong, sir, but it ain't particularly uplifting, and that's a fact. Are your stepmother and sister among this marble lot or on the table?"

Carradine dusted two photographs carefully with his handkerchief and handed them to Lintott, who received them with equal care, sensing they were precious.

Gabrielle Carradine was portrayed

63

in a ball gown of gleaming satin, complete with long gloves and jewels. The exquisite formality of her toilette could not subdue the vitality of face and body. Like many French-women, she was light-boned and well fleshed. The delicate features and small hands and feet contrasted with a superbly swelling bosom and rounded arms.

"She never needed a hairdresser except on special occasions," said Carradine quietly. "Berthe used to dress it. Her hair was naturally curly and reached down below her waist."

Nose, mouth, and eyes were narrow, clean-cut. The chin pointed, ears neat and close. A cat's closed face, self-aware.

"Mind of her own?" Lintott suggested, sensing a consciousness of purely feminine power.

"She was a queen," said Carradine. "My father would have laid down his life for her. He loved my mother, of course, who was his first wife, but that was a marriage of mutual affection and esteem. This was something much headier."

"I'd put my money on the affection

and esteem myself," said Lintott gravely. "A man can lose his head over a woman, and where does that get him in twenty years?"

"To Paradise, perhaps?"

You were in love with her too, Lintott thought. All that about little boys' feeling passions and being told to go back to their marbles.

"How old were you when your father married Miss Lasserre, sir?"

"Almost five, Inspector. She was the answer to our loneliness."

Lintott laid the photograph gently down and studied Odette. "Her mama's daughter, eh? They must have been a fetching pair together. French through and through. Do you take after your father at all, sir?"

"Yes, strangely enough. I say *strangely* not in any derogatory sense, but it is a fact that blood is thicker than water. In appearance we are — or were — totally un-like. His physique matched his temperament. He was tall, as I am, but broadly built, comfortably built. He was a generous man, simple, trusting, utterly reliable."

"And you don't think you are, eh?"

"I know myself to be generous of pocket but not of a faithful heart such as his was. My temperament is a vacillating one. I am neither simple nor trusting nor, I regret, particularly reliable."

He traced the dust on the floor with his stick and drew a clown.

"So where does the resemblance come in?" asked Lintott, head on one side, viewing the spare cleverness of the lines.

"There is a better man in here, somewhere," said Carradine. "I could be all those things, given the right woman."

"Ah, you think so, do you? It don't, perhaps, occur to you that if the man was there in the first place the lady would follow?"

Carradine stared at him and then at the drawing. "It had not occurred to me, Inspector. You may well be right." Slowly he ran the point of his cane over and over the clown until he was obliterated "Have you found a case yet, Inspector?"

"A lead or two," said Lintott.

The day's search and emotional toll

had exhausted Carradine. Now he saw that Lintott also was weary. "Come," he said courteously, "Let's talk over a cognac."

They did not speak again until their second brandy was warming the raw day from their bones. Lintott relaxed in his bamboo chair and soaked up the atmosphere with interest. Noise and smoke, fierce arguments over the *Paris Soir*, waxed mustaches, energetic gestures.

"Fascinating, aren't they, Inspector?" said Carradine, observing him. "I find them so, and particularly the women. They are so feminine. There is no woman on earth, in my opinion, to equal a Frenchwoman. They seem born knowing how best to please a man."

"That's as may be, sir. But pleasure is as pleasure does."

"You sound like my good housekeeper, Inspector. Thoroughly disapproving."

"Oh, I enjoy the sight of a pretty woman as well as the next man does," said Lintott frankly. "But if I'm reckoning in the long term I like character. Durability. Prettiness don't last. Prettiness is a night out — and you don't care for the look of the next morning."

"The words of a philosopher," said the more lightly to cover the emptiness within him.

"I wouldn't know about that, sir. But I've seen too much to be taken in by appearance. Now, sir, to business."

"To business," Carradine echoed dutifully.

"The little girl was traveling alone to see friends in Switzerland. I've put forward a reasonable explanation for that. What do you think?"

"Impossible," Carradine cried. "I don't care what explanation Berthe gave. I utterly and completely reject the idea. Odette was rarely apart from either Gabrielle or her nurse, and never from both. Even had they entertained the notion, my father would have opposed it absolutely."

"Very well, sir. Since we have to start from somewhere we'll start from there. Second, the child could only be identified by her gold bracelet. Would your father have kept that, do you think? They'd have been given her effects — that is, the bracelet." Delicately.

"He might have done. My solicitor put all his papers in order after his death. I've never had reason to look into them." Carradine was puzzled. "How would the bracelet help, Inspector?"

"It might not," said Lintott, "but I like to see everything, in case it comes in handy. Now, taking your supposition that they wouldn't have let the child travel alone, we have two lines of thought to follow. One being that she was never on the train at all, and they identified someone else. I'll have a knock at that, for a start. They *knew* Miss Odette was on the train, so had reason to look for her. Second, if she *hadn't* been she would have turned up somewhere else. Right?"

"Correct," Carradine agreed.

"So she must have been with somebody. Do you recognize any of the names on this here list we copied, sir?"

"None, I'm afraid."

"We're leaving a loophole here," said Lintott, enjoying tripping himself up, confident he could scramble back on his feet in any event. "We're assuming that a lad of thirteen knew every single

69

person his stepmother knew. So it *could* have been someone on this list. But we can't follow up because they're dead. Unless" — pointing a finger — "anyone connected with the late Mrs. Carradine is still alive. Brothers, sisters, relatives of any description, old friends?"

"Gabrielle was an only child. Her parents are dead. We dropped every connection with the family and their circle afterward, and that's another curious thing — "

"Never mind that for now," Lintott counseled. "We've got enough curious things to keep us busy for a bit. The train was crowded from end to end, according to the newspaper report — they said it could have been a regular holocaust. So we'll assume that every seat was filled. There were only seven passengers in that front coach and eight seats. The person who was with your sister might have been that eighth passenger and somehow got away. Now don't get wound up, sir. It's *if, if, if,* all the way — and one if gone wrong can upset all the others. Pure speculation and not a single hard fact so far. But my nose don't half twitch!"

70

They sat together, an ill-assorted couple with only an adventure in common. Carradine, in his wide-brimmed hat, admired the twilight through half-closed eyes. Lintott, stout and plain and gray, sought out ways and means by contemplation of the checked tablecloth.

"The nurse," Lintott murmured to himself. "Berthe Lecoq. If she's still alive. If I can find her. She's the key — if there's a lock to open. *If!* There's a heap of *ifs*."

"Only Whistler could capture this evening light," Carradine mused.

He recollected his position as host. "You must be hungry, Inspector."

Lintott would have given much for three cups of strong tea and a plate of hot buttered muffins, but these did not seem to be forthcoming. He nodded.

"Then let us pay tribute to the perishable and inimitable art of French cuisine. In short, dinner."

Lintott looked miserable.

"Soup? A good steak and vegetables? An iced pudding? Cheese? Something of that sort, Inspector?"

"Ah!" said Lintott, whose mind had

been conjuring up frogs' legs by the bushel. "That'd be capital, sir."

Carradine smiled, comprehending.

Lintott reached for his bowler hat. "If agreeable to you, sir," he said slowly, "I'd like to go back to England. I want to sift through every blessed paper your father or stepmother ever kept. Bills, receipts, letters, diaries, account books — you'd be surprised what you can find out about a household through an account book, sir. The lot."

"Then we'll go. As soon as you please. Tomorrow if you wish."

Lintott measured him and found him coming nicely up to standard. "I shan't need you on this stretch, sir, if you want to stay behind. Just put me on a train, with instructions as these folk can follow. I'll make my own way back."

"Allow me to see you onto the boat at least," Carradine said, surprised. "I can hardly leave you to ramble the Continent alone."

"Well, I would be obliged, sir. And could you write me a letter of introduction to your lady-housekeeper and another to your business manager, explaining?"

"Why to him — you are most welcome, of course, Inspector — but why to him?"

"I want to check the list of your father's customers. It might come in useful — you never know."

Carradine shrugged and laughed. "You're a regular British bulldog, Inspector. Set your teeth into a morsel and you never let go. You shall have the letters, with pleasure, naturally. You will be free to search the mice in the attics and the cobwebs in the cellars, and every cask of wine we possess, if you so desire, Inspector. Does that suit you?"

Lintott replied, grinning. "It'll do for a start, sir."

They strode along in high good humor.

"Tell me, Inspector, how do you find Paris? I should like to know."

Drawing on his woolen gloves, Lintott answered directly, "Like royalty, sir. I'm glad to know it's there, and to watch it go by, and I wouldn't have missed it for anything. But it's not my world, sir, and never will be."

Disappointed, Carradine frowned, and then he smiled. "It's one of mine,

Inspector. And since you have slighted the lady I must cherish her twice as much to make up for your coldness."

"Oh, Paris is a lady, is she?" said Lintott dryly.

He had caught sight of a pretty painted face, whose lips were beginning to pout an advance, and stared it down dreadfully. The girl shrugged, pulled her crimson feather boa seductively up to her chin, and sauntered past.

"Well, a woman anyway," Carradine replied, noting the exchange with amusement. "They have a saying, *Paris est une femme, et une femme nue.* Paris is a woman, and a naked woman. What do you think of that, Inspector?"

Lintott said, "Precious little!"

3

WALTER CARRADINE had been the son his father wanted: obedient, industrious, devoted to the family business. He began as his father's assistant, became his partner, and married according to his wishes. Emily Burgess, a few years older than himself, had money of her own. This was invested in Carradine's Superior Wines when she became Walter's wife. Bred to willing submission, Emily moved into her father-in-law's house and proved to be an excellent if uninspiring wife, her only deficiency being in the region of the nursery. For ten years they remained childless, and when at last she dragged Nicholas into the world the effort dragged her out of it. Old Carradine died shortly afterward, and Walter was left with a baby son, the business, and the home he had never deserted.

He was not an introspective man, so set down his dissatisfaction as grief or liver trouble. But beneath the layers of conformity beat a romantic heart. He had traveled to France for his father many times, in the noose of work. Now he traveled and looked about him as well. In the course of the next few years he met Gérard Lasserre, whose tastes and connections exceeded his capacity for money-making. Walter summed him up at once as a dilettante and drove a hard bargain over the contents of a small but promising vineyard. But Lasserre, divining the Englishman's simplicity, made a bargain on his own account: his eighteen-year-old daughter Gabrielle, whose only dowry was her beauty.

The Lasserres wined and dined the middle-aged merchant while their bait glittered opposite, and for the first time in his life Walter fell in love. He found it a glorious, a painful, an expensive awakening. He translated the girl's reluctance as modesty, and the Lasserres confirmed his view. He invited Gabrielle and her mother to his London home and introduced the child Nicholas. Mme. Lasserre inspected the house from cellar to attic and pronounced it worthy but inelegant. Gabrielle, in a final spurt of defiance, said she could not bear to live in such gloominess, so Mme. Lasserre suggested alterations and Walter agreed. Gabrielle insisted upon the engagement of a new nanny and housekeeper, rightly sensing that her position could be made difficult by the existing deities. Reluctantly, Walter agreed to this also. Every objection on Gabrielle's part was met until, at length, she offered no more resistance. Then, realizing she would have her way in all but inclination, pressured by her parents' desire for a rich match and by Walter's infatuation, she married him.

★ ★ ★

Lintott mounted the whitened steps of the Carradine residence. Though every house in the square was veiled in lace curtains, theirs were more elaborate than the rest. Inside, the usual opulent twilight of dark paint and heavy wallpaper had been lightened and cheered. No Highland scenes loomed from massive frames. Oval portraits, gilded mirrors, tempted Lintott with frivolous vanity. But frivolity and vanity only roused his suspicion, so he sat at the edge of a drawing-room chair while Mrs. Tilling put on her spectacles and read the letter from Nicholas.

He liked Mrs. Tilling. She was his sort, plain, steady, and comfortable. She pursed her mouth and frowned a little — the better to understand the message. He ventured to speculate. Father probably a butler, mother a parlor-maid, brought up in service and dedicated to it. A stickler for detail but able to keep her staff happy as well as efficient. Warmhearted without being woolly-headed. Sharp of tongue and eye. Capable of a loyalty and affection that could neither be deterred by human failings nor blinded by human charm. A tidy little body. A fine, up-right woman.

"Well, sir," said Mrs. Tilling, taking off her spectacles, folding the letter, and replacing it in the envelope, "Mr. Nicholas says to give you the run of the place, in a manner of speaking. Will you be wanting me to make a room ready for you?"

78

"No, thankee, ma'am. I have my home and good lady out at Richmond. I can come up and back as long as I have to. I shan't trouble you."

"Would you care for a glass of Madeira, sir, or a glass of Shrub to keep out the cold?"

"I'd relish a cup of tea, ma'am, if that's convenient. And somewhere more homely, if you don't mind me saying so." Fearful of small ornaments, thick, flowered carpets, and thin-legged chairs.

She smiled, taking in his stout, polished boots, the old suit immaculately brushed, the clean, inexpensive linen.

"I'll get Alice to fetch a pot of tea to my room, sir, Would you come this way, if you please?"

"Now this is more like it, ma'am," said Lintott in relief. "Your children, ma'am?" Inspecting the array of unpretentious photographs.

"My nephews and nieces, sir. I was widowed very young, and then coming to a good position here I never married again. But I've been able to help them to better themselves, and they don't forget me."

79

The family shored up by her savings. Lintott accorded her silent respect as he nursed his teacup.

"I daresay you know why Mr. Carradine's employed me, ma'am," he began, warmed. "And it's a regular rum notion, as I told him."

She nodded, hands folded in the lap of her black merino dress.

"There's precious little to go on, and you can probably tell me more than I'd find out for myself, if you'll be so good. I hope I needn't say," Lintott assured her, "that it'll be in the strictest confidence. It's not impertinence as makes me ferret round."

Her head shook in negation.

"Then I'll put it this way, ma'am. If you want to know the ins and outs of a case you must have the folk involved. People act as they do because of what they are. If you find out what they are, then you can more or less know how they'll act to a given situation. So I'll give us a start. Mr. Carradine is out of my line of country, I admit that. But I've formed one or two opinions, and I'll be glad to hear if they're right or wrong.

You're attached to the gentleman, of course?"

"I've known Mr. Nicholas since he was about five years old, sir."

Just so. He's one on his own, isn't he? Leastways, artists may be alike for all I know, but I've never come across one before."

"We entertain a great deal, sir, with Mr. Nicholas now being a member of the New English Art Club and that. I've had the honor of meeting Mr. Wilson Steer and Mr. Max Beerbohm, Mr. Roger Fry and a many others. Mr. Sickert left the country, on account of parting with his lady, two or three years since. But he's living in France now, and I believe Mr. Nicholas keeps in touch with him, and knows some of the French artists too. I'm running on, sir, but what I meant to say was this — they're all different, every one of them. Mr. Beerbohm is a proper gentleman, for all his fun. Mr. Sickert is a lovely mannered gentleman too, and well turned out, but he's a bit of a bohemian. He has a taste for queer places and queer folk, like Mr. Nicholas. Then that Mr. Whistler is a regular autocrat, very high-handed. Talks down to everybody."

"I see, ma'am," said Lintott, who did not. He pulled the conversation onto familiar ground. "The second Mrs. Carradine employed you, I believe?"

"Yes, sir, and was a good mistress though on the fussy side. Everything had to be as she liked it. I could have done without that Berthe Lecoq at my back, morning, noon, and night," Mrs. Tilling added frankly, "but beggars can't be choosers. Not meaning I was a beggar, coming with the best references, only I needed the position. I'll say this for Berthe, she could work. The house was in a rare pickle when I come to be interviewed. The workmen hadn't been as quick as Mr. Carradine hoped, and what with madame's trunks and boxes, and the paint pots, we were fair put about."

★ ★ ★

"Sit down, if you please, Madame Tilling," said Gabrielle.

"Thank you kindly, ma'am."

82

Mrs. Tilling sat correct and self-contained. Only the violets quivering slightly on her best bonnet, betrayed her nervousness. She was young, at twenty-seven, to be applying for the post of housekeeper, but she needed work quickly.

Gabrielle Carradine's black eyes rested briefly on the purple velvet flowers, studied the round, good-natured face and capable hands, noted the firm mouth and chin and the air that was respectful without being obsequious. Behind Gabrielle stood a tall, spare woman in her forties, whose eyes were harder and busier than those of the mistress.

"You feel you are able to direct this big house, Madame Tilling?"

"I have every confidence, ma'am, and would make it my business to please you."

"You are a widow? You have no little children?"

"We'd been married only a few months before he died, ma'am. No children."

"That is sad," Gabrielle said briefly. She turned to Berthe Lecoq and spoke in French. "Her references are excellent. What do you think of her?"

"She will work, madame. Look at her hands. She is strong. Also she is genteel. She knows her place. She won't chatter and idle. She is no *bavardeuse*."

"You prefer her to the others?"

"Yes, madame."

"Good. Madame Tilling, this is my maid, Berthe Lecoq. She has been with my family since I was born. I wish her to stay with me and take care of the little boy. There is work to do in this house, as you see. She will perhaps be able to help you. Only it is necessary that you like each other."

Mrs. Tilling studied the formidable figure clad in unrelieved black. Oh, well, in for a penny, in for a pound. The wages were generous. She had liked the look of Walter Carradine, exuding kindness and a dazzled bewilderment that aroused her sympathy.

"I don't make enemies, ma'am, and I'm reckoned to be easy to get on with. Does the lady speak English?"

"A very few words. You will teach her more."

"I'll do my best, ma'am, and work's work whether you're English or French, to my mind."

The small pointed face glanced at her imperiously, discerned her meaning, and smiled. She turned again to her maid, translating, and a phantom of a smile warmed Berthe's countenance as she replied.

"Berthe says you are a woman of good sense, Madame Tilling. So. When do you begin?"

"As soon as you like, ma'am. My mistress is going abroad, and we all have to find ourselves new places. She'll let me go and be glad to know that I'm settled."

"Then that is done. One moment, Madame Tilling. There are servants who are here a long time. It is necessary only to change the little boy's nurse and the housekeeper. But Berthe does not like all the servants. She says they are idle."

Oh Lor', thought Mrs. Tilling. I'm going to have my staff sorted out for me too. "Well, ma'am, perhaps you'd let me see how we go on for a few weeks? If any of them aren't worth their wages

85

they'll be sent off, you may be sure."

Gabrielle translated, and Berthe gave a grudging nod.

"One more small thing, Madame Tilling. I do not like that you call me 'ma'am'. That is well in England, but you will call me 'madame', if you please."

"Very well, ma'am . . . madame."

Then the charm broke through, and Gabrielle said, smiling, "And since you are so genteel I shall call you 'Mrs. Tilling'. Yes?"

The gleam of rapport was comforting. The newly appointed housekeeper bobbed a curtsy, which was repeated by the violets, and began a seven-year marathon, which she now summed up to Lintott.

"By the time I'd made myself understood, and kept everybody on an even keel, sir, I could've run the British Empire single-handed."

"I get the picture," said Lintott, "and it's a bit different from the one Mr. Carradine gave me. But not much different from the impression I got off Mrs. Carradine's photograph."

"You can tell more from her painted

86

portraits, and the house, sir. If you've finished your tea I'll show you round. Madame was only eighteen when she married, but she could have been a hundred the way she set her mind to something and got it. She'd been trained as few young brides are. She had her eyes on everything, and Berthe was right behind her. It must have cost poor Mr. Carradine a fortune. And she was a funny one with money. I've known her spend forty and fifty pounds on a piece of furniture she fancied, and then hunt a few pence short in the housekeeping accounts all morning.

"This was her own room that she called the 'petty salon'."

Very small, in shades of dark and pale rose, the white paintwork picked out in gold, the square, gilded mirror large upon one wall. A buttoned chaise longue stretched beneath the window. China elegancies cluttered little tables.

"The lady was fond of mirrors, wasn't she, ma'am?"

"Ah, well, she had the looks, sir, and she liked to look at herself. She was Catholic by faith, like most of these

French people. Went to Mass, and said her prayers with beads, and that. But she might have been a pagan for all the good religion did her. I've seen her properly down in the dumps over something. Then she'd jump up, look in the glass, set her hair to rights, and hum a tune to herself. The little girl, Miss Odette, was just the same. Here they are, sir, as like as peas in a pod."

Head to head in a painted prison. Mother and daughter. Willful, pretty mouths, narrow black eyes, straight noses, massed black curls. Odette in a white dress with a gold bracelet on her left wrist — was it *the* bracelet, perhaps?

"But madame really cared for that child. Oh, she was wonderful with Mr. Nicholas. I'd have thought, losing his own nanny and having that Berthe instead and a new stepmother, he'd be unhappy. But they treated him like a man, sir, even though he was only five. They treated him like royalty. His father never had the polish, though very affable and polite. He never had the easiness of Mr. Nicholas — *they* did that for him, the polish. Still, as I say, the one she loved was Miss Odette. There was a softness about her then that I never saw with anybody else. It was a picture to see them together, and they knew it. They had those two men besotted, I can tell you."

★ ★ ★

"Where is my Nicki? Does he wish to go for a drive with us or is he tired of our company?"

"Here, Mama!" cried the boy, flushed and handsome.

"But what does he work at so very hard?" Gabrielle asked the governess, who detested her.

"Latin, madame."

Gabrielle pursed her lips and raised her eyebrows, in comradeship with Nicholas, who 'hid a smile' and waited for the rout that would follow.

"But that is a dead language, Miss Bell, and so dull."

"If Mr. Nicholas is to enter Marlborough, madame, he will need to do a great deal better with Latin than he has done."

"But he speaks French as well as I,

Miss Bell, and that is more useful."

"Latin is compulsory, madame. French is an extra."

"How very sad. Come here, poor boy, and let me feel your head. You are fevered. Berthe! Feel this poor boy's fever. Does your head ache, my Nicki?"

Miss Bell's expression dared him to lie.

"No, Mama," he said regretfully.

"Worse and worse. A fever with no ache. What do you think, Berthe?" — to her maid, who was carrying Odette.

Berthe's smile only appeared when either her practical nature or love of battle was roused. The governess, who had proved a worthy combatant, set her spectacles straight and glared at Berthe.

"It is nothing, madame," said Gabrielle's champion laconically, "that fresh air will not cure."

"And what of his Latin?" Miss Bell demanded.

"We drive only for an hour in Hyde Park. He returns refreshed and works very hard. Do you not, Nicki?"

"Yes, Mama, I promise. I honestly do promise, Miss Bell" — placating her.

"And poor Miss Bell, who is red with fatigue, may rest also," said Gabrielle, smiling. "All the work and no play, as you English say, makes Jack a dull boy. And to be dull is to be a bore. Come, Nicki. Now what is it that you do when a lady asks you to accompany her?"

The boy bowed and kissed the extended hand smelling so deliciously of French perfume. Miss Bell, defeated, clicked her tongue and shook her head as they departed.

★ ★ ★

"She always dressed the little girl in white," said Mrs. Tilling, "and nothing but the best. They were off to Paris three or four months of the year, broken into separate visits. I looked after Mr. Carradine and the house. He'd join them when he could, but he was busy, poor gentleman. Off they'd go, Madame and Berthe and the two children, and an empty trunk as well as the other luggage. When they came back it'd be full of new clothes. She never shopped in London. Lace, made by the nuns, and everything stitched by hand. It was a good thing Mr. Nicholas was sent away to school or he'd never have learned his letters."

★ ★ ★

"I have only two things to say to you, my boy," said Walter Carradine kindly. "Take full advantage of the education you are being offered, and never do anything of which you would be ashamed to tell us."

"When do I begin, Papa?"

"At the end of September, my boy, so you have the summer before you."

He could only offer money, being unable to express his feelings, so patted Nicholas's shoulder and slipped a sovereign into his hand.

Upstairs, in feminine disarray, Gabrielle cried, "My poor Nicki! Come, sit here and amuse Odette while we pack. So you will be torn from us? Why do the English love to send their children away to school? What monsters! We shall he sad without you. What do you wish to say, Miss Bell?"

The governess was standing in suppressed

wrath at the bedroom door. "If you will excuse me, madame, I think it highly improper that a big boy of eleven should be in a lady's room at such a time."

"Improper?" said Gabrielle lazily, "but I am his maman, Miss Bell."

"English boys do not watch their mamas packing . . . garments," replied the governess, and her spectacles glared down at the lace-edged stays, flounced petticoats, and frilled drawers.

"Ah, Miss Bell, I shall not quarrel with you. I hold you in such respect. But I do not agree with your English education, and I do not speak of Latin, for that is your duty. I speak of the education of life. How shall a man learn anything of women if he is set apart from them always? Our Nicki will go to a school full of boys, and they will teach him to depise us and to be very polite. Much later, when they cannot hide his interest in women, they will teach him to esteem some and to use others — "

"Mrs. Carradine! Is this the way to speak in front of a maiden lady and an impressionable young boy?"

"I think so," Gabrielle replied composedly.

"I speak the truth. Is that so terrible? I do not wish my Nicki to think of women as goddesses or slaves. So he watches us pack? It is better that I let him watch than that he peeps through a keyhole. The peeping is improper, not the watching."

Imperturbably Berthe continued to shake out and fold underwear, to lay it between sheets of tissue.

"I have no further place in this establishment," said Miss Bell with dignity. "I should be obliged, Mrs. Carradine, if you would find a replacement. It has been difficult enough," she added, trembling, "to teach Mr. Nicholas with the amount of interference I have borne. To teach Miss Odette would be quite impossible."

Gabrielle, who had intended her to leave anyway, accepted her resignation with effusive regret and promised to give her the best of references.

"For she is very good, your poor red Miss Bell," she explained, handing Odette to Nicholas as he sat crosslegged on the fourposter bed. "I do not hate her."

"She hates you," said Nicholas

truthfully, "and I know why."

He had grown in more than stature under Gabrielle's six-year reign. His adoration of her was absolute, but the early, clinging, speechless worship had changed into companionable awareness. She treated him as she would treat any attractive and intelligent young man, and he responded with perception.

"I am damaged to hear it," Gabrielle cried, and he grinned at the expression. "Tell me why she hates me, Nicki. Do not spare me!" Knowing it would be a compliment.

"You're fishing for praises, Mama. Don't wriggle so, miss!" — as Odette tried to free herself and fall among the tissue paper and ribbons. "Poor old Bell! What a rotten life for a woman, teaching other people's beastly children and never having a home of her own."

"But you are not beastly, Nicki. I teach you to be charming. Perhaps it is the charm she hates. The beastliness she would comprehend."

"You're a fearful cynic, Mama."

"I am a realist. I shall fight this Marlborough of yours, nail and tooth.

They shall not turn you into a dull dog who knows nothing of women. I set myself against them!" And she laughed superbly and rumpled his hair. "Ah, but forgive me. You do not like that, now you are older."

"Papa is not a dull dog," said Nicholas, disquieted.

She divined that the statement was really a question and dismissed it with a gesture. "All rules are broken, Nicki. But he did not go to Marlborough, and that is why" — and she smiled as Walter knocked tentatively at the open door — "that is why he is so kind" — with a kiss that delighted him — "so generous, so nice, so good to us all. What is the matter, my heart?"

He had mounted the stairs to have a firm talk and found himself at a loss as usual.

"Miss Bell says she is leaving, my love."

Her hands flew to her cheeks. "I know, I know," she cried, "and I am desolated. But we shall give her a good letter to take with her, and she will he happy. Do not worry, because I shall teach Odette, and then you do not have to pay the wages."

"But poor Miss Bell seems to be very upset, my love."

"We are all distracted to lose her, but I teach Odette. *Bijou! Petite! Cherie!* Say to papa what mama has teached you."

The child slid from Nicholas's arms, ran to her father, and was swung to his shoulder.

"No, no. Stand up very tall and say the English poem for papa!"

"No. I shall stay here and *whisper* it to him."

"You're tickling my ear, miss," said Walter, bewitched, "and that's a French poem with some lines missed out. I may not be fluent, my love, but I know that much."

The child flung back her head and laughed, preening before the admiring circle of faces.

"Oh, you are a bad one," Gabrielle said mournfully. "Papa will not trust me, but," and she hung on his other arm, beseeching, "I teach her three verses from 'The Charge of the Light Brigades' because you like it."

Nicholas and his father exchanged a smile.

"There was only one Light Brigade, my love, but I'm sure it sounds even better in the plural."

"So," said Gabrielle, pouting, "we fail utterly."

"Not failed at all, my love," cried Walter briskly, confounded by the pair of them. "I think that's splendid, absolutely splendid. You don't want Nicholas here while you're packing, surely?"

"But why not? He is amusing Odette. And now, my dear one, please to go away because we are busy. I shall buy Miss Bell something very beautiful in Paris. Do not let us talk of her any more. I am too sad. Do not let her know how much she has made me sad. I wish us to be good friends."

"No, certainly not. Certainly not. Well, well . . . "

He made his way downstairs, having accomplished nothing and feeling that the governess truly had been a little unreasonable.

Berthe closed and locked the last trunk and disappeared. Gabrielle walked up and down the room, hands clasped behind her head, thinking. Nicholas held Odette's fingers away from his face.

"That's Odette," the child observed, finding her reflection in his eyes. "Two of her all at once. Tell me a story about two Odettes."

Nicholas had never discovered why a command from either his stepmother or half-sister should bring him to instant obedience, whereas a natural pride resisted orders from all other quarters.

"Once upon a time there were two awful pickles," he began, teasing.

"Not nice. Not a nice story. I want a nice story."

Gabrielle turned and watched them indulgently. Suddenly it occurred to Nicholas that he was leaving this wholly feminine world behind, and the masculine one seemed harsh and austere. His self-possession deserted him. He stared at his stepmother, horrified.

"I say, you won't half miss me!" he cried, riven. "I've a jolly good mind not to go."

Odette ceased to plague him, aware that his mood had changed. Gabrielle rustled toward him and touched his cheek. None of them said anything. Then Nicholas set the child carefully on the bed, swung his legs to the floor, and tried to whistle as he walked out.

"My friend," Gabrielle said quietly, "one moment."

He would not look at them, pausing by the door, head bent.

"Cherish the wound in your heart," she commanded, speaking in her own language. "It's good to feel so deeply. Don't betray yourself for what people call security. Don't be afraid to break rules. And remember us, always."

He lifted his head then. Seeing and treasuring the two faces together. Seemingly fragile, vulnerable, dependent, they wielded a power that set a mark on him for life.

4

"**M**R. NICHOLAS going to public school made a deal of difference, both to him and to them, sir," said Mrs. Tilling. "Old Mr. Carradine thought the world of his son, though he was never one to show his feelings except where madame was concerned. He might have had a ring in his nose, the way she led him. Meaning no disrespect. Still, he didn't want them all gallivanting off to Paris and taking Mr. Nicholas with them, the minute he came home for his holidays. So they waited, that spring of 1882, until he went back to school, and then the master saw the three of them onto the boat train at Victoria. Sometime in May, sir. Yes."

★ ★ ★

Walter Carradine had aged considerably over the past eight years, and the difference between himself and his wife was so marked that they appeared to be grandfather and granddaughter. He and the housekeeper had done everything they could to assure the travelers a comfortable journey. A picnic basket, containing everything from cold capon and white napkins to Malvern water and china cups, a little pile of ladies' periodicals for Gabrielle; the guard handsomely tipped to keep an eye on them and their baggage. Now he stood at the carriage window, feeling solitary and inadequate, hat in hand.

"Take care of madame and mam'selle, Berthe," he said in French, though the maid's English was now fair enough under Mrs. Tilling's tutelage.

Berthe, preferring silence, nodded briskly and held up Odette to be embraced. Neither of Walter's womenfolk ever failed to rouse his love and his pride. Tenderly he brushed the small cheek with his moustache. Reverently he kissed Gabrielle's extended hands. She was wearing a deep blue traveling costume trimmed with black braid, but the child as usual was clad in white, from bonnet to buttoned boots. The only flashes of color were her coral necklace and a narrow gold chain bracelet, from which swung a gold heart.

"My cordial regards to your parents, my love," said Walter to his wife. "And don't forget to telegraph me immediately you arrive in Paris."

"But of course. And I shall write also, my dearest."

She made a favor even of common courtesy.

"I shall miss you both," he cried involuntarily.

"And we shall be desolate without papa, shall we not, *mignonne?*" Gabrielle demanded of her daughter, who clasped her arms around his neck in answer.

He seemed gray and leaden beside their glowing good health.

"Until we meet again, dearest Walter," Gabrielle said softly. "You know I would not leave you if maman's heart was not unsure."

"No, of course not, my love."

Mme. Lasserre's heart had been the excuse or concern of her family for twenty years, though it would eventually outlast all of them.

The guard blew his whistle and swung down his green flag smartly. The station roof filled with steam. The train lurched.

"Take care!" Walter called. "Take care!"

The two sweet faces together, the gloved hands waving. White against lambent blue, and behind them Berthe's watchful black figure. He stood for a few moments, looking after them, then set his hat slowly on his head and walked away.

★ ★ ★

"It could have been two strangers coming back, sir, less than a month later," said Mrs. Tilling. "Mr. Walter spoke for both of them, what bit he told me, but madame said nothing for weeks. I ran the house like I always did, and saw she wasn't disturbed. She kept to her bed a great deal."

Sitting up against the lace-edged pillows, exquisite and empty.

"Mr. Walter just said that the little girl had died in a train accident on the Continent. Well, sir, it's a dangerous place to take a child, to my way of thinking. He said madame had been too shocked to attend the inquest. And he wanted Mr. Nicholas to be spared as much as possible, being so fond of Miss Odette, and we should say she'd died of a fever and Berthe had gone home. It was understandable. So the boy was told that, and asked not to talk to madame about it, along of her being upset."

"He specifically said that Berthe had gone home, Mrs. Tilling?"

"Well, sir, that's what we were to tell Mr. Nicholas. But Mr. Walter never actually said she *had*. Only, the little girl wouldn't be traveling without her nurse, would she? And if Berthe had been alive she would have come home with madame. They were very close. So I took it she died on the train with Miss Odette. Nobody ever mentioned her again. All the pictures and photographs in the house were put into the attic. But Mr. Nicholas had them out after his father's death. The clothes and toys and books are still there. I put mothballs with the clothes. It was as if the child had never been. Those were Mr. Walter's orders, for madame's sake.

And if you'd seen her, sir, you would have understood why."

"And you never told Mr. Nicholas the truth as he grew older?"

"There was no cause for that, sir. The child was dead, wasn't she? The truth could only have pained him." Her good-natured face was troubled. "And I must say, sir, as I don't know what good the truth *has* done him. Worriting over what's past and gone, and getting you to rummage up a lot of old memories for nothing but heartache."

"Did Mrs. Carradine die of heartache, ma'am?"

"Twenty months later, sir. She never recovered her spirits, and she never went back to France. Oh, she took up the reins again, as you might say. Gave her orders and looked through the account books and that. It was like talking to a stranger. There was no more entertaining or theater-going. Mr. Walter used to come home at six, punctual as usual, but I don't think they exchanged a dozen words the whole evening. Not that she was unpleasant or cold. She even seemed to cling to him a bit pathetic-like. She'd sit with her hands in her lap, like this, for hours. And she'd look at him from time to time, almost timid. But she'd no cause to fear him. He was as gentle with her as another woman would be."

"Did the boy not cheer her up, being fond of her, ma'am?"

"He got closer than anybody, I must say. They tried to make life more natural for him than for themselves. He'd play drafts and backgammon and cards with her and tell her his news. But she wasn't trully interested. She'd lost interest in living, sir, and that's the truth. She caught a cold the following January and didn't fight it. It developed into pneumonia, and she was gone. Then there was just poor Mr. Walter, and Mr. Nicholas in the holidays."

"Would you call father and son close, ma'am?"

"They had an affection and respect for one another, sir, no doubt of it. But Mr. Nicholas lived in a world of his own, and Mr. Walter never understood that. When the old gentleman died Mr. Nicholas gave up the wine trade and went in for art. There seems to be nothing of his father about him, except a kind nature. I never knew his mama, poor soul, so I can't say if he resembled her, but I doubt it. He belonged to madame more than most sons belong to their own mothers. He belonged to her more than he should, sir, in my opinion. And dead or alive she's never let go of him."

"He's been engaged twice, he tells me, ma'am."

"Lovely young ladies, sir, as God is my witness. Oh, he's fast enough to fall in love, but he don't stay in love. There's two well-known families in the best society, and connections of both, that'll pass him in the street without so much as a good day. He can't seem to settle."

She was wondering how much to say but decided on silent loyalty.

"Mr. Carradine said as much to me, of course," Lintott remarked easily. "He mentioned his work too, though that's a bit beyond me. I don't know it — though my good lady had his name off without so much as a by your leave."

"Well, sir, he's never satisfied with anything. I think he painted *Miss Lucy* lovely, and so did a great many people. But he gave all that up in a year or two, and did things different as he said was better. And still he's not satisfied. If you'd like to take a look at his studio, sir, it might explain more than I can."

★ ★ ★

He had tried all manner of pictures on them, in all moods and seasons, in a nostalgia of paint and pastel. It was the nostalgia that had captured the public. People preferred time held fast, rendered harmless, to time strange and unknown. Through Nicholas Carradine, in those first years, they had clutched their childhood to them, remembering the best that had been or that should have been. Lintott himself warmed to the sunlit beaches and tucked bloomers, the cold rush of waves and fragile shells; canaries in cages, fires behind brass-railed guards, faces pressed to winter windows, boot tracks in the snow; November

109

pyres, lamplight and nightlight and evening prayers. Carradine had painted security. Safe in a communal past, the viewer tended to lose detachment and to wallow. Oh, the artist delineated precisely, impeccably. He painted from the heart, but it was a heart in thrall, a heart immobilized inside a childhood dream.

"Then he broke away entirely, sir, and I was a bit sorry for it, to tell the truth."

Heavily influenced, though neither Lintott nor Mrs. Tilling could have known this, by Whistler. Symphonies in white, with hints of decoration in the Japanase style. Nocturnes, but never without people, of moonlight on water, of fireworks against a velvet sky, or shadows mysterious and exquisite.

"Although they were really pretty," said Mrs. Tilling. "You have to admit that. But they didn't tell a story. I do like a picture to tell a story."

Then the Expressionists had taken their toll. Splendor of pigment, a sweeping brush, planes of color, willful distortions of form. And still, at the center, that

110

preoccupation with the ideal woman, though he delineated her with savagery.

"I didn't like any of *them*," said the housekeeper.

Nor did Lintott. But he recognized a wild design, a restless striving after solution, which he had manifest in Paris.

Finally, and sadly, a picking here and there among all these attempts, pleasing no one. The craft shone through, and something else.

"Mr. Sickert was particularly good to Mr. Nicholas," said the housekeeper. "The master would take anything from him in the way of criticism. Not that I was eavesdropping, sir, it'd only be if I came into the studio or the drawing-room with refreshment. They'd be talking, with perhaps two or three of Mr. Sickert's pupils listening to them — as if it was a theater."

★ ★ ★

"Why aren't your figures *doing* something, my dear — Carradine? Let them misconduct themselves, if you please, but let them do *something*!"

111

"Why can't I walk about in your pictures? Why is nothing exciting happening?"

"At least, you don't maul your paint."

* * *

"And sometimes Mr. Sickert would come out with peculiar suggestions. I never knew whether he meant what he said. Once I asked Mr. Nicholas, and he said he did."

* * *

"Get another studio, my dear fellow. This is far too respectable. Somewhere mean and forbidding would be just the ticket. The sordid is a great source of inspiration."

Dandy facing faultless dandy over the port and walnuts.

"Have you ever dressed up as a tramp, Carradine? Do try it. It's my idea of heaven. Of course, people will think you a rummy old bloke, but what an *insight* you get."

"*Elegy in Green*, my dear chap. What

at title! Why not *I Threw It Up in the Channel?*"

Then they would rattle off a music-hall favorite, in riotous duet, on the grand piano.

★ ★ ★

Mrs. Tilling flung up her arms in remembrance and shook her head, smiling. "I didn't know what they were on about, most of the time, sir. I only know that Mr. Nicholas talks to me now and again. He said the other week he was in Purgatory. That's a Catholic expression, meaning neither one thing nor the other. He don't know what he wants, sir, and that's the truth."

"And the same in his private life, I understand, ma'am. Did his two fiancées resemble the late Mrs. Carradine at all?"

"One did, one didn't. When I met the second young lady I thought, 'Well, here's a change!' For he favors dark-haired ladies, and she was fair. It's as if he tried to . . . wrench himself out. But it made no difference. He wasn't suited in the end, the more's the pity. And he's a great ladies' man — and some of them aren't ladies either, if you'll excuse me. Models, he calls them. I know my place, but I won't have them downstairs — while they last. Madame taught him his ways. He knows just what to say to any woman, high or low. He needs to meet his match, but he don't pick his match. He goes for these little simpering things as can't answer him back."

The canvases glimmered in the evening light, projecting their own myth. Even in landscape, even in a few minute strokes of the brush, mother and child were present. He had sought to throw them off in a hundred ways. Odette was a child in the circus audience. Gabrielle the singer in the music hall. They permeated his imagination, and the artist in Carradine struggled against the man. His obsession had a life and will of its own, demanding more attention than he should give. His awareness did not help him. For to paint them was to love them again.

"He seems to have everything a man could want," said Lintott at last. "What's worriting him?"

114

They stood in the darkening room. Puzzled, simple people, content in that station of life to which it had pleased God to call them, pondering the willfulness of his discontent.

Part Two

REFLECTIONS IN A MIRROR

'In a life like this, are we not all fugitives?
You will have no peace, but to be
stripped of everything.'

Georges Rouault

5

THE girl intrigued Carradine because he couldn't make up his mind whether she was fleeing or inviting him. He had sauntered some distance behind her, on his way to Montmartre, simply because they were walking in the same direction. She seemed to be a respectable creature of the servant class, and he had been careful not to alarm her. But when he slowed down, so did she, and the frequent glances over her shoulder began to appear more hopeful than fearful. He stopped deliberately. She looked round, paused, and stood still. Amused, he crossed the street and heard her hurrying after him. He lengthened his stride until she was almost running. Then she called, softly and timidly, "M'sieu, if you please!"

"Mam'selle?" Turning back.

"I beg your pardon, sir, but would you be kind enough to let me walk with you? I'm feared to be out at night by myself, but madame would send me with her message."

He raised his hat, offered his arm. She came up with a rush and a gasp, and clung to him childishly. Her voice was light, her tone pathetic, her accent provincial.

"I was always afraid of the dark, sir, but madame will have her way."

"The pleasure is mine, mam'selle. Perhaps I should introduce myself? Nicholas Carradine, at your service. And whom have I the honor of escorting?"

"Valentine, sir. My name is Valentine. Leastways, it wasn't Valentine until I went into service with madame. It used to be Marie-Charlotte at the orphanage, but I never thought much of Marie or Charlotte myself, and madame thought Valentine was more like a lady's maid. Although I do more than any lady's maid for her, not that I mind, along of her being so good to me, and the life very different . . ."

She stopped for breath, and the thread of the conversation.

"An uncommonly pretty name, Miss Valentine, which suits you admirably. To where may I escort you?"

"Oh, we live near the Etoile, sir. Quite a step."

"More than a step, mam'selle, and you are walking away from it."

Bewildered, she murmured something about mistaking her direction.

"Let's find a cab, shall we? I can't allow a lady to tire herself further. Surely madame doesn't expect you to do such errands on foot?"

"Well, she did give me the fare, sir, but I lost it." Woefully.

Carradine smiled down on her, and she smiled back in confusion.

"I hope you didn't lose the message as well."

"Oh, no, sir. Madame pinned it to the inside of my pocket, and the answer is pinned back there this minute."

"I see."

He studied the fine olive skin, the dark hair escaping in tendrils on neck and forehead. Given spirit, the narrow eyes and full mouth would have been alluring. But Valentine's face was as guileless and unwritten as that of a child. She had the simplicity and trust, the directness, of a child. As he helped her into the cab, he resolved to warn her against talking to strangers, but Valentine was bent on confidences.

"Marie is a holy name, sir, don't think I'm saying anything against it. Only, in the orphanage we're all called Marie and then given another name as well, and you don't half get tired of hearing it. Marie-Jeanne, Marie-Louise, Marie-this and Marie-that, all day long. I don't know what my mama and papa would have called me, if they'd lived, but it would have been something very grand. They were members of the aristocracy, you see, sir.

"You can always tell from a person's hands and features, can't you? My hands are very small" — extending them in a pair of black cotton gloves — "and my features are fine, so I'm told."

"I've been admiring those features with an artist's eyes, Miss Valentine. Why" — seeing her expression change — "how have I offended you?"

Because she was suddenly so alarmed and dejected that he feared she might try to jump out of the moving cab, he grasped the hand that grasped the window ledge.

"I never knew you were an artist, sir. I thought you were a gentleman!"

"I hope I'm both, mam'selle. Allow me to give you my card."

She clutched this, as she had clutched the ledge, as she would clutch a solitary spar in a furious sea.

"Oh, and you're foreign too," she cried, further distressed. "But you speak like a French gentleman, sir."

"I'm English," said Carradine patiently. "But my stepmother was French and taught me the language. I'm very rich, you see, mam'selle, and have nothing to do but spend money and amuse myself. So I paint pictures. I should like to paint a picture of you, in that pretty hat. And because I am rich I shall pay you one franc an hour."

She stared at him, frightened and tempted at once.

"I shall, of course, ask permission of madame, and assure her you will be quite safe with me. I can write her a letter, or call on her tomorrow, if you wish."

Valentine shook her head until the

crimson feathers trembled. The hat had belonged to someone more fashionable, and perched over her plain gray cloak and mocked her mended gloves like a rich relation. In a self-possessed girl it would have seemed ravishing. On Valentine it had an air both sad and rakish. A child dressing up.

"No, no, sir. Not madame. She'll give me such a tell-off as never was. I know I'm safe with you, sir. I knew the minute I saw you that you were a gentleman. The only thing is, sir, would it be all right to come in the afternoons when she rests? I could slip out and back and she'd never notice."

"I should prefer you to ask your mistress," said Carradine, fearing too much responsibility.

But Valentine became so incoherent and repetitive that he reassured her with a handclasp.

"Only," he insisted, "you must come in a cab. Here is my address. Show it to the cab driver. Tell him I will pay him when he delivers you safely. Then I shall send you back in another cab. Have you a further safety pin on your person, Miss Valentine, so that we can secure the address to the inside of your other pocket? And shall we say Monday?"

He had thought of everything. Her gratitude and excitement were boundless. She alighted, with a flourish of white petticoats and black-stockinged ankles, and caught up his hand and kissed it vehemently. Then her expression altered from one of radiance to one of doubt.

"You do believe that my mama and papa were members of the aristocracy, sir, don't you? It's the features you can tell by, sir."

"I know it, Miss Valentine. I know also that they would be proud to acknowledge their daughter as a beautiful young lady."

Her lips moved slightly, as though she tried out his meaning. Then she smiled again.

"Good-night, mam'selle. Until we meet again."

He watched her assume the air and carriage of a great personage as she swept away. Her gracious mounting of the steps revealed a hole in the heel of one stocking and the tattered lace edging of a cast-off underskirt. He felt amused and sorry.

* * *

The excitement of a secret assignation with a gentleman-artist, the grandeur of arriving in a cab, sustained Valentine until she entered the studio. Then old terrors seized her between their teeth and worried the truth from her, even as she unpinned her crimson hat and allowed Carradine to take her gray mantle.

"Madame says somebody must have dropped me on my head when I was a child, sir," she said, troubled.

"Madame says I'm full of foolishness. But I don't really tell lies, sir. Only I get confused about things."

Carradine, elegant even in his old clothes and streaked smock, a cheroot in his mouth, watched her walk to the window. Carefully he folded the cloak and laid it on a chair, smiled over the outrageous hat.

"I get confused too," he assured her. "We'll confuse each other, shall we? Did madame give you this wonderful piece of millinery, Miss Valentine?"

She turned hurriedly from her contemplation of Montmartre. "Oh, yes, sir. She can be kind. Something bad happened to me and I was very ill, and she came to the foot of my bed and hung the hat on the post. And she said, 'You have always wanted this, *petite*. Get well quickly and you can wear it'. So I got well, and now it's my very own."

Carradine spun it until the feathers were twirling flame.

"How do you feel when you wear this hat, mam'selle?"

She had forgotten her fears, or hopes, of seduction; of the scene that would certainly follow if madame found her absent. Her gentle eyes concentrated.

"Oh, I feel like madame in that, sir. Very brilliant. Very beautiful."

"Then I'll paint you in it, shall I?"

She glanced down at her plain black dress.

"Your gown will provide the contrast I need, Miss Valentine. I mean, of course" — as her face lengthened — "the contrast in color. Here, put it on for me. We'll pull this chair up to the table, and stand a looking-glass on the table. Then look at yourself in the glass as though you had just put on the hat. I shall have two Valentines to paint, and be twice honored."

"Do you wish me to pin it, sir?" Hopefully.

"Did Madame give you the hatpins, too?"

"No, sir, I bought them. They're very grand, aren't they?"

"Most striking" said Carradine, delighted by the incongruity of flaking imitation pearls the size of small tomatoes.

He drew the first white space of paper toward him and picked up his stick of charcoal.

"Ah! Stay like that, will you, mam'selle?"

Slim arms raised to the hat brim, pretty face intent.

"I shall only be a few minutes with this first sketch. I know it's tiring to pose in that way. You said you were brought up in an orphanage. Do you remember anything of your parents?"

For she was pursing her mouth in a most ridiculous manner, imitating portraits of society beauties, and he

128

wanted her to forget her image.

Valentine became shy and uncertain.

"Do you know what I mean, sir, if I say I can't exactly remember them but I know what they were like?"

"Perfectly. There are different kinds of truths."

She was relieved, and garrulous.

"Well then, sir, my maman was something like madame to look at. Very beautiful, very clever, very much admired by gentlemen. Gentlemen admire me too, sir, for all I'm a working girl. She had cupboards full of dresses and cloaks and a long feather boa . . ."

The boa meant much, and was slightly ahead of its time. Carradine suspected that madame had one, and Valentine coveted it.

" . . . and drawers full of gloves and silk stockings and lace handkerchiefs and fans, and one cupboard with racks and racks of shoes. And she never scolded me and she always gave me presents, not just when I was ill or she was pleased with me for dressing her hair. And my papa was tall, very tall, with thick white hair and black eyes that could read right into

129

my heart. Very rich, very strong. And he loved me better than anyone else except my maman."

"How lucky you are, Miss Valentine, to have had so much, to have loved and been loved so well. Love leaves us, you know, even when we lose it. We always know that we are special people because we have been so blessed. Where did you live? Can you remember the house?"

But she had no aptitude for mental architecture. Her sketch could have been a museum in the Tuileries. Small immediate possessions stirred her most: silk sheets, pillows edged with lace, velvet chairs, chandeliers.

"They wished me to marry a gentleman, naturally," said Valentine with a touch of hauteur. Then, tiring, "If you please, sir, might I rest my arms?"

"Certainly. Would you care for a glass of wine, mam'selle?"

She took the stem delicately between her fingers and sipped, delighted with the attention and courtesy.

"But how should I marry without a dowry?" she asked, pausing, suddenly disturbed by the practical.

"That is a difficulty without doubt. And a lady of your perception and warmth would have to find a gentleman she cared for. That is another difficulty. But all things are possible. We must hope. For myself," he added, careful to discourage any personal inclinations with a compliment, "I should not hesitate to pay court to such a pretty girl, except that I am in love already."

A little silence. The feathers drooped. His surmise had been correct.

"I daresay the lady's ever so pretty, sir," she said wretchedly.

"As pretty as you, mam'selle."

"She's lucky, isn't she?"

"You're more than gracious to say so. Shall we try another pose, with your hands in your lap, part turned toward me? No, just your body turned, and you still look into the glass. It should be no hardship. Your face is your fortune, Miss Valentine."

A woeful fortune, with real trouble behind it.

"Sir, you've been ever so kind. Might I ask you something?"

"Anything at all, mam'selle, and you

may be sure I shall not betray your confidences."

"Sir, I did meet a gentleman, but he's already married, and attached to another lady too."

"How very French of him," Carradine remarked, delighted as always with the national zest for living. "A wife, a mistress, and a charming friend. Where do you figure in his picture, Miss Valentine?"

"I don't rightly know, sir. But he loves me as I love him, only we just meet in passing, so's to speak."

Carradine laid down his charcoal and motioned her to rest. "You haven't met him alone, I hope?"

"Oh, we meet most days, sir. But though his heart's mine he isn't free."

"Let me advise you, Valentine," said Carradine firmly. "The gentleman is already doubly committed, and afflicted with a wandering eye. Don't allow your virtue to wander after it."

Two tears rolled slowly down her cheeks.

"Or has it already wandered?"

She nodded.

"My dear child, you're playing with fire, and you should keep well away from it."

"I'm expecting," said Valentine, "and I daren't tell madame."

He left his sketching block, stuck his hands in the pockets of his trousers, and paced the room in a leisurely fashion, thinking. Her eyes followed him everywhere, hoping for a miracle.

"He must give you money, of course," said Carradine at last. "And you must certainly tell madame, because these matters become apparent with time. Are you afraid she will turn you out?"

She was not sure. The scolding, being more immediate, ranked higher.

"Would it help you if I told madame? She must be told."

Valentine considered, tears following one upon the next, silently.

"What will you do otherwise, my dear girl?"

"Run away?" she suggested, as though it were a good idea.

"That would be both foolish and impractical. To where, or to whom, would you run?"

He saw that she was hoping to find protection with him.

It was typical of her naïveté.

"Trust is an excellent thing," he said bluntly, "but it can be taken too far. For instance, Valentine, you asked me to escort you home the other night. You were fortunate that I am as I am. It might have turned out very differently."

"But you're a gentleman, sir. I can always tell a gentleman when I see one," said Valentine, secure in her own brand of logic.

"So is this gentleman of yours a gentleman. Has that prevented him from acting irresponsibly, even heartlessly, in my opinion?"

She could find no answer to any of it.

"Look, let me plead with madame and take your scolding for you."

"You see, he won't give me any money, sir. He'll say it wasn't his."

"Well, suppose *I* offered her money? Would that make a difference?"

She blew her nose with a handkerchief that Carradine could only think had been borrowed from madame without her knowledge. He hoped she didn't lose it. It must have been worth several francs.

"There's another difficulty you see, sir, only I don't hardly know how to tell you."

"You wish to keep the infant? How would that be possible?"

"Oh, no, sir. I know the baby has to go. But the gentleman, sir. Madame will want to know who he is and I daren't say."

"Why not? He seems more than able to look after his own interests, even with madame likely to be after him."

"It's her protector. M'sieu Emile Roche. The Minister."

He stared at her, bemused, then threw back his head and laughed outright. She blinked at him, woebegone, the tear marks still on her cheeks.

"Oh, Valentine, Valentine! The ultimate mistake."

"You do see, don't you, sir?"

"I suggest you forget the Minister's part in this affair," Carradine counseled. "Presumably he maintains your little establishment? Well, then he is not to be embarrassed. Or you and madame might find yourselves in need of another protector. Allow me to inform your mistress that an unknown gentleman took advantage of your innocence, offer something handsome to take care of expenses, and leave it at that. And you say the same, Valentine, or we're both for the guillotine — no, I didn't mean that, I was joking! An unknown gentleman. One evening. When you were out alone. Perhaps madame will spare you errands in the dark after this revelation."

She held out both small hands, crying, "You're a good friend, sir!"

He kissed them gently, replaced them in her lap, and replied, "Now, if you are ready. One more sketch, and then you can go home. Give me an idea of madame, so that I might know how to approach her."

He had solved her problems, and her face was clear and simple once more. All was well. She could chatter without fear.

"Madame is inscrutable!"

As she spoke, her eyes narrowed in imitation and became those of a remote sphinx, and yet of an approachable alley cat.

"Incredible!"

Her fingers spread and slowly closed in admiration.

"Passionate!"

Arms akimbo, body half turned. Smiling an invitation that was wholly impersonal.

He would not for worlds have brought her roughly to reality. So, once more, the pose destroyed, he laid aside his work and smoked while Valentine became Mme. Natalie Picard. Her simple mind and pliable nature were no vehicles for the ambition that possessed her, and so she dreamed of power by means of her mistress. Power that depended upon attractiveness, wit, and cunning. Power that time would weaken. So much was evident in her portrait, which Valentine reproduced faithfully without comprehending it. Mme. Picard had reckoned on all eventualities, and prepared for them. A foolish woman would have spent her youth and beauty. Madame had invested it and would retire on the proceeds. Meanwhile, in full and glorious spate, she triumphed.

Valentine's exultant face gradually returned to its bewildered triangle. Her arms drifted to her sides. She sat, passive, mute, and stared ahead of her. The relationship between mistress and maid became evident.

"She is severe, sir. She can be very severe. And especially with me."

"Why with you, Valentine?"

Her sadness vanished.

"Will your picture of me hang in a salon, sir?"

"Perhaps. I may prefer to keep it to myself. No, I mustn't be so selfish." Seeing her disappointment. "It will be admired by thousands. Not for my work, Valentine, but for the loveliness of the sitter."

Instantly enchanted, she assumed another role.

"And perhaps a gentleman will admire it, sir, and ask who I am. At first we shan't tell him, of course." Withdrawing a little, head lifted in serene indifference. "Then I shall allow you to tell him, sir." Gracefully permitting the introduction. "Perhaps it will be my father?"

Carradine forbore to remind her

that her father was dead, and nodded encouragement.

"Or some aristocratic relative," Valentine mused, uncertain on whom to spring the glory of her identity. "Then I shall leave madame. Only I'd give her a lot of presents and invite her to dinner once a month. Yes, that'd only be right. She'd be my friend then, because we'd be as good as one another. She wouldn't be able to scold me, would she, sir?"

"Of course not, Valentine. And now I do think you should go home."

Sensitive to every intonation, she tumbled back to stern reality. Her chin quivered. She was being dismissed, and the hour, on the whole, had been a golden one.

"You shall come again," he promised. "We shall need several sittings, so that the portrait is perfect. To hang in a great gallery," he added kindly, "and to be much admired."

He set the old mantle round her small shoulders, handed her the cotton gloves. He wondered which particular fantasy he might raise to comfort her until their next meeting. But Valentine was adept at drawing dreams around herself for every occasion.

"The Minister'll have to divorce his wife and marry me when he knows who my papa is. Otherwise he might be challenged. But I'll refuse, very polite-like, of course.

"Do you know why I'll refuse him, sir?"

"I am at a loss to imagine, mam'selle."

"Because of madame, don't you see?" And she clapped her hands and laughed at his missing the subtlety of this point. "I couldn't steal madame's protector from her, now could I? I'm not ungrateful. I love madame."

"A noble sentiment," said Carradine, ushering her down the stairs, "and one which does you honor. Now, please remember to say nothing to madame of this other matter. I'll call on her myself. And recollect what we said, my dear girl. An unknown gentleman, one night, took advantage of your innocence."

Regally she held out her hand. Carradine kissed it, under the irreverent eyes of the cab driver, who had drawn his own conclusions.

"Do you know how my papa will recognize me, sir?" she cried, poking her rakish hat from the window.

"How else, mam'selle, than by your sweet countenance? No doubt the image of your mother's beauty."

"I've waited ever so long for somebody to know who I really am," said Valentine. "It'll be such a lovely day, won't it, sir?"

"You will give as much joy as you receive, Valentine, I assure you."

She was radiant, grateful.

"It'll all come right in the end, sir. God knows best, don't He?"

"Let's hope so. His ways are often mysterious to the point of sheer incomprehension."

He watched the cab hurtle recklessly away, and wondered whether life was simply a joke in extremely bad taste.

6

THE lady who reclined in the elegant clutter of her salon seemed less imposing than Valentine's reflection. Carradine had expected a mature woman of statuesque proportions, but Natalie Picard was small-boned, plump, and of a certain youth. Her years were a secret between herself and her mirror, and animation removed a few of them in a moment. She had already embarked on the losing battle between beauty and time; lying abed in the morning, coming to easy life in the afternoon, flowering exuberantly in the discreet light of evening. She aimed at twenty in dress and vivacity but could have been thirty when shrewdness took the place of coquetry. And judging by the richness of experience in those knowledgeable black eyes, the careful painting of that handsome face, her femininity was as old as time itself.

Bending over her ringed and scented

fingers, Carradine suffered nostalgia and kissed them reverently. Parisian women, he thought, sitting in the chair she indicated, make an art of being women. He began to explain the object of his visit in fluent French, at which Natalie raised both eyebrows and one rounded arm. She spoke English, she explained, and had so little opportunity to practice the language. His command of the French tongue needed no improvement. Would he be so gallant as to bear with her many imperfections?

He guessed, correctly, that she chose to speak English because her accent was ravishing. And, though she knew better than to endanger her relationship with the Minister, Carradine was a man and therefore material to be charmed. Smiling into her smiling eyes, he inclined his head and complimented her on her pronunciation. There was a further brief delay while she begged him to talk more slowly. Then she subsided into the lilac bower of her tea gown, one olive-skinned arm lying as if by chance along the back of her sofa.

She was an excellent listener and

received the account of meeting with Valentine by slight, expressive movements of face and shoulders. Clearly, his romanticism amused her. As he progressed to the girl's pregnancy she became watchful, and at the mention of money alert. When he had finished, she studied her rings and said softly but firmly that the sum mentioned would not be sufficient.

"My action is one of disinterested generosity, madame," he said coldly and translated with some impatience as she looked bewildered.

She laughed then, unamused. "Disinterested, M'sieu Carradine? When you have seduced a simple girl whose only hope is a dowry large enough to attract some peasant in the provinces?"

"You mistake my meaning, madame."

She sat up, abandoning her pose of relaxed gentility. "I mistake nothing," she said. "Nothing. I understand too well. I know men like you too well. You take pleasure and pay little for it. So, I tell you this. My poor Valentine has no friend but myself. I stand for her maman, for her papa, for them all. All of them."

She rose and paced the room, hands on hips, firing sentences at him.

"Ah, yes! You think I thank you, do you not? That I take your miserable francs?" The *r*s were rolled like a fusillade. "That I am pleased with your dis-interest? What do you know of her suffering, now and when the child is born and when she must part with it? Dis-interest is a good word, very good. You *are* dis-interested, M'sieur Carradine. You feeling nothing. Nothing. You are like the rest. *L'appetit vorace, le coeur vide!*" She flung her arms wide, reminding him of Bernhardt in *Phèdre*. "Empty! Empty! Empty!"

She paused at the gold cage by the window, where two lovebirds crooned, and surveyed them with considerable irony.

"This is not life as we know it, is it? Is it?" She observed his discomfiture and his growing anger and adjusted her mood to his. "Well, well. Forgive my enragement, M'sieu Carradine, but the girl is dear to me and cannot speak for herself."

She was now as composed as she had been furious, and returned to business.

"Come, we need not haggle, you and I. Let us say twice as much."

The roundness of her vivid face did not disguise its resolution. She would bargain if she were on her deathbed — and probably win. She knew the cost of everything.

"Madame," said Carradine, hardening, "I am not the father of Valentine's child. I promise you that. I merely wished to help the girl. The suggestion of six hundred francs on your part is a gross exaggeration, and well you know it."

Natalie reclined once more on her sofa and studied him intently. "You are not the father, no? You swear it, yes?" She shrugged, convinced and completely at a loss. "Why do you offer money if this is so?"

"Because Valentine is a child. Do you comprehend that, madame?"

She frowned, considering him. Looked round at her white-and-gold room, at the Persian cat stretched before the fire, at the little griffon on his cushion, at the love-birds in their bright cage. Substitutes for the children she must not have. Dependents she could afford to possess.

Small warmths to replace the great warmths.

"I comprehend you very well, m'sieu."

Then she reflected that seriousness ages a woman and smiled brilliantly. "You are very strange," she said on another track. "Full of sentiment. That is dangerous and can be expensive. As in this case."

"I am only too pleased to offer my original sum of three hundred francs, madame, if that is what you want."

"A thousand thanks. So my poor Valentine will bear her child in comfort. I accept for her. But I feel you bite off more than you chew — that is a good phrase, is it not? Has she confided to you the name of the father?"

He hesitated. She laughed, a rich, soft sound calculated to rouse answering laughter.

"Did she say it was M'sieu Roche?" She laughed again. "Do not be embarrassed, M'sieu Carradine. There is much you do not know of Valentine. Her world is not as this one. She is not practical like me. She is romantic, like you."

"That's something of which I am

aware, madame. I may be sentimental but I am not a total imbecile."

"So? Well then, all things in Valentine's world must be as these two foolish, pretty birds. Life must be beautiful, and it is not. Always, the father of her child is a gentleman. Ah, yes. She has been pregnated before. One still-borned, one in the country. It is difficult for me. Twice she says M'sieu Roche seduces her. For she wishes to be Natalie Picard, you comprehend, M'sieu Carradine? She loves, she fears, she envies me. Who shall know the truth? Perhaps it was a gentleman, perhaps not. But this is the first time that someone offers money. I am grateful to you. Does she tell you of her parents?"

"She mentioned they were of the aristocracy, but she seems unable to decide whether they are dead or not."

"Another dream," said Natalie calmly. "Valentine is an orphan. She is abandoned. The nuns take her in from pity. No one knows where she origins. I bring her from the *orphelinat* to be my maid. Like many orphans, she makes the family she wishes to possess. But she is also simple.

Not mad but simple. Perhaps her life is too bad to remember. Perhaps she is borned a fool. But let us speak of other matters."

She passed smoothly from one topic to another, subtly searching him out.

He touched on the matter of Odette, became involved, expansive.

"But you make a mystery of a dead sister, m'sieu? Why? She is dead. So? Pff! You are rich, naturally? Ah, yes. When one is rich one can amuse oneself. Indeed, one must. For what else does one do with time when one has everything? You are married, of course? No? Extraordinary. Such men as you marry young and regret. But do not think I have no heart. You loved your sister. It is foolish, but I comprehend. I too have a sister. She is with me since our dear papa and mama died of the *choléra. Mon bijou!"* Her face softened momentarily, then became matter-of-fact. "M'sieu Carradine, the hour of five approaches, and I expect a friend. Perhaps one evening you like to meet with my little circle? I have connections which may please you, which may be of use. We must amuse you in Paris. But, one moment, m'sieu. You must meet with my jewel. We have much in common, you and me, M'sieu Carradine, with our gentle hearts and love of our sisters."

She rose, smiling, and tugged a beaded rope. Valentine appeared, trembling.

"So you've been stupid once more, my child?" said Natalie in French, maternal. "We'll talk of this later. Don't be afraid. This gentleman has pleaded for you. Tell Mam'selle Claire I have a most charming Englishman here who would like to be introduced." As Valentine whisked out, relieved, she explained, "Claire is a little *gauche*. You have a word for it in English?"

"Shy? Modest? Awkward?"

"All these things," Natalie said vaguely. "She fears men. But you, with your heart of sentiment, will not offend her. Ah, you are here, *bijou*. M'sieu Carradine is departing, but he is so kind that you must thank him also. Our poor Valentine is pregnated again. Yes, it is foolish of her. Very sad. But since he is not the father M'sieu Carradine gives money for her *accouchement*."

As she spoke she drew the girl towards her, smiling encouragement.

"Honored, mam'selle," said Carradine, kissing the barely proffered hand.

"M'sieu Carradine makes friends with Valentine, our silly one. He has — how do you call it, m'sieu? — disinterested generousness. Just so."

In an era that obliged women either to be or to seem pliable, Claire Picard vaunted a defiant independence. Tracing their kinship, in coloring and features, Carradine guessed the girl to be some years younger. In contrast to Natalie's flamboyance, Claire was dressed with girlish severity in a high-necked blouse and skirt that showed her ankles to advantage. Where Natalie was willfully provocative, Claire was simply willful. Where Natalie was seductive, Claire was reserved. Carradine suspected that if her defensiveness did not mar a man's interest her tongue probably would. But of this he had no proof, since she spoke not a single word.

"A broken engagement. A broken heart," Natalie confided in a whisper as she escorted him to the door of her apartment. "Ah, we Frenchwomen! We are all heart."

Carradine reflected that there was nothing amiss with their heads either, but did not say so. He murmured a suitably sympathetic remark and promised to attend a soirée soon.

He was almost thrown aside in the hallway by the impetuous entrance of a very young man. They exchanged apologies and compliments, while Valentine smiled and curtsied.

"And who is he?" Carradine asked, watching the boy take the stairs three at a time. "A visitor for Mam'selle Claire?"

"Oh, no, sir. For madame. He is madame's little friend. M'sieu Paul Roche, the Minister's son."

"Madame's obsession with children is quite extraordinary," said Carradine, grinning.

Valentine stood on tiptoe and confided softly to his ear.

"Sir, M'sieu Paul is not what he seems. It was he who . . . " She spread her little hand over the gentle rounding of her abdomen.

"You may trust me not to speak of

this," Carradine assured her solemnly. "Madame must never know. It will be our secret, Valentine."

His gravity and kindness kept this dream, too, safe for her. Impulsively she kissed his hand.

The weather was cold but fine. He decided to walk. Gradually the compassion he felt for Valentine was replaced by his amused admiration for Natalie, his amused curiosity over Claire. Suddenly he whirled his cane in the air and laughed aloud. He adored them all.

7

"THE trunks are all locked, sir, but I'll find the keys. Mr. Nicholas has one set. I have the other. Not that anybody'd want to steal them. It's just habit on my part," said Mrs. Tilling. "You'll get yourself in a rare mess up here, sir. You can't keep an attic like the rest of the house. Let me find you an overall, and of course if you want to take a bath afterward . . . "

"A bit of dust won't hurt me," Lintott replied, eyes keen, face lifted, as though he scented something. "Thankee kindly, ma'am."

"There we are!" she cried in triumph, selecting keys. "Twenty years after, sir, and I still know where everything is. Now I'll leave you to it, and if you should require anything you know where to find me."

She departed, leaving Lintott in his candle-lit treasure house. The Inspector placed a square hand on the rocking

154

horse and set it in motion, childishly. It began to move nowhere, nostrils arched, head bent. He opened the nearest trunk, then another and another, gauging their contents. Then he set to work in earnest, burrowing like a mole in the profusion.

Walter Carradine had thrown nothing away. A small fortune in clothes was packed in tissue, lavender sachets, and mothballs. Lintott spread several old copies of *The Times*, furnished by Mrs. Tilling, and laid out the contents with care. Nothing escaped him. A crumpled lace handkerchief thrust into a pocket, a note in a netted purse from Odette to her mother. *Maman chérie, je t'aime toujours, Odette.* A family of wax-faced dolls, exquisitely dressed in pin-tucked gowns and underwear, in plush bonnets and mantles, staring at their surroundings after a long incarceration. Exercise books scrawled in French and English. Reading primers in both languages. *Dear Papa, I am clever. Love from your Odette.* The child was alive again in the attic, demanding and vital.

"Poor little lass," said Lintott to himself. "I could never see the sense of a child dying. Never."

A story, written and illustrated by Carradine for his sister. Sewn together to form a book of five pages.

Once upon a time there was an enchanted princess called Odette. She did not know she was a princess. She thought she was someone else . . .

"That's him all over!" Lintott snorted. "She'd have to be something different, now wouldn't she?"

A fair likeness of the child had been used for the cover. The Inspector surveyed it, head on one side, critically.

"Very good!" he commented and put it aside and pulled out a bundle of letters. "I suppose these are from Mr. Walter Carradine when they were courting."

But they were not. Written in French, signed "Papa" or "Maman." Daily news, political news, remembrances of the last holiday, hopes for the next holiday, were imprisoned in a language unknown to him. But he formed an impression by their bulk.

"They didn't half stick together. Not a sheet, not a line, from her husband? Did she throw them away then? Probably.

156

This here divine marriage seems a bit one-sided to me."

Gabrielle's housekeeping books, immaculately and minutely kept. Paid bills that made Lintott's eyebrows climb. And then six locked volumes and one unlocked bound in blue leather. None of the keys was small enough. Dexterously Lintott picked all the locks with a hairpin lying in the dust and opened the top volume. All he could make out were the dates. He applied himself to the others and guessed them to be the diaries kept from Gabrielle's marriage to the death of the child in 1882. The last entry was made in June of that year, the rest of the book was blank.

Confounded, he stared at the elegant foreign hand. It was like watching a criminal escape down a street while you stood at a high window. He collected them and placed them with the letters. After further thought he added the account books, though he had not much hope of them. Still, you never knew.

"I shall need help with these," he said, puzzled. "I can't hardly ask him to come back home, and yet I'm foxed. It'll have to be somebody as I trust too."

He straightened up slowly. You couldn't call it rheumatism, but his joints were stiff and reluctant to perform. He looked round at the luxurious disarray, then went to find the housekeeper. Helpless and guilty. Under his arm, wrapped in newspaper, was tucked possible evidence.

★ ★ ★

Lintott finished his stew with considerable relish and drew a slice of bread round his plate to sop up the last of the gravy.

"Is that good enough for you then, John," Bessie inquired with a hint of sarcasm, "after all the foreign cooking?"

He shook his head slowly from side to side, grinning at her tone, and watched her move from oven to table and back. Currant pudding and custard.

"That was capital, my lass. Capital. Bess, do you recollect our Lizzie learning French?"

"Oh, she not worriting with that nonsense now."

"An inquiring mind," said Lintott pensively.

For the girl had tried to teach herself, and he had found tuppence for a secondhand primer.

"She's best off with a family of her own, and well she knows it. I never saw the sense of learning for learning's sake."

An old problem, sorely felt and insoluble. He would have been glad to shelve it.

"You don't suppose, Bessie, as she might still know enough to help me out with these French diaries, do you?"

"I can slip round after supper and ask her if you like."

"No, no. Sit yourself down. I'll take a turn in the air myself, I think. I haven't seen her in a week or two."

Communing with his pipe, knowing he could have done no more for the girl than he had done, knowing it was not enough.

Bessie, divining his trouble, said, "Water under the bridge, John. That's what you always say. She couldn't have a better husband than Eddie. I daresay he'll set with the children while she comes here."

So Lizzie washed her hands and sat at the parlor table, a little flustered with importance and pleasure, while her father untied the parcel of diaries. A battered French dictionary stood by to refresh her memory.

"Now then," Lintott began awkwardly, "if you can't help me, my dear, I'll have to fetch Mr. Carradine from Paris, and I'd rather not do that. I needn't say," he added, becoming a policeman, "as this is all confidential."

Lizzie shook her head, picked up the first volume, ran her fingers lightly over the embossed blue leather, and sniffed the pages.

"You're a regular detective yourself, my dear!" he said, admiring.

"I always do that, Father. I like the feel and smell of a book."

There was no reproach, but he sat humbly beside her, hands knotted between his knees, as she scanned the pages.

"Can you make it out, my love? It don't matter if you're on the rusty side."

"Oh, I'm not rusty," said Lizzie. "I've kept it up, Father, along of teaching the children as they get older."

"Waste of time!" Bessie pronounced, slightly jealous of their closeness, though she loved them both.

Lintott recognized himself in his daughter as she raised a strong, plain face.

"We'll never agree on that, Mother, so let it be."

Bessie sniffed and opened her mending basket ostentatiously. Lintott and Lizzie exchanged a smile.

"Shall you write it out, Father, while I read it? I shall be slow enough."

He nodded and reached for pen and paper. Became a policeman once more.

"You're not to repeat a word of this, mind, either of you," he warned his womenfolk. "Now, Lizzie, I'm not interested in chit-chat about society and the weather. So read it out until I stop you, then go slow. We might have to put a night or two in on this lot, if Eddie don't mind, but we'll see. Start away, my love."

Then he settled down to frequent dips in the inkwell, while Lizzie brought Gabrielle Carradine to life.

The socks had long since been darned

161

and folded by the time Lintott leaned back and stretched and ordered a pot of tea for all. As Lizzie had translated, he had edited ruthlessly, making notes and comments. Now he lit his pipe and watched the two women pondering on a world unknown to them.

"And *I* pulled him up about thinking wild," he remarked in the silence.

★ ★ ★

Gabrielle's triannual flights from respectability and a dull, devoted husband. Meetings with D. chaperoned by Berthe. Unchaperoned meetings with D. in a rendezvous previously arranged. Sauntering in the Tuileries, parasol against a glittering sun. Conversations whispered on spindly iron chairs as Paris took the spring air. The city, cold with snow, warm with promise. The long lazings in bed while the first fire of autumn soared in the grate and cast shadows on a high ceiling. Happiness, until he stole the child.

★ ★ ★

162

"Where's the list of passengers?" Lintott asked himself and ferreted it out while his tea cooled. "No go. The only D. in the lot is a Miss Damien, sixty. He must have got away. But he took the little girl on that train all right! I swear it!"

"I wonder it her poor husband ever read those diaries after she passed over," said Bessie, nursing her cup.

"Well, if he did he never said anything," Lintott replied dryly. "He was like those three monkeys, meaning no disrespect to the gentleman. Neither heard, saw, nor spoke evil."

"He couldn't afford to face the truth," said Lizzie unexpectedly. "She was an angel to his mind. You don't question angels, in case they turn out to be something worse. I'll bet he just had everything locked up and put away without looking."

"She was a proper bad lot," Bessie pronounced judgment.

"Was she beautiful, Father?" Lizzie asked wistfully.

"A regular bobby-dazzler. Not my style, of course," he added hastily.

"She seemed to be other men's style,

from all account." Bessie sniffed.

But the revelation had been richer, more titillating than a novelette. She would have liked to read it by herself, all over again, in delicious secrecy, and condemned every word. Lizzie was quiet, knowing that passion belonged to favored women, and always would.

"I still don't see why she took against Berthe," Lintott mused. "She gives no details of this here . . . kidnapping. Just says D. *has* her."

"If he got her away from the nurse on a pretext of some sort, wouldn't Mrs. Carradine blame her, Father?"

"The nurse might've been in the plot," said Bessie, well versed in paper romance. "He might've bribed her to let the child go, and Mrs. Carradine found out."

"Mother! Don't talk so soft! That nurse had been with Mrs. Carradine all those years. She wouldn't do a thing like that."

"She's a foreigner, isn't she?" said Bessie indignantly. "We don't know how they might behave."

"Now, now, now," Lintott ordered. "Stop your clatter. No, Bessie, I can't go along with that ingenious notion of yours, my dear. I've got a fair idea of old Berthe, and bribes don't come into it. I daresay Lizzie's nearer the mark. Mrs. Carradine thought the world of that little girl. I can see her flying up and striking out, right and left — and Berthe was the nearest to hand and probably guilty of neglect. Let the child go off for a walk with Mr. D., or something of that sort. She'd known him after all for — when does the first entry come in? — five years."

"Disgusting!" said Bessie. "She must've gone straight off as soon as the baby was born."

"*Mon beau printemps,*" said Lizzie quietly, without condemnation. "He must have thought the world of her, Father. He didn't mean the little girl any harm. He was only using her to fetch Mrs. Carradine after him."

Lintott removed his pipe from his mouth, astonished.

"*Only?*" he cried. "What's come over you, Lizzie? You don't kidnap a six-year-old girl, get killed on a train, and spoil folk's lives, and somebody says *only*!"

165

"I don't know what you were thinking about, love," said Bessie, frowning and shushing.

"Anyhow," said Lintott, mollified, "that's beside the point. "When I tell Mr. Carradine this little batch of news he'll have me haring after that Berthe. And there wasn't a mention of where she lived, or a letter from her to the lady, in those papers."

"There wouldn't be," said Lizzie, silenced on one opinion but offering another. "She was a peasant, Father. She couldn't read or write, I expect."

"Oh," said Lintott.

Skirmishes between Bessie and Lizzie, with the Inspector acting as a peaceful referee, had been frequent. Skirmishes between Lintott and Lizzie were to be avoided.

"Have you been through Mr. Carradine's papers, John?" Bessie asked quickly.

"Not yet." He recollected his double position, as head of the family and confidential detective. "I'll fetch your mantle, Lizzie. Time you went home."

Escorting her through the quiet of a Richmond midnight, he said shyly, "I'm much obliged to you, my love."

"I enjoyed it, Father. It makes a change."

Her intelligence had always been a block over which the family stumbled: unable to comprehend the use of it, financially helpless to encourage it.

"You should have been a man," said Lintott uneasily. "A woman with a brain is like a race horse in a farmyard, neither use nor ornament."

"You know my views on that, Father. We'd best not argue."

"Just don't get mixed up with this suffragette business, my girl. You know what the old Queen thought of it, God rest her."

"If a woman is fit to rule a country, why isn't she fit to vote?"

"Well, well, well. If women are to do men's work, what are the men to do? We can't all be earning a living. That's common sense, that is, Lizzie."

She was silent, needing his affection more than his approbation. He patted her shoulder, inadequate for once.

"Nothing's wasted," he comforted her. "Look how your French turned out

167

tonight. I'd have been lost without you. Think of that, my love."

She kissed his left muttonchop whisker, then opened her garden gate.

"A woman's place is in the home," said Lintott stoutly. "Always has been, always will be. The hand that rocks the cradle rules the world, my love. You've more influence over us, and a better influence, that way."

Her nod was mere good manners.

"How should we manage without you looking out for us?" he cried after the faded violet mantle.

"You needn't fret, Father," said Lizzie, trapped by love and circumstance. "We need looking after just as much."

"That's all right then. God bless you, my love, and good night."

But he shook his head now and again on the way home.

"That's one case as I've never got to the bottom of," he said to himself. "I can't always understand a woman when she's being a woman. When she's trying to be a man I'm floored."

* * *

Lintott sat at Walter Carradine's mahogany roll-top desk and marveled at love's patience and blindness. The diary entries were tender, brief, stating fact and commenting on it with affection. Gabrielle's letters, tied with a ribbon, were her only concession to romance.

"I hope he got more out of them than I have," Lintott commented. "They seem pretty cold stuff to me. If he'd stopped to think — well, he didn't want to think, did he? — he'd have seen she was being coerced by both sides. I daresay he put it down to maidenly modesty. After the marriage she could have told him night was day, and he'd have reckoned she was right."

The recorder that was his mind set Gabrielle's diary against Walter's and found deception.

Walter: *My dear wife telegraphed me today, advising me to postpone my visit for the coming weekend. Odette is staying with a friend of the family, and Gabrielle wishes me to avoid the disappointment of her absence. She thinks for us all.*

Gabrielle: *D. has her. I have questioned Berthe continually, but she has no cause to distrust him. Today I telegraphed Walter. How should I explain her absence? I cannot endure his patience and his questions. It is difficult enough to explain to my parents. Such thread-bare reasons, and yet they accept them, and Berthe, of course, supports me in everything.*

"There you are, you see," said Lintott, puzzled. "Still the confidential maid. No sign of a rift there."

Walter: *I received the terrible, the incredible news that Odette has been killed in a train accident. Gabrielle is prostrate with grief. I am waiting for a cab to take me to Victoria.*
Gabrielle: *Gone, both gone. I am dismissing Berthe, I cannot bear even to see her. Maman arranges everything. But, gone, gone, gone. All gone.*

Then blank entries in her diary until June 1882. And two lines:

This must be the new life. What emptiness! The child died as I live, by fire.

But Walter had recorded with loving care and kindness the weeks between:

We returned last night. Gabrielle has sent Berthe back — to her village. She says she can bear no one near her who reminds her of Odette. I spoke with the poor creature before she left Paris and assured her she should not want. I wished to remonstrate, in the kindliest fashion, with Gabrielle, but she was too unwell.

Gabrielle seemed a little better today and came downstairs for dinner, though she ate nothing.

Gabrielle rose at noon today but retired early with a headache.

Gabrielle and I sat together this evening, and once or twice she spoke to me with quite a composed aspect. I believe she is recovering a little.

Nick comes home tomorrow. I have great hopes for his visit, since Gabrielle was always fond of him. Perhaps he can help her as I evidently cannot.

And then, in January 1884, the simple words: *She died today. 2:55 p.m.*

Afterwards, comments on Nicholas Carradine's progress at school, his hopes for the boy's career in the family business. Only two references to his loss. He had written to inform Berthe, and he had asked Gerard Lasserre to allow him to be buried in Paris when his own time came.

Lintott was not a fanciful person, but the thought of a good Englishman lying in foreign soil beside an unfaithful wife disturbed his notion of propriety.

He turned to Walter's account books and traced a payment, equivalent to £200, care of M. le Curé, Paimpol, Brittany, for Berthe Lecoq.

"Mrs. Tilling" — as the housekeeper appeared with a laden tea tray — "how old would Berthe be now, at a guess? Oh, I do enjoy a hot muffin."

"I can only reckon by guessing, sir, and that's the truth. She never mentioned her age. She'd be around forty when madame — first engaged me, and that was — bless me! — twenty-eight years ago. Close to seventy, sir."

"A strong woman, Mrs. Tilling? Hardy constitution?"

172

"Oh, yes, sir. She had the constitution of an ox, if you'll excuse the expression."

"Then she could still be alive. Mrs. Tilling, I have to ask you this though I don't like to. Could anyone have bribed Berthe, in any way, to betray either her mistress or Miss Odette?"

"Oh, no, sir! She'd have laid down her life for madame or the child. I'll say that for Berthe. She might have been difficult, but she *was* loyal."

"Mrs. Carradine sent her back to her village, you know," Lintott continued conversationally, "just like that. Said she couldn't bear anyone round her who reminded her of the child. How does it strike you, knowing them both?"

The housekeeper's face was a struggle between curiosity and respect.

"Very peculiar, sir. I never realized. Nobody said anything to that effect, but it was all confusion and trouble. We had to be careful not to say anything to madame, except about the running of the house."

"What would you have expected Mrs. Carradine to do when she lost her daughter?"

173

"Cling to an old friend as spoke her own language, sir."

"That's what I thought. Well, Berthe offended her some way. I don't know how. It'll be my job to find out."

"Madame could fire up, sir, but she was never what I'd call cold-blooded. And that's what it does seem, don't it, to send Berthe back? You see, sir, Berthe had been nearly thirty years with madame. There'd be nobody left as she knew in her village. If Mr. Nicholas was to pension me off this minute and send me back to Shropshire — where I was born and raised until I got wed — it'd be like a death sentence."

Lintott had revealed as little as he wanted to and gained as much as he expected.

"Well, well, well, ma'am. There may have been a good reason as we know nothing about. She might even have asked Mrs. Carradine if she could go back. Thankee kindly, just the same. I don't mean to upset you, you know, ma'am."

For the housekeeper was suffering from a vision of being returned to

Shropshire in her old age.

"You're like my Bessie," said Lintott kindly, chiding her. "I've only to mention matches for her to think the blessed house is afire."

8

"MY dear Natalie has not given this soirée without good reason," said Emile Roche, bowing to Nicholas, "and I am delighted to meet the object of it."

His diction was correct to the point of pedantry, his accent so pure that only the pedantry betrayed him. A short and dapper man of sixty, with a head of thick silver hair, a thin-bridged nose, and heavy-lidded brown eyes, he surveyed Carradine. His air of ironic amusement was habitual.

"I should warn you, my friend, that Madame Picard never, in fact, gives anything without demanding some return. And here it is, arrayed — as Count Montesquieu said to Bernhardt at La Duse's première — like Iphigenia brought to sacrifice. My sweet Claire, I kiss your little hand."

Natalie's sister was in the sort of mood that Mrs. Tilling would have denounced briskly as 'a paddy.' Behind her, Natalie smiled enough for both of them.

"My Claire speaks of nothing but M'sieu Carradine since three days. His generousness, his disinterest, the small sister. You capture our hearts, m'sieu."

Claire had apparently talked her admiration out, because she found nothing to say at the appropriate moment.

"You are an artist of considerable repute, sir," said Emile Roche, though he had never personally heard of him. "Do you perhaps accept commissions? Madame Picard, I feel, would grace any canvas — "

"Ah, no, my dear! Claire, now, is a better matter — "

"Oh, it is to be Claire, is it? I knew it was to be one of you. I beg your pardon, madame."

But he had made the mistake on purpose, out of mischief.

"Forgive me," Carradine replied, "but I don't accept commissions. They place demands upon me which I find unacceptable. But if Miss Claire would consent to my portraying her as I see her, that is another affair entirely."

"But what delight!" Natalie cried. "She accepts at once, do you not, my angel?"

The girl's voice was unexpectedly rich, low-pitched, and decisive, her frankness even less expected, and she spoke deliberately in her own language.

"Let's not pretend I have a choice, Natalie. Let's at least be honest with each other."

Natalie was piqued, Roche amused, Carradine surprised and a little sorry. She was trapped in this situation, or others like it, however defiant. Her absurdly virginal white dress, with its discreet sprinkling of pink rosebuds, became as bizarre as Valentine's hat. It was a costume, not a part of her.

"You mistake me, mamselle," he said, good-natured. "I wish to paint you."

She shrugged, disbelieving him.

"Your maid will be an excellent chaperon," he suggested.

"But that is not necessary," said Natalie. "We do not insult our guest this way. Besides, I have need of Valentine myself. So that is settled. Please to make your rendezvous. Thursday will be excellent for us. And for you,

M'sieu Carradine? That is good. Come, Emile, Madame Villard wishes to speak with you."

She smiled brilliantly as she turned away, but Claire said vehemently to Nicholas, "Don't trouble to pay me compliments. They are useless, I assure you."

He could have laughed out loud, and his inner enjoyment must have conveyed itself. Her eyebrows contracted, her lips thinned. She left them without another word.

Roche, admiring the girl's long back and narrow waist, said, "Make sure of your goods before you purchase them, my friend. More than one man has thought her spirited and found her cold. Natalie is the only head among the three of them. I see her, in ten years' time, giving yet another evening for Claire, putting out yet another of the unfortunate Valentine's mistakes to foster parents. And so it will go on, until we are too old to care. You find our little Claire interesting?"

She was mentally and physically apart from everyone. The back, so resolutely presented to Carradine, looked arrogant.

But in the mirror on the wall her face seemed pale and lost. The coquetry of one silk rosebud, perched an inch above her right ear, mocked her reflection. In obedience to a nod from Natalie she moved away to speak to someone else, and the glass filled with other faces.

"I find her very sad," Carradine replied and addressed himself to the wine, which was good but not excellent.

"I am sure Madame Villard has no need of my compliments," said Roche, nodding toward a group of men who concealed everything but an animated green ostrich feather. "Now there is a woman who has made a triumph of her ugliness. Her wit is quite superb. M'sieu Carradine, Natalie keeps her best wine elsewhere. Let us seek a little privacy in the *petit salon* and take a bottle with us. There is nothing for you here." Observing him shrewdly. "We need have no pretense, as our charming Claire remarked. This is a flesh market, my friend, and you would prefer conversation, would you not? I too. When one has dined and made love one becomes weary of the flesh."

Sitting together in the small gold and white-paneled room, they relaxed over their first bottle. The second loosened their tongues, and the truth.

"You met my son Paul the other day, I believe? Another of Natalie's favorites. She is his mistress, of course. Were you about to say something polite and innocuous?"

Carradine laughed suddenly, throwing back his head.

"I am a realist," Roche continued, smiling. "Why should I mind? No, my friend. The boy wishes to become a man. I am saved the expense of keeping a mistress for him as well as for myself. There is no harm in this little affair. He will leave her eventually, but she knows that. She is very sensible. Naturally I say nothing either to him or to her. I do nothing. I appear to know nothing. But we understand each other very well, she and I."

He had seen most things in his sixty years, looking at life ironically down his fine nose, brown eyes unsurprised. Life was an untidy business. He had turned it into art.

181

"As for Claire, I have some knowledge of women, but I assure you she is a mystery to me. Sometimes I have wondered whether she inclined toward women rather than men. You understand me? But I think not. No. She may well be cold, of course, but so was Pompadour. Yet Pompadour was practical and made pretense of passion. This one is impractical. But if you are interested in solving riddles, my friend . . . "

Carradine said, "Perhaps Mam'selle Claire is searching for love?"

The Minister dismissed this notion with a gesture. "What is love?" he asked and did not wait for an answer. "Natalie can scarcely keep up the image of the virgin sister for much longer. Virginity sours with keeping. Claire is young, but not so young, and time is on the side of no woman. One does not ask, but one does speculate how old she might be. They have been in Paris for six years. She was then said to be seventeen — though Madame Picard now furiously denies this. Shall we broach another bottle?"

Carradine shook his head. The room

was too warm, the disclosures too sincere, for comfort.

"So Madame Picard is trying to find some honest farmer in the provinces who will marry Valentine for the consideration you so kindly provided, my friend. The girl is a constant embarrassment."

"I can't imagine a farmer being Valentine's idea of a husband," said Carradine with some compassion.

"Oh, she is resisting the suggestion with what little power she possesses, certainly. But it is her weakness that fights best for her. The balance here is a delicate one" — Roche tapped his forehead. "If one presses too hard it may shatter, and then . . . " He spread his hands and pursed his lips. "So Madame Picard dare not go too far, and the situation remains the same. I am told," he went on in a different tone, "that you are uncovering the secrets of the past, m'sieu."

"Which must have struck you as a highly impractical procedure, M'sieu Roche."

Roche shrugged. "Impractical, yes. But also dangerous, my friend. Is life not perilous enough for you without challenging it to do its worst? I believe you are trying to discard a dream. But why? A dream should be cherished because it can never be realized. That is its beauty."

Carradine judged them to be amicable enough for personal revelation.

"May I ask what dream you may possibly cherish, M'sieu Roche?"

"One that would be ruined if ever I met her again. She will be a stout and handsome grandmother by now. I was enraptured, as a young man, with this lovely creature whose parents discouraged my courtship. They found her a better match. Had she been my daughter I should no doubt have done the same."

He spoke of his youth as he spoke of his son, with a wry and affectionate detachment.

"But how I suffered," he observed quietly. "With that infinite capacity for suffering that only the young possess. Much later I discovered that I had a choice in life — to suffer or to compromise." The peaked eyebrows, the heavy lids, the well-kept hand holding the stem of his wine-glass. "Keep your sister in your heart and memory, my friend, where she and you are safe."

"Your advice, m'sieu, is excellent. But like most good advice it is often given and seldom taken. My Nimrod, in the shape of an English detective, is already tracking down his ghostly quarry."

"A pity. The Fates are notoriously mischievous." He smiled, connecting them with someone else. "What a fascinating woman Madame Picard is! A glorious set of contradictions. For instance, she poses as one who has no illusions, and yet enjoys the pretense of family grandeur. After six years, my friend, and much tenderness, I have never succeeded in discovering her origins. It is a matter of no consequence, as it would be in a wife, and frankly I do not *care*. But sometimes it amuses me to question her and receive yet another embellishment of the dream. When I catch her out in an inconsistency she either denies it or repeats the inconsistency even more firmly than before." He spread his arms. "And I do not care, my friend. She could tell me anything about herself and I would not care. Ah, how infinitely amusing I find her!"

Both men turned guiltily as the door opened.

"Madame Picard has sent us a more exquisite reproach?" said Roche easily. "Is she terribly angry with us, Claire? You will pardon me, M'sieu Carradine, I must make my excuses to her. I have been enchanted to make your acquaintance."

He smiled and bowed to both of them and sauntered out.

"I wish," said Carradine spontaneously, "that Whistler hadn't painted a girl in a white dress reflected in a mirror. He has stolen you from me. Do you know the picture to which I refer?"

An evening's resistance had wearied her. She stood, mute and pretty, against the door. She shook her head.

"Won't you sit down and talk, or listen, for a few minutes?" he asked, knowing they would remain undisturbed, realizing that Natalie and Roche had maneuvered them together.

With his customary detachment he saw that the wine, conversation, and flattering confidences had been merely bait. Roche had appealed to his inmost weaknesses: masculine vanity, the desire to solve mysteries, the belief that he could face truths unacceptable to most people. And ruefully he admitted that Roche had been successful: that he, Nicholas Carradine, wanted to reach this remote and angry girl, to find her out in flesh and mind and spirit, knowing all her circumstances, and to say, "This was simple, with me." He regretted his vulnerability. He regretted that Roche had apparently used rather than befriended him. He would have liked to believe there was a genuine rapport between them. There might be, but he would never know.

Claire was making the effort to speak in English. Natalie must have cowed her temporarily.

"I am fatigued and shall not be very amusing for you, m'sieu."

"If you're tired, mam'selle, then sit down. Oh, over there if you wish. I'm not in the habit of making love to unwilling young ladies." He added, with considerable irony, "Particularly so publicly, and especially because those round us want it to happen."

He had unconsciously adopted her earlier attitude, and she looked startled.

"You needn't worry," he said, annoyed by everyone, including himself. "I am in no mood for compliments, mam'selle."

And indeed he was already bored by the situation. She would become another pretty girl, and there had been so many. He lived, with the clarity bestowed by wine, through the whole affair from start to finish, and no longer desired it. He desired a woman who could be that passion, that completion, that at-last-contentment be achieved with paint and brush. He desired a woman who could make him her servant, who could show him his inadequacies, who could transcend him and yet love him. He desired a woman brighter, better, more powerful than himself. He desired Galatea, made flesh by his own hand.

This sorrowful, virginal coquette whose only interest lay in the defiance he might melt — if he were cunning enough — was no answer to his needs. She was there if he cared to amuse himself, and amusement had grown stale long since with repetition. How would he paint her?

As he had painted girls in the past, faults hidden that they might not destroy his ideal? What were her faults, that he might explore them for a change?

"Smile for me," he commanded.

Her eyes narrowed. She grimaced, and he saw that her teeth, though white and even, sloped slightly inward. Absorbed, he walked all round her chair, and she sat tensely, staring at nothing — or at something terrible and inevitable that only she could see. Her corset was cleverly padded. He perceived the line of velvet that gave an extra inch to her bust. Her arms were faintly freckled; there was a mole beneath the hairline at the back of her neck. Her curls were natural enough and strong enough to prevent a perfectly smooth chignon. He visualized them as wires, rough and uncontrolled. Her body scent, beneath the docile, flowery perfume, was green and sharp.

"You wear the wrong perfume," he stated impersonally. "Your dress is wrong too. But I should like to paint you. Regard it simply as a professional consideration. If not you, then another. I am never short of models."

She drew a long breath and said in her controlled, dark voice, "I am not a cattle market, m'sieu," then her control deserted her. She spat something at him in French. Not an obscenity, but the worst that she was able to put into words at that moment.

He stood indicted of bad manners and a fundamental unworthiness.

"Leper!" she said, standing up and facing him.

Social leper. Spoiler of good bargains in the marriage market. Cut by a brother and an uncle in the Garrick Club. That chap Carradine, something wrong there, you know. They made their money in the wine trade. Not a gentleman.

"Woman-hater!"

He had never thought of the girls involved, except to be genuinely sorry for them, except to assure them that he was not good enough and they would be happier with a better man. So they had been, all of them, eventually. Now he saw them as the discarded, and sensed what it must have meant to them personally. Two had been sent abroad to recover and returned for the next season. He had felt each imagined stroke of the pen, in his mind, as the mamas crossed him off the list of eligibles. For he minded, though he always said he did not, what people thought of him. And he admitted, in this instance, that their distrust was justified. Had he hated those girls? He had never remotely considered it. Then he remembered the distinct flash of relief beneath the self-reproach, the beautiful apologies, the brilliant explanations. Perhaps, in an odd way, he had enjoyed hurting their feminine esteem. He had reached them, that way, as he never reached them in courtship.

Claire recollected the English term and delivered it a couple of tones richer and more deliberate than usual.

"Bastard!"

None of them, of course, had challenged him in this fashion. Not even Evie Harrison. They had grown paler and somewhat smaller. He pictured them in the only abandonment open to young ladies, the abandonment of shamed and bewildered tears in the privacy of a girlish bedroom. It took a failed French courtesan to swear at him.

Boyhood phrases came unexpectedly to his lips.

"Steady on," Carradine cautioned. "Hush up."

He had halted her simply because she didn't know the idiom. They looked at each other warily. She made a face. He smiled. Then they both laughed.

"What is that 'hush up'?" she asked, hands over mouth.

"It means talk a little less forcibly, mam'selle. But I must ask your pardon for my own behavior — "

"No, no, no. Not the English gentleman, if you please. I mislike him. So stiff, so polite, so nothing."

"All right. I'm sorry. I really am very sorry. Won't you let me paint you? You don't have to be my mistress, you know," he added charmingly. "If I made love to every girl I painted I'd never do any painting."

She assessed him slowly and shrewdly. "We shall make a contract, you and I, m'sieu. Let us be friends. That way we are all happy. They need not know. Let them think as they please themselves."

"The bond of artist and sitter, mam'selle.

Did you know there was one? Oh, yes, indeed. So very close, and so very far. The immediate and the untouchable. That should suit us both."

He was back in an old and delicious habit, speaking partly in English, partly in French. For Gabrielle's command of the language had never been more than adequate, and he had learned her tongue out of love, so that he might explain himself fully. Claire, stumbling, guessing, correcting herself, followed him. He sensed there was no coquetry in this. She was unlike the imperious deity, his stepmother, who had accepted his tribute and never sought to improve herself. Claire was trying out words and phrases, to catch up with him.

"Who buys your clothes, mam'selle?"

"My sister. You knew that? Then why did you ask? And my perfume that you say is wrong, she buys that too. So that the gentlemen think I am silly and pretty. A pretty fool. Is that what you paint. m'sieu? Pretty fools?"

"I did," said Carradine, "but I'll try to change. Perhaps that was part of my problem."

"Perhaps my problem is not to be a pretty fool."

She was as absorbed, as contemplative of this idea as he of his work. She had puzzled about herself and her place in the scheme of things and found no solution.

"They will hope," she said, warning him. "They hope you will take me away, and then they need not keep me."

"That will be their amusement. Are we agreed on friendship?" He held out his hand.

Half smiling, half frowning, she took it and pledged herself in an English handshake. Now that he had promised not to court her she wanted to make him betray his interest in her as a woman. But he bowed and bade her good night.

By herself, she wandered over to the glass and scrutinized her reflection. The silk rosebud struck her as ridiculous. She unpinned it in a leisurely fashion, tried it in different positions, then moved away and sat with it in her hand for a long time. Yet she resented his taking her at her word. For six years she had played the part, however sincerely, of a woman who was both desirable and unobtainable. For six years other men had played a supporting role to this remote princess. The rules had been broken in a matter of moments, and she must find herself in another role, that of a friend.

Natalie, seeing her bemused and softened, said, "So you like our impractical M'sieu Carradine?"

"I think him interesting."

"Keep your head, *bijou*. This is one who runs away from reality and from women. Make sure that his gifts are not all flowers and compliments. Ah, what it is to have an honest man who accepts the truth about himself and you — and pays for it."

She meant Emile Roche.

9

"**I** CAME over to see the Incoherent Group, as they were nicknamed, some thirteen years ago. They were exhibiting in a café on the Champ-de-Mars. Gauguin, Emile Bernard, young painters who had worked with them in Brittany. They were one of the attractions of the Great Fair of 1889, and in my opinion surpassed the more popular attraction of the Eiffel Tower. I prefer internal views to external ones, and in any case I detest iron skeletons — am I boring you?"

No, she was expanding as he talked, realizing he was well away from her.

"Have you seen Paris from the top of the Tower, mam'selle?"

"Oh, yes." As part payment for her company, with a a man she preferred to forget.

"How much does art interest you, mam'selle? How much do you know about it?" Sketching rapidly as he spoke.

"I like my portrait to be painted. I like to hear you speak. I visit exhibitions. Some I like, some I do not. I cannot remember names of artists and pictures."

"As a matter of interest, and purely for my entertainment, what did Madame Picard say to you before you left today?"

"She sends you her affectionate remembrances," Claire replied with a caution strange to her.

"Oh, come on," said Carradine, grinning. "She told you not to be a fool. She reminded you that you are no longer a child. She underlined security, in the form of jewels. She advised you to be compliant at least, and responsive at best."

Claire was silent.

"I thought we were supposed to be friends," he continued, "and friends speak the truth — a commodity your establishment regards either with suspicion or as a future investment."

He had recovered from the smart of being manipulated by Emile Roche and even enjoyed it in retrospect.

"I am never afraid of the truth, m'sieu" — with a touch of temper.

"Good. Then tell me about yourself, and no fibs. I shall know if you're fibbing. I am an expert fibber myself."

"Tell *me* what you wish to know, and I tell *you*."

"Don't point your finger at me, Claire, it spoils the position. Thank you. Tell me about your childhood, your parents, why you are so different in character from your sister."

"You shall not tell Natalie what I say?"

"Certainly not. Friendship implies trust."

She had been formal in her amber velvet gown, consciously posturing. Now, little by little, she relaxed. Her careful prettiness gave way to intelligence. Her dress ceased to wear her.

"Of course, we are orphans together as long as I remember. Natalie knows our parents, but I am very small when they die. So we go to the orphanage, and Valentine is there too. Always, Valentine was the servant. Natalie made her fetch our boots and button them, though this is not allowed."

Kneeling in a worship that dared not admit of envy or anger. The buttonhook grazing her knuckles as it sprang back. They had made a compact against the tight world of nuns and looked to the world outside for freedom and pleasure. It was to be their oyster, and Natalie would find the oyster knife.

"They make us all wear the same clothes. A blue uniform, very plain, very coarse. Our hair was scraped back in plaits, our faces were scrubbed with soap until they shone, so that we would not be vain. There were no looking-glasses. Natalie found a piece of broken mirror once and hid it. She would let us use it if we pleased her. She was always the *chef de bande* — how do you say that?"

"The ringleader."

He crumpled the first Rosetti-like pose and concentrated on this new person. As a model she was fascinating, as a woman he had been right to ignore her. That pointed chin suddenly insistent, that soft mouth suddenly incisive, those dark eyes narrowing in recollection. Not Natalie, certainly, but a woman with a mind and will of her own, which might well not be his mind or his will. A prospective thrower of tantrums, an arguer, an acute observer and recorder (and with a memory for unpleasant facts). She would be an intolerable nuisance as a mistress, but as a companion she delighted him. He admired her too. He had to admire the long years of subordination, the tenacity that opposed Natalie's plans for her future.

"What did they intend to do for you at the orphanage, Claire? I may call you 'Claire', may I not? And you must call me 'Nicholas'."

"But of course."

She had forgotten Natalie's Madame Récamier attitude and leaned forward, hugging her knees, head bent.

"Valentine is simple and good, so they would keep her in the kitchen. I am quite clever. I do as they tell me, not because I want to but because it is easier like that. So they will make me a governess. But Natalie, they called her the bad one, they did not know what to do with her. Always, from sixteen, she has love affairs. Once a soldier climbs into the bedroom through the window. How we were afraid! I pull the blanket over my head so I shall not see them. Natalie was a *voluptueuse*."

"Even in a dormitory full of Catholic orphans?"

"Even there."

"What a woman!"

"You like her to be like that?"

"From a distance, yes. For myself, not in the least. What happened?"

"She run away with another soldier, a captain. I do not know what becomes of him. For two, three years we hear nothing. We think she has forgotten us. Valentine works in the kitchen. I work in the schoolroom. I wished to go, not with a captain but by myself. I do not like what Natalie does with the soldiers."

"I can imagine," said Carradine, comprehending, and he put down his stick of charcoal. "Natalie has probably warped a whole dormitory full of impressionable virgins. How did she manage to avoid becoming pregnant?" He saw her shocked hesitation. "I really shouldn't have asked that, mam'selle. I was speaking as I would speak to a friend, and I forgot that you are a lady. You see how quickly friendship brings barriers down."

She glanced from him to her clasped hands, pursed her mouth.

"The soldiers know how not," she said finally, making up her mind to pursue friendship in all its curious forms. "Later Natalie knows how not, and she tell me. I do not like that either."

"No, well, it's a pity she didn't inform Valentine. That would have saved a heap of trouble."

She laughed as they had laughed together some evenings ago, and he watched her in pleased astonishment. Friendship obviously suited her temperament. He reflected that she had probably gone very short on friendship. Alliance through necessity, even learned by affection, was not the same thing.

"But how if you tell Valentine?" she cried, hands over mouth like a child. "She forgets. She forgets everything."

"We'll leave it at that, mam'selle. Friendship has its limits. We were at the orphanage and you wanted to leave by yourself."

"I am a coward. Always I tell myself I am a coward. I am afraid to go. I am afraid to trust myself." She was sobered by her apparent cowardice. "So we wait. Then one day Natalie comes back."

In a carriage, elegantly gowned and discreetly painted, with unimpeachable credentials from M. Emile Roche. Offering the post of maidservant to Valentine, of governess for his ward to Claire. Natalie told the nuns she was Madame Roche's personal companion.

"I do not know how much they believe her, but they cannot doubt the letter. We come to Paris, to the apartment near the Etoile. We stay here ever since."

"What an incredible disappointment you must both have been," Carradine remarked, amused.

She considered this, frowning. "I should like to be free," she admitted, "but how can that be? I tell you I am a coward. With Natalie I am nothing, but if I am a governess I am nothing also." She observed his irony with resentment. "There are worse lives," she said defiantly: "Natalie is hard, you think? That is not true. She loves us. We love her. We are a little afraid of her, but we love her. And so we live." She shrugged. "Is your life so much better,

203

M'sieu Nicholas?"

"I work. That is infinitely better."

Her brows drew together. The work threatened her as a woman. It could and did replace her in his estimation. And she was facing a totally new problem in his detachment. She did not want him as her lover, but she wanted him to want her as his mistress. Not to have but to want. For what else could she offer any man? And what could any woman offer this man, whose work lay always between himself and her?

"Perhaps you should make love to a lady that paints?" she suggested.

"God forbid!"

"You are afraid that she paints better than you?"

"I'm afraid that lady painters bore me to death."

"I am tired now," she said. "I wish to rest. Let me see what you have done to me. Ah, how ugly you find me!"

She worried over the intent woman, hands hugging her knees, whose formal gown seemed both costume and contradiction.

"Not ugly, highly interesting. In fact,"

said Carradine, holding the sketch at arm's length, "I find it an improvement on my usually vacuous efforts."

"But she is so sad," said Claire sadly. "Why do you not draw me nice?"

And immediately she smiled and became ravishing.

"Do you not draw nice things?"

"I always draw nice things. Come and look."

She was his old public: exclaiming over past joys.

"Do you paint what is real or do you make them up?"

"Oh, they're real enough. They're things I remember. This one, for instance, was an afternoon many years ago when my stepmother took us to the park outside the Hotel Carnavalet. I went back to draw the square, for accuracy, and then put us all into it. Here is Gabrielle, and Odette in her baby carriage, and there am I."

Sunlight and leaf shadow, the repose of the young mother, the sleeping baby, the abandonment of the small boy chasing his hoop with a stick.

"How happy you must have been, Nicholas. Are children so happy?"

The blue uniform, the plain diet, the prayers and suppression, the sudden terror of two urgent bodies beneath a dormitory blanket.

"I certainly was."

"What is this picture called?"

He was staring at it abstractedly and answered with a reluctance he could not explain, "*The Children in the Square.*"

And it was all wrong. Something to do with gravel, with a badly grazed knee, with a perfumed handkerchief round his leg, with interruption, with shattering. The picture stopped short before that man entered it; otherwise it would have become a terrible thing. It had not been the first time he was there, apparently by chance, in a public square or park. His manner was always correct. He addressed Gabrielle as 'madame', he patted Nicholas's head, he bent over the carriage and said Odette would be almost as beautiful as her maman. He kissed the extended hand in its little glove. He chatted. "Play your hoop, my Nicki!"

What did they talk about as he glanced over his shoulder jealously? Something that constricted his breathing, even though he could not hear it, something only for the two of them, something so important that he felt himself barred. An invisible circle was about them; they shone from within it, unreachable. A magic circle from which his physical body would rebound if he tried to enter it.

An electric current whose touch would shock him.

Then, fury only to be conquered by speed. He had run and run and run, hoop spinning madly, and at last fallen and lain still. That had been the right thing to do, because Gabrielle flew to him with cries of alarm and took him home immediately, and the man was forgotten. They had left him standing there, hat in hand, forlorn, his power shorn from him. Forgotten.

Claire was forgotten too. She touched his shoulder, spoke his name. He hardly heard her. She must go away so that he could think this out. He must get rid of her.

As though he had spoken his thoughts she picked up her cloak, dispossessed. Repentantly he placed it about her shoulders, thanked her, suggested another day. He even suggested she should come back to England with him for a holiday. No, no, not as his light of love but as a model or a companion, a friend — whatever she wished. Anything, so long as she would leave him alone with his revelation.

I painted the wrong picture, he reflected.

The simplicity of the solution amazed him. He pursued it further, handing Claire her feathered hat.

I painted what I wanted to think, not what I knew. I've always painted the wrong pictures because the right ones were unbearable. And I prided myself on facing unpalatable truths! I painted tawdry circuses and music halls to avoid painting the truly tawdry. I painted innocence to disguise my lack of it. I idealized or denigrated women because women as they are terrify me. And I courted them and slept with them and made them fall in love with me because I couldn't have Gabrielle and I wanted her. What did I tell Lintott? *I speak not of the flesh — which is another matter — but of the emotions.* No, I speak of the flesh. She roused me, blast her, as no other woman has ever done.

Who was that man? Her lover, either in fact or fancy? Whichever it was, she was faithless to my father. So I was afraid of faithlessness. I was faithless and uncommitted so that I shouldn't be hurt again, as she hurt me with him. Who *was* he?

"You would like to keep this, Nicholas?" Claire reached for the sketch.

"No, no. Take it away with you if you like. I'll do several studies before I decide on the final one. Tell Natalie. She'll be delighted. Tell her we need time together, a great deal of time."

Time to digest and absorb, not Claire but Gabrielle. The looking-glass hit and shattered at last. And yet what a sense of freedom rose from fragments. And pity too.

Pity for the boy who experienced too much, too early.

Pity for the father who had been betrayed and who had loved dumbly. Pity for Gabrielle, a trapped thing beating against the glass. What a coil! What a rotten, beastly coil for all of them!

And this was why the painting seemed so insipid. He had painted perfection perfectly, and there was no such thing. Wrong colors. Too light, too . . . easy. He needed a new palette, a darker palette. Sepias, somber greens — no grass on earth was that luscious shade. The park had been gritty. He must convey the grit, the dust, the heat of that summer afternoon. A heat both moist and heavy.

The hatred and the heat had made him sweat. Who was this little fellow with the hoop, so fresh and cool in his sailor suit? Fresh and cool from Berthe's hands.

Not me, thought Carradine, never me.

"Thank you," said Claire, bereft.

He kissed her hand and then on an impulse, simply because he knew he was rejecting her, and she knew she was being rejected, he kissed her cheek.

The casual affection, the sop, infuriated her. He should not rid himself so easily. She placed her hands lightly on either side of his face and as lightly kissed first the left and then the right cheek. An expression of Natalie's left her lips before she could suppress it.

"We say in French that we kiss all four cheeks, but that is not among good friends, Nicholas."

She saw the remark had not registered and crossed herself involuntarily. "Until we meet again," she cried, running down the stairs.

Much later, when he had torn up innumerable sketches of the new square, he felt the kisses as indentations. He even walked over to the mirror and stared into it, almost expecting two hollows. And later still, waking in the early hours with the notion of painting the park as though he observed it from the air, infinitely remote, those kisses were still with him. Two small, warm, invisible sensations.

Part Three

'Between you and the world I am a veil
for a divine instant. I am love.'

Georges Roualt

10

THIS time, feeling a seasoned traveler, Lintott made his way to Paris alone, and was mollified by the courtesy extended to visitors. He did not, however, feel it incumbent upon him as an Englishman to communicate with his few French words or (heaven forbid!) gestures of explanation. Instead he set down his notebook of names, addresses, times, and connections; handed over his mystery of French currency and hoped they were honest, patiently waited until they moved him one stage farther toward his goal; then lifted his bowler hat and thanked them in English.

Winter was receding into cold spring. Lighter skies, washed by rain, lightened to washed blues and grays the roofs of Montmartre. Skeleton trees subtly promised future green. And this particular quarter of the city, countrified by windmills and vineyards, appealed to Lintott in spite of himself. The hubbub and color dazzled him. The crowds were not a mass personality, anonymous, hurrying, withdrawn, but a company of separate individuals clamoring for attention. Uplifted faces, sideways glances, a thrust of a jaunty elbow or a careless, shoulder, demanded the recognition even of a passing moment.

He deplored their self-sufficiency, their egotism, their insistence on the joys of today. But then, just as he was feeling his own man again, the turn of a corner would display Paris at his feet, and his heart stopped. He clicked his tongue in reproof and shook his head.

The studio was untenanted, but Lintott found the key under the mat. (Silly sort of place to put it. Everyone knew that dodge.) He let in himself and his Gladstone bag, and a thin cat followed him and made itself at home on the window seat. He found, and offered it, a saucer of milk. No language difficulty here. He brewed a pot of tea from the packet Bessie had given him and savored his solitude and temporary possession.

Empty rooms fascinated him. So much to be discovered and divined about those who lived in them. He unwrapped the last of Bessie's sandwiches and chewed stolidly as he looked about him. Nothing new in the dust and exotic carelessness. Mr. Carradine still hadn't found a woman to clean for him, or hadn't tried. Nothing new in the squeezed and draggled tubes of paint. The artist was still at work. The larder was still depleted. Either he was still snacking or eating out. Lintott swept the crumbs from his trousers tidily into his handkerchief, took a last delicious swallow of hot tea, and stood up.

"What's this then?" he asked himself and put on his spectacles for a closer look. The childish face beneath the garish hat, arms lifted, eyes intent. "Fancies herself as a fine lady," said Lintott, holding Valentine at arm's length. "But he did ought to tidy it up a bit. Those big streaks, as if he was drawing with thick chalk. Bessie wouldn't think much of that. And what about these?"

The sheaf of sketches formed a sequence of events that Lintott registered immediately. Another girl this time, hugging her knees, head bent, frowning. The same girl, head thrown back, laughing, caught in a few swift strokes.

Head turned, brooding. Hunched in the window seat where the thin cat purred, unaware of her watcher and recorder. A similar posture, only this time aware of him and looking provocatively away. A full-shaded portrait, sad-mouthed, defensive. Then half-a-dozen poses in what appeared to be a chemise.

Interested and shocked, Lintott studied slim, taut arms, a knife-edged corset cutting against soft lawn, ghostly lace over soft breasts. He could find no shred of evidence to back up his sense of immorality. The girl was no more unclothed than she would have been in an evening gown. By no stretch of his imagination could the pose be called saucy or even indiscreet. But there was something pretty near the bone there, if only he could put a name to it.

"Makes me feel as if I was peeping through a bedroom window," said Lintott reproachfully and put the drawings away from him. "Much use *he'd* be to a wife. Turning the glad eye on somebody else, more like."

He marched over to the canvas on the easel and peered at this too: gray head poked forward like an inquiring turtle. He did not hear the key in the lock.

"I shall make an art critic of you yet," said Carradine, smiling by the door, "as I appear to have made a regular traveler of you, Inspector. Welcome back to Paris."

Lintott shook Carradine's hand shyly, caught out.

"I'm sorry I wasn't at home to greet you, but I had a lady to escort back, and the city is so crowded at this hour. In despair of a cab, I walked."

Carradine was always vivid in any company. Now he exuded vitality. Lintott experienced a gust of cold spring air, brilliant hazel eyes, an energetic handshake, as though it were a delightful infection. He almost believed himself to be the cultured Gypsy of Carradine's imagination, then clapped irons on fancy. Steady, lad, he cautioned himself. One of us has to keep his flat feet on the ground.

"Admiring your work, sir. A very charming young lady."

"Oh, more than that, I assure you." Skimming his wide-brimmed black hat across to the window seat, where it flopped near the cat. "Let's have coffee and the talk you promised me in your letter. Then we can eat." His cape followed the hat, and the animal leaped down outraged. "How was your journey? Good! How do you like my Mrs. Tilling? I thought you and she would find a rapport somehow. Excellent." He loosened his collar and flowing tie and set the enamel coffeepot on a small portable stove. "What news from the past, Inspector? Have a cheroot."

"I'll take a pull at my pipe, sir, if it's all the same to you," said Lintott and sat comfortably with his legs apart on the model's dais.

"The day I can draw you just as you are," said Carradine on another line of thought, "I shall know I have achieved something worthwhile."

"And what might that be, sir?" asked Lintott, shrewd and amiable.

"Reality, Inspector."

With a flick of wit he had not known he possessed, Lintott replied dryly, "Ah, that's out of your usual line of country, ain't it, sir?"

Carradine extended one arm, delighted. "Touché," he said, and then, "Startle me with reality, Inspector."

Lintott sucked his pipe stem, unsure how to make truth acceptable.

"Well, sir, I've turned up a lot of information as we weren't expecting. Thankee. A little more milk, if you please. It tastes too bitter else. Well, difficult to know where to start, sir."

"Say it all at once then."

Lintott took a deep breath. "Your stepmother, the late Mrs. Carradine, was carrying on with a Frenchman for about five years unbeknown to your late father, I'm glad to say. And thank God for that. He was an honest gentleman."

Carradine's face was somber. He strolled over to the easel, cheroot between his teeth. Confirmation held more sting than he had expected.

"The nurse, Berthe Lecoq, was dismissed for no good reason as either Mrs. Tilling or me could see. Your father sent two hundred pounds to the curate in Paimpol as a sort of compensation. So we've got some sort of an address. I suppose he'd be acting for her much as our vicars do, sir?"

"Yes. Berthe may well have lived in

some outlying village. My father would send the money to someone who could be trusted to see she received it safely."

"And now we come to the nutty bit," said Lintott. "Adding two and two together, this here Frenchman of Mrs. Canadine's kidnaped your sister and took her on the train."

Carradine sank into a chair, utterly silenced.

"I thought that'd take the wind out of your sails, sir," said Lintott, obscurely satisfied by the impression he had made. "As far as I can gather, they were pretty keen on one another. And somehow he must have got the child away from Berthe — offered to buy ice cream or took her for a walk perhaps. Berthe was hand-in-glove with Mrs. Carradine and knew all about this here affair. So it could have been done easy enough. She wasn't sent away for that, any road. Mrs. Carradine took against her *after* the accident. Now I don't know his name. Your step-mother just referred to him as D. And there ain't a man in that railway carriage with a *D*, either Christian name or surname. So he must have got away somehow."

"Was he asking for ransom, do you think?" Carradine asked, the light gone from him. He was merely making responses.

"No, sir. I think he was using the child to fetch the lady after him. I even went through a list of your father's regular customers, in case a Frenchman with a *D* in his name cropped up. I checked them all out. All living, or dead, in London, and no connection. This man lived in Paris. She went to his apartment frequently. No address, no indication of where it might be. She covered up like a professional," said Lintott with some admiration. "But if Berthe's alive, and I can find her, *she* knows."

"I remember the man," said Carradine with difficulty. "But this was more than twenty years ago, and the description would fit a thousand Frenchmen, and he will have changed."

"Been digging inside your head sir?" Lintott inquired humorously. But he was concerned by Carradine's immobility.

"Oh, into my head, and my work, and my divided self. Yes, Inspector."

He recollected courtesy. "You have done remarkably well. Where did you find this particular family skeleton?"

"In the attic, in that collection of diaries belonging to your stepmother. Written in French. I had to get my daughter to translate," he added with pride.

"She must be highly accomplished," Carradine replied automatically. "My father didn't read them, did he?"

"No, sir. I made sure of that. He just said he'd asked Mrs. Tilling to put everything safely away, and they were locked. Not much of a lock but enough to stop anyone peeping."

"Thank God for something. To live a lie of that magnitude with a man who loves and trusts you. What a wretched business."

"Look here, sir, do you want me to stop?" Lintott asked outright. "It ain't a police matter, you know. You don't have to go on."

Carradine pondered over his clasped hands, a frown between his brows. Then he stood up, resolved.

"No, Inspector. We may as well

uncover the lot, and then perhaps I can live with it. We shall see." He sought for distraction. "Let's put your undoubted talents to a little artistic detection, Inspector." He spoke more heartily than he felt. "Come, tell me what you think of my latest efforts. You must have thought something. You were studying them so very thoroughly."

Lintott heaved himself patiently to his feet, stood beside his employer, scratched his head, puffed his pipe, and assumed a reverent aspect.

Carradine smiled involuntarily. "Say what you think, Inspector. I'm not begging for compliments."

Lintott's scandalized eyes rested on the sheaf of sketches. "There's something not . . . wholesome . . . about them," he ventured.

"And this?" Bringing out the original *Children in the Square*.

"Now that's capital," said Lintott, delighted to praise.

"How about this?" Showing him the new version.

"Is it the — yes, so it is. The same place. Why don't you paint it as neat, sir, if you don't mind me saying?"

"Inspector, don't for a moment imagine I am criticizing your likes and dislikes. But if you could put morality and technique behind you and consider the *effect*. What effect had — where the devil are they? — this on you, and this and this" — fetching out in rapid succession three early idylls — "and then, this?" His first sketch of Claire, which Natalie had returned with the comment, *Why not draw her nice?*

Lintott struggled toward enlightenment and was relieved to see that Carradine's own light had returned. He hesitated. He plunged.

"That one looks like Bessie when she's fretting. It ain't pretty but it's . . . right. I've seen many a woman carrying on inside herself like that. More like my Lizzie," he added to himself in a lower tone. "Wants what she can't have." He beamed paternally on the untouched, the unattainable. "Young men's fancies, sir, for all they're so nice. Couldn't boil a kettle if they tried. That's not what life's about. I daresay that's why folk like art, and I don't, to be honest. It gives them a minute off, looking at a jolly picture, thinking it might be them if they were luckier, or richer, or handsomer, or a bit more dashing."

He sensed that he had hit upon something important to Carradine and flowered. He walked round, picking up canvases and drawings, using eyes and mind. Impartial, objective.

"Did you know as there was a heap of stuff in that attic of yours, sir? You should look it all up when you get back. You used to write stories for your sister and make pictures up round them and stitch them into little books."

Carradine sat down, smiling, eyes clear and remote.

"No guts to them," said Lintott suddenly. Carradine's eyes lit and narrowed. "No, sir. Very pretty, very fanciful. Not flesh and blood and character. Shadows, that's what they were — and what some of these are too. That's why you won't put *me* on a canvas in a hurry." He was horrified by his loquacity and daring. "Not that you'd want to," he murmured and applied himself to his pipe.

"It's only what you'd expect of a young lad, mind you," he softened the rebuke. "Only, a man wants to do a man's work. I had a constable like you once, as promised to be a smart chap. But he wanted to solve a case in his head without getting his hands dirty. I had a talk with him one day." He succeeded in lighting the tobacco and shook out the match. "I told him he was dealing with human nature, not crossword puzzles. And human nature is good, bad, and indifferent. You can't take out a section of it as you fancy and pretend the rest don't exist. You've got to take all of it, see it for what it is, and deal with it. There's a lot we can't explain. That's why the women take to religion as they do. It's harder on them than on us. Although I call myself a Christian, and I'd fight to the last drop to defend folks' right to worship, I'm more of a realist. I've seen too much to say 'God's Will' so easily."

He studied the first sketch of Claire

again. "That's human nature," he said and laid it down.

Carradine's silent satisfaction transformed the studio. A catalyst, Lintott puffed and commented, untouched. The late sun was luminous in the dust.

"I know what it is," Lintott said, echoing Carradine's feeling on a humble level. He was deep in the unwholesome sketches. "Something between you and her. And it should be kept private, what's more."

"Nonsense," said Carradine, laughing. "You've picked up the emotional bond between artist and sitter."

"Emotional, yes," said Lintott, removing his spectacles in great satisfaction, "but there's a good deal of old Adam and Eve in it, mark my words."

Carradine clapped him affectionately on the shoulder. "You shall meet her this evening and judge for yourself. She's not Eve, Inspector. And now I am going to show you Paris at the altar."

"Church, sir?" Lintott inquired, bewildered.

"No, no. Paris at the comestible altar — the one that really matters. Paris worshiping fine food. In company with two charming French ladies."

"I thought the ladies might come into it somewhere," Lintott observed. "I'd best have a wash and brush up."

11

CARRADINE had chosen a table for four, at Chez la Mère Catherine in the Place du Tertre, instead of taking his chance with the benches along the wall. This was for Lintott's insular sake. He placed Natalie and Claire opposite them because, as he explained, they could see and talk to them better in that position. The Inspector, doing his best to avoid gaping at the ladies' decolletage, wished himself back in Richmond and stared suspiciously at the menu.

Natalie, magnificent in flaming velvet and diamonds, had insisted on Claire's appearing in ivory silk and pearls. The diamonds were real. Furthermore, since Carradine and Claire must be given every opportunity to court each other, she took upon herself the doughty challenge of Inspector Lintott. He replied, when he had to, in gruff monosyllables.

"This is not like your English food,

231

no? You must try the *langoustine*. It is very good. This is not like your English restaurant, no? I have dined at your Claridges. It is very dull."

"Claridges is not comparable to this, Natalie," said Carradine. "It is a highly reputable hotel for very respectable people. We have others, I assure you."

She laughed in a way Lintott considered too robust for a lady. The jewels shivered and quickened against a neck that was now voluptuous and would be fat. Then she returned to the fray.

"You do not have lovers in English restaurants like this, no?" She indicated an elderly man talking fondly to a young girl, who hung upon him like a borrowed medal.

"We do in some places," said Lintott, disapproving.

"You are not so . . . honest . . . as us, no?"

"About what?" said Lintott sharply.

Her eyes widened. She was enjoying herself. "Look there, m'sieu. Do you see the gross gentleman with two ladies?"

Rubicund, good-natured, his napkin tucked into his collar, the man was

232

inspecting all three plates and discoursing on their contents earnestly. He cut off a sliver of chicken and offered it to the younger, more fashionable woman. He sopped a bit of bread in his sauce and offered it to the older, quieter woman. Both were eating tranquilly, hugely. He beckoned the waiter, tasted the wine, urged them to drink. He beamed upon their appetites, feeding them.

"What are they, m'sieu? You are a . . . detection. Tell me of them."

"Bachelor gentleman taking his sisters out to dinner," Lintott guessed.

Natalie clapped her hands together and laughed even more robustly. "How English you are! The dull one is his wife, the pretty one is his mistress."

"We have no proof of that, Inspector," said Carradine, keeping a straight face, "but from long observation of the French I would agree with Madame Picard."

"Don't the wife suspect?" asked Lintott, astounded.

"But she knows," cried Natalie, enchanted. "Pff! What matter? She has his name, his home, his protection, his children perhaps. When he dies she has his money, all but a little gift to the mistress. If he wishes to make love with another woman, what of that? They are all content. They accept. They are honest. They enjoy their dinner with good appetite."

And she applied herself to hers with zest.

"I'm sorry about that, Inspector," said Carradine gravely, "but the French act upon your own principles. They face up to life."

Outwitted and outraged, Lintott tackled the steak that had been ordered for him.

After a few delectable mouthfuls he said sturdily, "Oh, well, we live and we learn, sir," and tried the wine.

Keep your feet on the floor, lad, he advised himself. Keep your eyes and ears open and your mouth shut. You might find something out that way.

"And what do you know of the little sister?" Natalie asked, cleaning up her sauce with half a roll, wiping her fingers on the napkin.

The guillotine would have drawn a word from Lintott, but Carradine had no such professional inhibitions and expressed himself with a baldness that surprised the Inspector.

"It appears that Odette was kidnapped by my step-mother's French lover."

Natalie was greatly intrigued. "So your goddess is thrown down, my dear Nicholas. How many more of idols will fall, I wonder?"

"I'm endeavouring to live without any idols at all," he replied lightly, but Lintott saw his face change momentarily.

Claire said, touching Carradine's wrist, "Women are not idols, Nicholas. We like that you treat us as women." Mocking and serious at once.

"Nicholas knows well how to make love, though he have not make love to me," said Natalie, expert in such matters. "Perhaps he make love to you?"

So that's the way the wind blows, Lintott thought. Not Eve, my foot! And the other one egging her on like a blessed serpent. He'd better watch out or he'll get caught. Madame here has her eye on a good match as well as the grub.

"How long is he her lover?" Natalie demanded of the Inspector.

"About five years," said Lintott reluctantly.

"An affair of passion — I shall have Creme Chantilly — I understand all. She is his life. He wishes her to elopement with him so they are happy always. She is this way and that way. She cannot decide" — acting out every expression, to Lintott's acute discomfort — "so, pff! he steal the little one and say to meet on the train. The message come too late. She is to depart the house when the train accidents itself . . . "

By Jove! Lintott thought, though mentally discarding this dramatic theory. I must be getting a regular old dummy. How *did* she know the child was on that particular train?

" . . . and she lose her lover, her child. She dies. Ah, we Frenchwomen! We die for love very easy."

She really believes that, thought Lintott. *And* it's sharpened her appetite. Observing the busy spoon, even though her eyes were full of tears.

Aloud he said, "If the lady will excuse me mentioning it, Mrs. Carradine was very happy with the arrangement she

236

had. Why should she give up a good home and a good husband for the sake of a fly-by-night love affair as had gone on for years?"

"Fly . . . by . . . night?" Natalie and Claire said together.

Their English was agreeably inaccurate rather than idiomatic.

"A shot in the dark," Lintott explained. "Catch-as-catch-can. Here today and gone tomorrow."

"A dilettante," Carradine said.

Their black eyes focused flatteringly on Lintott's plain countenance.

"Ah!" They comprehended.

"Besides, the gentleman hadn't any money," Lintott continued. "He was an old flame who wanted to marry the lady years before, and the family wouldn't let him . . ."

Carradine translated 'old flame' for the ladies, and thought of Emile Roche. Still, no *D* in his name.

"An old flame," Lintott repeated heavily, "as couldn't provide for the lady, let alone the little girl, in the manner to which she was accustomed. Now if you value money — I'm not saying I think it's right — you don't throw it up in a hurry."

Natalie looked at him with new respect. "You have right, m'sieu. Why shall she throw herself on a rubbish person? Unless she is a mad."

Avaricious foreigner, Lintott thought, and was comforted.

"It's all to be looked into anyway," he said firmly. "We shan't find anything out by talking."

His tone silenced them and might have made a hole in the conversation but for a timely interruption.

A young man had entered and hung up his shabby cloak, which had once belonged to a larger and stouter man. He emerged in a secondhand dress suit and frilled shirt. The suit was too small, the frills too tattered, but he lent an innate elegance to the outfit. He stood at his ease, assessing his audience. A head of tight brown curls, mournful eyes, an air of arrogance that could only be based on self-belief. Conversation faltered and ceased as the diners observed him. While they turned and craned he found the right face to address. Placing both hands on Carradine's table, he leaned forward and recited softly but distinctly to Claire. Suddenly vulnerable, she flushed and looked down as he declaimed earnestly and reverently into the listening silence. When he had finished there was a spatter of handclaps. Carradine gave him money, which he accepted with serene indifference.

"What was that about then, sir?" asked Lintott, bemused.

"The young man is a poet who calls himself Le Jallu. I have seen him before. I daresay, since he is a student and poor, he ekes out a living this way. Possibly he will be given a meal in Mère Catherine's kitchen, as well as the tips he earns, for lending an ambiance to the restaurant."

"He recited one of his poems to the young lady, did he?"

"Can you remember it, Claire?" Carradine asked, smiling.

"A little bit." She had recovered her composure and spoke in her usual low, measured tone. "He speaks of the passing of love and beauty, and that we shall live this moment as if the next moment does not come."

"Oh, well, each to his own taste," said Lintott expansively. "The food's solid enough anyway."

"But also transitory, Inspector. You have just devoured it."

"So we live and love?" Natalie remarked, selecting cheeses. "That is not a poetry. That is the common sense."

The boy was jealous of his craft and would only bestow it where his fancy lay. No use for that stout French matron, this rich American widow, to preen and glance. He would not court them. As he passed their table again, Carradine laid a hand on his sleeve and asked a question. Le Jallu bowed, then brought up a wooden chair.

"Is he going to say another poem, sir?" Lintott inquired, patient and polite with his host's whims.

"No, Inspector. The young man needs to find work for the Easter vacation. I am about to persuade him to accompany you, as paid guide and translator, to Brittany, to find Berthe."

"Oh, my Gawd!" Lintott murmured and applied himself to the wine. "But he don't speak English, sir."

"I speak excellent English," said Le Jallu, remote but courteous.

"And he needs the money, m'sieu," Natalie added, regarding the poet's beauty with a maternal and acquisitive eye. "And he is famish, Nicholas."

The whole affair was beyond Lintott. The evening swam round him. Five of them, elbow to elbow, at a table meant for four. Carradine drinking cognac and talking art. Le Jallu eating enormously and talking poetry. Natalie devouring a second helping of Crème Chantilly to keep him company, and talking of love. A jumble of French and English, the English for the Inspector's benefit and none of it appearing to connect. The sheen of Natalie's energetic arms and rising bosom, far too close. Claire flinging caution to whatever winds might carry it away, kissing Carradine on both cheeks and then on the mouth, calling him her good friend. The restaurant emptying gradually. God knew what o'clock it was. Claire in fiery argument, first with Carradine, then with Natalie. Silent, half an hour later, under the influence of Jallu reciting Rimbaud: her arms round

Carradine's neck, her face against his, gentle and quiescent.

Like a blooming weathercock, thought Lintott fuzzily, and covered his eyes.

When he opened them he was being helped into a cab. They jolted along in a heady crush of feminine flesh and perfume until the ladies were deposited. At some stage the poet disappeared. Much later Carradine pushed black, bitter coffee into Lintott's hands.

"I seem to have made a fool of myself," the Inspector said, disconcerted. "I'm used to English beer and a quiet life, sir."

"Your behavior was impeccable, if a little blurred at times, Inspector, I assure you."

The smile on Carradine's face was the smile on the face of the evening: enigmatic.

"You needn't worry about Le Jallu, Inspector. He's far too proud to be dishonest. You'll be in charge, and he won't be paid until he delivers you safely back. I'm not totally irresponsible."

"That's all right then, sir," said Lintott, faintly relieved, "but I seem to have got myself into queer company, and no mistake."

"A remark you made frequently during the course of the evening."

"No offense meant, sir, and none taken, I hope?"

"None whatsoever, Inspector. We cherished your judgment of us as we would cherish truth itself. We enjoy our frivolities but respect your more durable quality. As Le Jallu would put it, very roughly translated, 'The mayfly dances for a day. But how long has the sun shone?'"

Feeling obscurely complimented, Lintott murmured, "So long as I didn't spoil the party."

12

THOUGH Lintott had not carried his wine as well as Carradine had, he was first up and spruced before setting water to boil. Nicholas found him standing in front of the canvas, studying Claire.

"A serious young lady," Lintott observed. "Not like her sister, sir. You can't help feeling a bit sorry for her. She's seen and known more than she liked — and more than she should." He eyed Carradine's brown velvet dressing gown. "Do you mind me speaking out, sir? With no disrespect intended to any party."

"Speak on, Inspector."

"Mrs. Pickered is a lady with an eye to the main chance. I take it she isn't a married lady in the usual sense of the word, sir?"

"Not as far as I know. She has a protector."

Lintott snorted. "I wonder who protects

him?" he said. "And has this here sister of Mrs. Pickered got a protector too? Because, if she hasn't, I think they might have marked you down for the job." He raised one blunt hand as Carradine opened his mouth in protest. "It's not for me to judge whether that's right or wrong, sir, but a gentleman *is* known by the company he keeps."

"Not in my profession, Inspector. I keep all kinds of company."

"Very good, sir. Point taken. But if you're keeping company with those ladies you'd do well not to mix money with sentiment. Else you might find yourself permanently landed with that younger sister, and that wouldn't do. Wouldn't do at all."

"I've avoided permanent attachments so far, Inspector."

"Ah, yes, sir. Thankee — there's nothing like a cup of English tea when you're in foreign parts. Yes, sir, but then you've taken up so far with ladies as know the score and don't fuss when it comes to a good-by, or with the ladies of good family whose family can take care of them. This Miss Claire Pickered is something of a lame dog, and you're partial to lame dogs, sir. You might be caught by feeling sorry for her — as I do, sir, I admit it. I feel, given a fair chance, she'd have made a worthwhile woman. But she's been soiled, sir, and that's a fact not to be overlooked before you leap."

"I don't particularly care for the word *soiled*," said Carradine stiffly.

"I'm sorry for that, sir, but I speaks as I find."

"Her background is tawdry, I agree. But she has put up considerable resistance to her sister's plans for her. I believe there was an engagement of some kind which fell through and occasioned her suffering — "

"Oh, be your age, sir," Lintott chided. "That girl's been on the French merry-go-round, as God's my judge. You ain't the first. I'm surprised at you, sir, I really am."

"Are you assuming she's my mistress?" Carradine cried, furious.

"I wasn't born yesterday, sir. No, no, no." Lintott shook his head sagely from side to side in a most infuriating manner. "She was all over you last night. I wasn't so stupid that I couldn't use my eyes. And what about those drawings?" He flourished toward the sheaf of sketches.

"I see you haven't wasted your time in the detection of my private affairs."

"If I did wrong to look about me and draw the obvious conclusions, then I beg your pardon, sir. I wasn't prying. You was the one that said an artist gave himself away more in his paintings than he did in real life, or something of that sort. I applied the principle."

Carradine's wrath ebbed. Lintott stirred his tea industriously, hurt.

"Only your assumption was wrong, Inspector. Miss Claire poses for me. I haven't seduced her. I respect lame dogs, as well as caring about them."

"She's pretty fond of you, sir."

"Another good reason for leaving her strictly alone. I'm not a scoundrel."

"Well, well," said Lintott, only partly satisfied, "so long as you've got the situation clear and don't make more trouble for yourself. I'm only speaking for your own good."

A few moments of silence closed the subject.

He's only told me a half-truth, Lintott thought.

"Inspector, I met Madame Picard's friend, Emile Roche, one evening, and I have been indulging in a little speculation. He told me he had once fallen in love with a girl of eighteen, whose parents refused to let them marry because of his financial circumstances. She then married a man far older and richer than himself, but he holds a sentimental recollection of her."

"Plenty of men like that, I reckon, sir — if you're thinking he might be our suspect."

"Oh, yes. But Madame Picard revealed even more about him in the course of several conversations. And I think you will agree that he fits the bill to a surprising extent. He is now sixty. His romance occurred around 1873, the year before Gabrielle married my father. M'sieu Roche speaks as though it were a brief affair, conducted at a distance. But Madame Picard tells me it was carried on in a far more intimate capacity for about ten years. Not until he found the situation hopeless did he marry, in 1883, just before Gabrielle died." As

Lintott remained unimpressed, Carradine emphasized, "Madame Picard said he almost wrecked his career with a scandal in 1882. He told her he had escaped ruin by a hairbreadth. But he didn't say what the scandal was or how he had escaped it."

"A good thing too, if she chatters like that to everybody she meets."

"Oh, he is highly judicious. He gives away no hard facts. He said the past was safely buried. Buried, mark you."

Lintott considered his empty mug. "Well, if you find some way for me to question him, go ahead, sir. I take it he's in some high position, to keep Mrs. Pickered in diamonds? A Minister, eh? Forget it, sir. He's too fly to be tapped His name ain't a *D*, neither."

"He could have changed it."

"I doubt it. Sixty now and forty then. You don't drop into a Minister's post without being checked. They'd want to know why he changed his name, wouldn't they? Besides, he'll have worked his way up the ladder from twenty, not forty."

"Gabrielle could have referred to him

by a nickname beginning with D, couldn't she?" Persistent.

"Yes, sir, she *could*. And it *could* be this Mr. Roach. But you don't leap to conclusions of that sort without a mort of questions. I want the answer to a few points as escape me. Such as, how did he get out of that carriage and in what condition? Was he perhaps so badly burned and disfigured that he stayed in hospital several months? And how did your stepmother know that the little girl was on that train? Perhaps he sent her a letter, to say when they'd gone and where to follow him? Whatever it was, she *thought* he was dead. And he never showed up again."

Impatient, obsessed, Carradine strode the studio, rumpling his hair.

"Berthe's our best bet," said Lintott. "But if you can find out anything about Mr. Roach while I'm away, it all helps."

"Do you know what else worries me about the inquest, Inspector? Odette was only identified by a bracelet. God, what a fearful thought! Suppose, in the shock of that identification, Gabrielle mistook the bracelet? Suppose they were not on that

250

train at all, but on another? Suppose he took her away and then, hearing about the consequences of his action, he stayed away?"

"Saddled with a little girl for life, sir? Besides, Mrs. Carradine didn't die for twenty months after."

"She never returned to France, though."

"He could have written," said Lintott sensibly. "He must have known her address even if she never used it. No, sir, you're talking wild."

"Two things remain in my mind — the identity bracelet and his escape. If he escaped scot-free I shall find him. I shall find him and confront him."

"Oh, we're on the vengeance tack now, are we?" said Lintott dryly. "If you're thinking you could clap him in prison on this lot, you're mistaken, sir. It'd never even get to court. Besides, I don't see how he could have got off scot-free." He felt inside his breast pocket. "I wasn't going to show you this, sir, unless it seemed needful. I just want you to understand what I mean."

He produced a little packet, an envelope folded over and over, that he had found tucked in a far corner of Walter Carradine's desk. Something that had been thrust away as though it had burned the fingers that had handled it.

Slowly Carradine unfolded the envelope and shook out its contents. A chain bracelet, whose links were jammed and distorted with heat, and from the chain hung a mis-shapen heart.

Lintott handed him a penknife. "It opens," he said.

Inside, two portraits had once been placed. Unrecognizable.

Carradine touched the bracelet and was silent.

"Would you call that identification, sir?" Lintott asked quietly.

"Yes," Carradine said at last. "I remember this. The portraits were of my father and Gabrielle. I had forgotten. I remember."

"She *didn't* make a mistake," said Lintott. "And he *didn't* get off scot-free."

Carradine walked slowly to the window and stared out. Montmartre was flame. He covered his eyes.

"Just suppose it was Mr. Roach, sir,"

said Lintott, trying to distract Carradine, because it was useless for the man to torment himself after so long. "What good will it do to know? Except that you won't want to see him again in a hurry."

"I shall hound him," said Carradine in a low voice. "I shall see he suffers retribution, of whatever kind."

"'Vengeance is mine, sayeth the Lord,'" Lintott reminded him.

Carradine spun round, colorless. "The Lord won't get as much satisfaction as I shall, Inspector."

"Now, now, now, sir. Folks as try to take the law into their own hands find the law coming pretty heavily on *them* afore they're done."

"Oh, I have no intention of killing him. That would be too easy. I shall see that he lives with their deaths."

"You might find yourself landed with those two ladies to support," said Lintott, deliberately humorous, for Carradine's obsession troubled him. "That'd be vengeance of another sort."

A faint smile warmed Carradine's mouth. "You're a good fellow, Inspector.

And not two ladies, but three, are under the Minister's protection."

And he gave a brief summary of Valentine, a sad little thumbnail sketch, lightened by affectionate amusement.

"Well, there you are then," said Lintott, relieved. "You don't half go looking for trouble, sir. I can see you lumbered in London for life, with madame entertaining your friends on the sly, and Miss Valentine getting herself in the family way every twelve-month." He omitted mention of Claire out of delicacy. "I'd like to hear Mrs. Tilling on that subject, I would indeed."

"Oh, she would insist that I kept them all upstairs and pretend they didn't exist."

Lintott grinned, and Carradine smiled.

"If you'll take a piece of advice from me, sir, you'll wait until I get back from Brittany. You haven't a shred of evidence to go on, and the gentleman has a reputation to keep up. And he hasn't got where he is without knowing whose back to scratch. He'll be fly, sir. And, meaning no disrespect, you're a babby in arms compared with him. Besides, if he's innocent you'll look a proper fool and offend him into the bargain."

"I take your point, Inspector."

"Now, *if* I find Berthe, and *if* she says, 'Oh, his name was Mr. Emile Roach, and Mrs. Carradine used to call him *D* for darling', or something of that sort — it'll be a different matter. Are you with me, sir?"

"I'm with you, Inspector."

"And would you lend me that bracelet, sir? There's something about it worries me. And I don't want you to go drawing pictures of it or anything of that sort. I believe in facing facts, but there's no use mauling yourself with them."

A timid knock at the door closed the subject.

"Would you mind, Inspector? I must dress."

"But I don't know the lingo, sir," Lintott protested, suddenly at a loss.

"I shall be in the next room with the door open. They can bawl French at me past your shoulder, Inspector." And he disappeared. Don't look much of the bawling sort, Lintott thought, shyly saying, *"Bonjour, madame,"* to

255

a childish figure in gray mantle and mended gloves.

"Ever so sorry to trouble you, sir, but could I speak to M'sieu Carradine, if you please?"

"Hello, Valentine," Carradine called. "Come in and sit down."

Lintott stood embarrassed as they exchanged news through the open door. In a few moments Carradine entered, kissed her hand, paid compliments, and escorted her out.

"So that's Mr. Roach's third lady?" said Lintott. "He's a brave man, sir, you have to say that."

"A pity you don't speak French, Inspector. She would undoubtedly have confided to you that I was the father of her child. I see that honor ahead of me in her imagination. The ladies sent her to inquire how we had survived last night's orgy. I wish Natalie wouldn't let her out. She gets lost. And but for pinning the main news to her pocket we should be working in the dark." He held out a note. "This is Le Jallu's address, which Madame Picard was practical enough to extract from him. I should have had to return to Mère Catherine's and ask. These little matters are inclined to escape me. Fortunate poet! He will find a warm welcome from our madame if he cares to visit at the right hour."

"I'm not so sure, sir," said Lintott. "I have a feeling he tends in the gentlemen's direction, but I could be wrong, of course."

13

AND now Lintott was indeed cut adrift and cast forth.

Jallu, clad in an outlandish assortment of garments that combined warmth with drama, led him into the flowering wilderness of the French provinces. Berthe Lecoq was no longer in Paimpol or its environs. The priest to whom Walter Carradine had sent her compensation money was retired to Sarlac in the Perigord. After three days of inquiry they set off to find him.

"Truffles, sir," Le Jallu promised. "Truffles in such abundance that the peasants roast them over the fire for breakfast."

"Don't they melt?" asked Lintott, whose only acquaintance with truffles had been the chocolate variety resembling walnut-sized hedgehogs. "No, don't trouble to explain, lad. I shan't try them anyhow."

Trains were rattling them from one

exile to the next, farther and farther south. They stayed that night in a farmhouse, where Lintott examined the goose-feather bed for fleas, and woke sweating and suffocating simultaneously.

The priest, old and nearly blind, could give them no information other than Berthe's taking a post as housekeeper with an attorney called M. Cluny, who practiced in Lyons. On this thread of a clue they wound their way to Lyons, tracked down every attorney in the place, and discovered that this particular one had retired too. The son of his former partner believed the house to be near Orange. They took a train to Orange.

Lintott's stomach had ceased to protest at its change of diet, though he would have given much for a wedge of Cheddar cheese. He now eyed the evening bottle of wine with the wariness of a connoisseur rather than of a beer drinker. He watched Le Jallu haggle over prices, silently applauding him when he won, shrugging when he did not. He sympathized as the poet explained the difficulty of different dialects. And he found another France: a place of frugal living and plain thinking, of poverty and beauty, of tight morals and traditional attitudes, with an excellent habit of going to bed early to save light and fuel. He liked that.

Le Jallu, exotic and egocentric, was less at home here than Lintott. It was at Lintott that the old women in dusty black directed their rare smiles, Lintott to whom leathery farmers and gregarious shopkeepers nodded in salutation. The language barrier blocked only one method of communication; the other flowed together. A tacit approval warmed their brief acquaintances.

Unconcerned with anyone's opinion of him, the poet imposed his presence and his questions on those who seemed likely to be useful. In between he was silent, or he ate and slept. Clearly he regarded the expedition as akin to the mills of God, which grind exceeding small, and Lintott as the miller in charge of a long, slow process. He addressed the Inspector with polite indifference. He allowed himself to be used because he would be paid eventually and meanwhile was living well at no expense. Lintott comprehended this, but it made him feel lonely.

They arrived in Orange to find, as the Inspector had feared, that no one knew anything about the attorney or Berthe Lecoq. But the country grapevine, in its metaphorical sense, promised to yield fruit. Time and patience were yet again required of them. So they 'holed up', as Lintott put it, let it be known that information equaled francs, and waited.

"These people have no excitement in their lives," said Le Jallu carelessly. "A Parisian poet, an English inspector, a mystery. They shall speak of it until they die. They shall discover Berthe for you. Fear not."

"I'm feared of precious little," said Lintott stoutly. "I'll just take a turn outside."

His solitary figure, bowler hat square on, plaid cape defying the evening breeze, strode mournfully about the town, taking note of landmarks so he might find his way back. That night, by the light of an oil lamp, he wrote laboriously to Bessie, and surveyed the result with less than satisfaction. His had been a small world after all. He spoke only the langauge of his birth and could not express himself fluently on paper even in that.

My dear wife, I hope this letter finds you as well as it leaves me at present. The folk outside Paris are homely enough like our neighbors in Richmond. Mr. Carradine has sent me here with a young student who does the talking for me. We are hoping to find the little girl's nurse. I am pretty comfortable and the landladies make a good stew which they call pot-o-fer.

He reread this line, scented domestic danger, and added to it: *It reminds me of home, and is near as tasty as your Irish stew but not quite.*

He then set down two profound truths: *Tell Lizzie that Paris is only part of France even if it is a fancy place. I shall be glad to get home.*

He signed himself, *your loving husband, John.*

He printed the address very large and clear, handed the letter to Le Jallu, and extracted a promise to see it safely posted. He watched it disappear into the boy's pocket with profound regret. The writing had been a link, and he could not hope for a reply in his present state of

262

transit. Besides, Bessie was even less of a hand with the pen than he. Suddenly he was so homesick that he would have welcomed the sight of Carradine striding in, demolishing his solitude with charm, with wild notions that Lintott could dispel, with self-mockery, with a breath of England.

"I'd best send another word to Mr. Carradine while I'm about it," he remarked, and was comforted, though this missive would be briefer and more wooden than the one he sent to Bessie.

"Keeps him in touch," he said and attacked the inkwell with renewed energy.

* * *

On the fifth day of their sojourn a very small woman carrying a very large basket arrived. Though they were just breakfasting, she had broken her fast before dawn, walking from a village some miles away with her message.

"It is the Old One," their landlady announced with some pride. "The Old One knows everything."

The Old One evidently wished to share

her universal knowledge in detail, and Le Jallu was lost in the first round. Lintott experienced in questioning, watched and fretted as the boy resolutely interrupted her, and she as resolutely began again at the beginning.

"Half a minute, lad," Lintott commanded. "Excusey-mah, madame. Now lookee here, lad" — as the ancient wisp laughed and pointed at him — "I've met this sort of lady afore. Lives alone, friendly nature, getting on in her years, needs a bit of a chit. Savvy? Sit yourself down and listen. She'll be a while reaching the point, and we may as well be comfortable while we're waiting."

Le Jallu's melancholy face lengthened. "She tells me all, but she tells me nothing."

"I know, I know, but that's her way. Just do as I say, lad. Bonjure, madame. Give her a cup of coffee and a croissant."

The Old One ate and drank with noisy appreciation. Their landlady launched into a rapid biography. Her staff gathered round for a convivial half hour.

"What's she got in that there basket?"

"A little goat's milk, a little cheese, a little butter, a few eggs. She sells them. They say she is one hundred years old. I do not believe them."

"I do," said Lintott. "I've never seen an older Old One in all my born days."

Age had shrunk and withered her without obliterating one jot of her zest for living. The eyes in that brown landscape of a countenance were bright and inquisitive. The hard hands gesticulated. She crouched on her stool by the fire, drinking in coffee and company. Only life was left her, but it sparkled still and was precious.

"If I lived hereabouts," said Lintott, "which God forbid, she'd be my Number One, she would indeed. I'd sit and have a chat with her, quite apart from professional reasons. She'd be fine gold to me as far as information went. Hears the lot and forgets nothing. Fire away, lad, and give me the gist of it."

"Her husband fought with Napoleon. He died many years ago. She has a goat and a cow and six hens. She collects fuel from the wood nearby. Everyone is kind to her. The miller gives her flour, and she bakes bread once a week. What use is this, sir?"

"Let her talk, lad, let her talk," said Lintott, lighting his pipe.

And so she did, slapping her knees in amusement, faltering over losses, stoical over hardships, momentarily illuminated by past joys: a human epic, looking forward to tomorrow's humble chapter.

"Fine old lady," said Lintott. "Let her talk, lad, let her talk."

The chain of circumstances leading to Berthe was enumerated link by link — what had been heard, been said, been surmised.

"My friends and I do not talk like this," cried Le Jallu, exhausted. "We speak of the great truths of life, of poetry and philosophy."

"This *is* poetry and philosophy," said Lintott. "You and your friends have got a deal to learn yet."

Berthe Lecoq had found, as Mrs. Tilling prophesied, that a thirty-year absence meant too much change. Time, of which there had never seemed enough, became a desert. A solitary cottage and no attachments seemed poor exchange for a busy, prosperous household and the beloved. She asked the curé to inquire about domestic service and eventually heard that an attorney in Lyons needed a housekeeper. A country peasant would never have moved more than a mile or so beyond the home boundaries, but Berthe was used to Paris and London. Lyons beckoned, and she took her chances with the Cluny family. He was a man of such morality that his sons left home and his daughters allowed themselves to be married as soon as they decently could. When his wife died, Berthe took over the household. Her references were splendid.

Mrs. Carradine must have given her a letter of sorts before they parted in Paris, Lintott registered. For he had found nothing to suggest such a paper, not even a request for one.

Berthe had come into the wide-ranging sphere of the Old One when the attorney had retired five years before, owing to ill health. She and M. Cluny were both reported to be rich. An English lord had given Berthe a fortune, and the old man had been mean enough to save every sou of his own. They saw no one and wished to see no one. They lived in complete seclusion, and Berthe reigned over his senility, a devoted despot.

"Where is she?" asked Lintott, quietly jubilant.

"Only eighteen miles away, but we must hire a carriage to get there," Le Jallu replied. "It is an isolated house in a small village with a long name. I shall make arrangement."

He sprang up, released.

"You do that, lad. I'll have a word with the Old One here. Give her the money she's been promised."

As she bestowed it in different parts of her petticoats, Le Jallu demanded arrogantly, "How can *you* speak to her?"

"I don't have to talk," said Lintott briskly. "Off you go, lad."

He drew his chair close to the stool, knocked out his pipe bowl on the bars of the grate, refilled it. Their landlady was scolding her servants back to their tasks and posts and recommending someone (probably a relative, Lintott thought) who could drive them there and back in a day.

"Bonjour, madame," Lintott bawled, jerking his chin up and down in a friendly fashion.

"Bonjou' bonjou' . . . " She was off again on that long, exhilarating adventure which most people would have named cruel existence.

Lintott nodded and smoked, and understood not a single word, and comprehended everything.

★ ★ ★

The house was secluded, walled and shuttered. Inquiries in the village, over bowls of soup and hunks of bread, had brought inhospitable response. Berthe emerged only for shopping purposes. No one had seen the old man since his arrival there five years previously. Visitors were discouraged. Public opinion felt they might keep a large fierce dog, except that they were too mean to feed it.

"Well, we'll have to manage without encouragement," said Lintott briefly. "At least, with all that time on their hands, we shan't be interrupting anything."

So he sounded intrusion with the iron

bell. A warm breeze riffled newly fledged leaves. A starling ran through his program of mimicry. A gate creaked apology.

"Proper old dungeon," said Lintott and rang again and again.

Steps trod the stone passage reluctantly. The door was unbolted top and bottom, unlocked, and opened two inches. A stout chain barred entrance.

"Say something quick and fancy, lad."

Le Jallu launched into courtesies, which were as unwelcome as themselves. The door showed signs of closing on them.

"Mention the name of Mr. Carradine, and tell her I'll ring this bell all day if needs be, lad."

And there she was, evidence come to life, and much as Lintott had expected. White-headed now, but spare and straight and obdurate as ever. Lintott regretted the starling, who had at least been cheerful.

Perhaps the kitchen at the back was more homely, but Berthe's sense of propriety led them into a tomb of a parlor. Dust sheets over cold furniture, a spotted mirror over the cold fireplace, four cracked porcelain cups lying in their saucers across the mantelpiece, a stopped clock rearing from floor to ceiling against one wall, the long dead glowering from sepia photographs. Berthe removed two covers and motioned them to sit. She offered no refreshments. She stood, hands folded in front of her decent black dress and black apron. They were not wanted.

"Tell madame," Lintott ordered, holding her gaze as he spoke, "that I'm here to stay until I've found out what I want to know. That I don't mind how long I wait in order to get it. And that there's money involved."

She looked at Lintott as though he were a cockroach. He made himself as comfortable as he could on the slippery horsehair settee, and took out his notebook and pencil.

"Tell madame, for a start, that we know about Mrs. Carradine's love affair. That *I* know *she* knows even more. And I want names and details."

"She says *never*, sir. She spits on your money."

"Oh Lord," said Lintott humorously, "oh, dearie me! Tell madame that she's an accessory to a kidnapping, which might mean a prison sentence."

"She says you may kill her if you wish. She tells you nothing."

"Tell her that Mr. Nicholas Carradine sends her his kindest regards and asks her to help him for old times' sake. Show her this card of his in case she doesn't believe me."

Berthe read the card and the message scrawled on its other side, put it in her pocket, nodded.

"Ask the lady to sit down, lad," said Lintott, satisfied.

"She says that M'sieu Cluny cannot be left alone so long, that he is now like a child and it is not always pleasant."

"Then ask madame to take us where he is. Bless you," said Lintott, "*I* don't mind sitting in the old gentleman's room. I've seen silly old folks afore."

The attorney was in the kitchen by the fire, a rug over his knees, firmly bound to his chair by a stout strip of linen. He had completed the circle from first to second childhood, resembling a very old hairless baby. The visitors delighted him, and he commented on them to himself in an excited undertone. Le Jallu was disgusted, Lintott imperturbable. Berthe scolded her charge automatically and offered him a biscuit, which he sucked in vast contentment.

"Tell the lady that nobody's going to be hurt or upset by her information, and Mr. Carradine could be helped by it — leastways, I hope he can."

Recollection was an old wound laid open.

Berthe Lecoq had come to Paris as a country girl, ignorant of everything except the raising of children, since she was the eldest of a large family. M. Lasserre had heard of her because her father worked in one of his small vineyards. Berthe had disgraced herself by bringing an illegitimate baby into the world. That it died within days of its birth simply meant she had milk to give and an abundance of balked affection. The stigma remained.

So, M. Lasserre engaged her, and Mme. Lasserre put Gabrielle into her arms. They kept her comfortably, paid her very little, and supplied a great want. Gabrielle grew into a young woman. Whatever desire Berthe could grant her was granted. They were closer to each other than to anyone else, until the girl fell in love with a young man and they wished to be married. By this time M. Lasserre was nibbling at his capital, keeping up appearances, and retreating behind a steady sale of small properties. He had no dowry to give his daughter, and the young man had nothing but his salary and his prospects. Ambitious, clever, close to thirty, Gabrielle's lover stood as yet on the lower rungs of the great French civic ladder.

"What was his name?" Lintott asked.

"Lucien Fauvel."

"Did your mistress have a nickname for him, beginning with *D*?"

"She may have. I don't know of one."

"Just do me a service, will you, lad?" said Lintott. He opened the Gladstone bag from which he had not been parted since he left Paris. He found the paper he was looking for. "It's the list of passengers killed on that train, lad. Can you see if Mr. Fovell's name is among them? I don't know how to spell it. It is?" He was dumbfounded. So much for Carradine's story. "Show me, will you, lad? *F-a-u-v-e-l* — I'll remember that. Thankee. All right, let her carry on."

Then Walter Carradine had appeared, offering what the Lasserres regarded as being of prime importance: *un bon parti*, a good match, and no demand for dowry. Only Berthe knew what the girl suffered before she gave her consent. But M. Carradine was kind and generous, accepted all her conditions, took Berthe along with her mistress and paid her handsomely. They were content. The little boy Nicholas was charming. In the first year or so of the marriage the little girl Odette was born. And on this child Gabrielle poured the same enraptured love Berthe had lavished on her charge twenty years before.

"I understood how madame felt because I had known it," Berthe said.

But madame was restless. She found London dull, she found her husband duller. She made frequent trips to Paris. She bought her clothes there. Then Lucien Fauvel turned up, still in love with her, still hopeful.

Berthe had never experienced passion — a peasant's by-blow could hardly rank in that exalted category — but she recognized it. So madame did wrong to become his mistress? So Berthe did wrong to act as cover and go-between? Well then, they did wrong! She wanted madame's happiness above all else, but they were careful. The little Nicholas was with them, his eyes and ears were sharp. Naturally neither M. Carradine nor the Lasserres must suspect. So M. Fauvel met them as if by chance, in public places, and chatted as though he were a friendly acquaintance, and made his assignations. Letters exchanged between them were immediately destroyed. Madame went abroad at certain times of the year, and he would wait until Berthe brought the news of her arrival. Gabrielle had invented an old friend, a Mme. David, who was childless and often lonely — lest Nicholas should mention the man. And M. Fauvel was M. David, come to beg madame to console the lady for a few hours.

"That's the *D*," cried Lintott. "My word, she covered up even in a private diary."

But the boy never said anything,

nor questioned the man's presence, nor discussed him, nor mentioned the fictitious name.

"Better if he had, to my mind," Lintott observed. "Better all the way round. Children know without being told. The quiet ones bottle it up inside them. It can do a deal of damage. It *did* do a deal of damage."

The affair lengthened, deepened, became their all-in-all.

"Lucky she didn't find herself in the family way," Lintott said to himself.

Le Jallu translated this also, rather more delicately, and brought a national reprimand on the Inspector's head.

"Frenchmen are not so uncontrolled as Englishmen," said Berthe scathingly. "They are more careful."

"Lucky she didn't have any more children by her husband, then," Lintott retorted, annoyed. "That would have spoiled her game."

But Walter's desire apparently surpassed his achievements. Lintott was mortified in the name of England.

Then Fauvel was offered his first good post, in Switzerland. The strength of their liaison, the knowledge of final parting, brought them to crisis point. He begged her to bring the child and come with him.

"And where did the late Mr. Carradine figure in this plan?" Lintott demanded, shocked and forthright.

"M. Carradine worshiped madame. He could be persuaded to come to some arrangement in time, for her sake."

"And what about his daughter?" Lintott cried. "Translate for me sharpish, lad, and don't sound so polite about it. Sound angry, like I am!"

Le Jallu slapped the question down.

But Berthe only said composedly that it would be very difficult, very sad, but M. Carradine adored madame. In the end he would do as she wished.

"Poor fellow," said Lintott. "A born loser, every time."

Still Gabrielle hesitated. She was too much the product of her upbringing and environment to cast it so willfully aside. Her position as Fauvel's mistress would reflect adversely on herself and Odette. Even with Walter complaisantly agreeing to divorce, which he might well not, her future seemed perilous. Besides, though the child was fond of Fauvel she loved her father. Gabrielle saw good society turning its back, whispering. She saw Odette barred from the privileges of wealth and connections that were hers by right. She feared scandal, ostracism, insecurity.

Fauvel waited three months for her to make up her mind. Desperate, he approached Berthe. He offered her a permanent place at Gabrielle's side. He protested that his intentions were honorable, his future assured and promising. He would provide for all of them. He would eventually make Gabrielle his wife. He asked for trust, for faith, for a last risk in the name of love.

"He pleaded his cause to some effect," Lintott commented dryly.

"He promised I should die in their loving arms," said Berthe. "I believed him. Madame wept and prayed and would move neither backward nor forward. I made up her mind for her. I knew what was best. I gave him the child, so we should follow him."

The silence in the kitchen was so intense that Lintott recorded every tick of the clock on the wall. The old man sucked another biscuit and contemplated the fire. Le Jallu sat, head bowed before this saga of human passions, and awaited further instructions. Berthe stared beyond them into immeasurable sorrow.

"I can guess what happened," said Lintott finally, "but get her to tell me, lad."

Berthe took Odette for the walk from which she would not return, and came home with a half-truth. Fauvel had met them, sent Berthe on an errand while he amused the child, and disappeared. In her hands she held the proofs of his excuse: a packet of cigarettes, a carton of sweets tied with a ribbon.

"Madame was distracted. I had to think for us all. I advised her to tell M'sieu and Madame Lasserre that Odette was staying for a few days with Madame David. Madame sent me to M'sieu Fauvel's lodgings. I knew he had gone. I knew which hotel he was staying in with the child. I went to him to ask what I should say. He gave me a letter for her, which was supposed to have been left with his landlady. Again he insisted that he loved her, that he meant well by all of us. He told her the child was cared for but longing for her maman. He gave her his address in Swizterland and begged her to follow them."

Gabrielle, trapped and hysterical, forced to hide her 'feelings from everyone' but Berthe, faced yet another problem. Walter had promised to join them for the coming weekend. She could not endure a further crisis. She telegraphed him to postpone the visit. She thought of a private detective, of the police, of a part confession to her husband — and discarded the ideas as impossible.

"I knew madame was at breaking point," said Berthe implacably. "My heart was heavy for her, but I knew where she would find happiness."

"Did you?" shouted Lintott. "Did you? What gave you the right to play God Almighty, I wonder?"

Unmoved by his outburst, Berthe continued. "The child had been gone a week. The Lasserres were curious, the situation was becoming desperate.

I knew which train was taking M'sieu Fauvel and the child to Switzerland. On the morning of its departure I took madame her breakfast tray. I told her what I had done. Madame stared at me for a long time. Then, vanquished, she said, 'So be it'.

"News of the accident came hours later. We could not conceal everything, except from the one madame now needed most — her husband. I told Madame Lasserre the essential details so that she and M'sieu Lasserre could act for us, advise us. They were distressed, they were shocked, but they were practical. We had to find out whether the child was alive, injured, dead. M'sieu Fauvel's mother was his only relative. We had to confide in her too. M'sieu Lasserre took all upon himself, all." She lifted her arms and let them drop in terrible resignation. "It was he who thought of saying that the child was visiting friends who would meet her. Then we heard that M'sieu Fauvel and the child were killed. M'sieu Carradine was informed. By the time he arrived the Lasserres had thought of everything. And madame was so ill that we feared for her life too. So M'sieu Carradine was content with what they told him, thinking now only of madame."

"They closed ranks," Lintott said quietly. "Covered up. Made it look right, so there wasn't a scandal. Is that it?"

Berthe nodded. "They were practical. It was all they could do for madame. We buried the truth with the child."

"You never bury the truth," Lintott replied with conviction. "It comes up and catches you unawares, one way or another. Aye, twenty years after. It's like the law. It might seem a bit on the slow side, but it's dogged, it don't give up, and it never shuts its files until the case is finished."

She cared nothing for his philosophy.

"And so Mrs. Carradine turned against you when she'd lost them both, eh? Blamed you for the lot, told her husband some cock-and-bull story about not having you round her because you reminded her of the child? Gave you a letter of recommendation so you shouldn't starve, and your fare home?

But Mr. Carradine turned up trumps, didn't he? Sorry for you, sending you money — and you accepted it, after the dirty tricks you'd played him."

Her obsession shielded her from Lintott's contempt.

"How she suffered. How she suffered. I traveled with her and with M'sieu Lasserre to identify the child. It was a dark time. Many others were there, searching for those who belonged to them. Sometimes I thought the dead were fortunate, when I heard the injured. We spoke little. Only a few words. We were in a dream from which we would not wake. There was a mark on us that would not be washed away, as though we were unclean . . . "

"You wish me to translate still, sir?" Le Jallu asked in a low voice.

"Yes, carry on, lad. It may not be evidence, but it's merciful."

" . . . they identified the nun by her cross. They did not weep. They said it was the Will of God. I heard those who cried against Him, but I did not cry. Who was I to complain to Him? He had punished me, and I was cast out. And yet there were those saved who should have been taken. I heard stories of pity and terror. Of a criminal, badly burned, whom they healed for the guillotine. Of a child nobody wanted, whose reason had been impaired, taken to an orphanage. The nuns, whose sister had been killed, stayed on to comfort those who were in trouble. I never saw them weep. I did not weep, but that was because my heart was frozen. God tormented me, through the child, through madame. I died a thousand times, watching her. She would not believe, you see, sir. Even when they showed her the bracelet. We took her home. She would not let me see her, touch her, speak to her. Only M'sieu Carradine spoke kindly to me, and Madame Lasserre was practical. I was a year in that dream. I woke to nothing. I was nothing. I am nothing."

Suddenly she wailed, hands over eyes, heedless of them.

"I think we'd best go, lad," Lintott said quietly. "No good thanking her, or giving her money or the old bonjour. It'd be out of place."

They breathed in the spring air

simultaneously and looked at each other.

"God is not mocked," Lintott observed reverently, "and whatsoever a man shall sow that shall he reap. *He's* a regular old harvest for her sins, ain't he?" Jerking a thumb toward the shrouded house.

"You find poetry and philosophy in this also, sir?"

"Of a very dark sort, lad. Yes. You stick to your sunshine and mayflies and the passing of love and beauty. It might be a bit on the flightly side, but it's a deal more palatable."

14

LINTOTT'S departure from Paris removed a sense of restraint. His rare letters, written stiffly in a stiff hand, took care of Carradine's earlier concerns, but they were no longer signposts pointing to a hidden answer. Nicholas had found himself without Lintott's assistance. The Inspector's search simply reminded him that he had tried to uncover a truth, to come to terms with the past. And truth had been discovered, as it usually is, in an unlikely place; and was very simple, as it usually is, being in this case self-deception.

His revelation in the studio during Claire's first visit, rousing forgotten hurts, forgotten angers, also promised new growth. He saw his obsession with Gabrielle as a childish thing, and with many falterings and regressions was putting it away from him. New attitudes were developing, and with them new work was possible. He had been saved, and recognized this unexpected growth with humility.

Only the thought of the dead child, played as pawn by Gabrielle's lover, wounded him. She had been innocent and had died fearfully. He had wanted to throw that terrible bracelet into the Seine, to bury it, to put it irrevocably from him. Then he realized that this too must be accepted. So he was careful to remember mother and daughter with compassion and regret, and to remember that they were yesterday.

Today was that intimate distance between sitter and painter. Today was exasperation and laughter, argument and tenderness. Today was a woman self-willed and vulnerable, who could be defeated by nothing but personal truths — and so utterly routed by these that he dared not speak them. Today was a Parisian coquette who knew everything about men in theory and nothing in practice. Today was a half-educated mind picking up and examining every crumb of knowledge he fed to it and asking for more. *Continuez!* Today was wanting this woman so much that he could not contemplate another, and this woman keeping him at a distance even though she wanted him too. Today, in a name, was Claire.

The pose had wearied her. She arched her back and yawned. Clasped both hands behind her neck, stretched again, and lapsed into smiling immobility. She was thinking of something other than Carradine, so easy with him and sure of him that she could forget his presence. He was entranced by her faults: the defensive manner in which she tucked both thumbs into her palms; the fine lines of temper that drew her brows together; her insistence on reason when she was at her most irrational. He was enchanted with a voice that could be velvet or steel; with a face that could be sallow and plain in anger, gentle in repose, lovely in pleasure, comical in pique.

As a painter he absorbed the folds of her absurd dress, the light pulse at the base of her throat, the rebel fringe and sober chignon. He became the hundred contradictions that were Claire.

As a man he had tirelessly attempted to rid himself of her by comparing her with other women who had temporarily moved him. He pictured her in middle and old age, when the rocks of character showed through, and knew that a placid life was out of the question. She would be handsome, determined, and armed with experience. With regard to beauty she came somewhere in the middle of his ideal, and lacked Natalie's vanity, which set beauty above expressiveness and so preserved it. She could be utterly charming and discard charm when it no longer served her. She could be exquisitely tactful and shatteringly honest. She leaped to false conclusions and fought for them. She created situations and blamed him for them. She was instantly and sincerely repentant when her errors were pointed out — and committed them again in spite of herself. And yet her absence left him incomplete.

He said slowly, "I have decided to love you." And knew it was no decision.

She opened contemplative eyes suddenly. He stared back as he must have done in his boyhood, knowing he had dared something unmentionable and would stand by it. His guilty obstinacy disarmed her.

Mildly she said, "I need time to love you. Wait."

He bent over his work again, and she resumed her pose.

★ ★ ★

In the garden of the Tuileries she said happily, "The chairs are out again!" Flinging her arms wide with a rapturous lack of restraint.

"It's far too cool to sit down, Claire."

"What matter? I do not wish to sit down. I like to see them so. In the autumn they are sad."

Stacked spindles beneath leafless trees, their summer concert done.

"Why have you brought your parasol?" he asked.

She sighed and took his arm and sauntered on. "So that the sun will see me and shine. Do not laugh at me, please."

"I thought it was to attract attention, or perhaps because it is particularly pretty."

"You are not polite."

"You once reprimanded me for being too polite. I am endeavoring to change. I am endeavoring to please you in all things. And I am also endeavoring to be patient, which is hardest of all."

"But what endeavor," she said lightly and smiled to herself.

"Are you coming with me to London, Claire? I must go soon."

"I have not made up my mind. Perhaps we are better good friends."

"I can think of several striking improvements on friendship."

"Because you have known much friendship. I have only you. I do not wish to lose you."

"Why on earth should you?"

"Oh!" The face of disillusion. "You want me. You have me. You grow tired of me. Then there is no more love and no more friendship. It is so."

They stopped as if in accord and looked about them since they could not look at each other. Fashionable Paris was strolling before and behind, courting spring with delicate ensembles, flowered hats, foppish escorts. Families wended their slower way: papa smoothing his mustache and glancing elsewhere, maman superbly fleshed and handsome, a gaggle of children trailing them in their Sunday best. High baby carriages wheeled by country nursemaids, their occupants sleeping or protesting in laundered white. A middle-aged Frenchman, bow-tied, bowler hat tipped gallantly, conversing with a middle-aged woman taller and heavier than himself. She turned and glanced at Carradine and Claire, smirking a little, well pleased with the rendezvous. *Moi et toi,* her expression indicated.

"Beside," said Claire slowly, "how shall I come with you to London? As your little French mistress? Your Madame Tilling will not speak to me. Your friends will joke me. They will say you are a jolly fellow and look me down their noses."

He was silent, tracing a pattern in the gravel with the point of his cane. He was not ready to commit himself further than loving.

Now she did look at him, and sadly. "I am right. We stay good friends, Nicholas."

"Do you intend to be solitary for

the rest of your life," Carradine asked, "whether you love or not? You are asking for marriage, aren't you?"

"*I* do not ask!" she cried, so passionately that even the Parisians raised eyebrows and smiled. "It is for you to ask, and you do not. Now I shall go home to Natalie. Take me!" Imperiously.

"Oh, the devil!" he said, defeated. "How can I explain myself?"

She watched him with tremendous irony.

"You explain yourself very well, always. You wish all of me. You give me a little part of yourself."

"Your parasol has brought out the sun," he observed, relieved by this distraction. The legs of the iron chairs slanted suddenly, new leaves became transparent. "Let us sit down for a few moments. If you're cold you can have my coat."

"But how polite! I am a fool to listen. You talk the ear off a donkey."

Yet she sat down, and he sat by her, studying her averted face.

"I love you," he began, "so stupidly that I say your name into silences,

294

conjuring you up like a callow schoolboy. I love you so intensely that I treasure your faults above your virtues. I love your ridiculous stubborn chastity, your irrational fits of temper. You are utterly impossible, neither taking me nor letting me be. I often wonder why I don't pick up a girl to amuse me and leave you to tease somebody else. In short, you are a damned nuisance, and I still love you."

She pursed her lips.

"I can't believe you are playing with me," he continued, "and if you are not, if you want me as I want you, then why complicate something so very simple and desirable?"

"Making love is simple. Loving is not. I wish to go home now."

"And have an inquisition with Natalie? I've told her I want to take you to London. I've promised to provide for you to care for you — "

"*Care?*" she cried, rising. "If you care, then I come tomorrow, but you do not. I care. And how do you dare talk of us to Natalie?"

"For heaven's sake, let's not have a scene in public," he begged, and generations of Englishmen spoke through him. A Frenchman would have joined in. "Don't make a theater!"

"I make a thousand theaters if I wish! I do as I wish!"

"How the devil did I get myself into this mess?" he asked himself, incredulous.

For he had always controlled the situation, and this one was beyond him and hauled him after it, however unwillingly.

"Bring me a cab. I go home alone now. You have offended me. I tell you and Natalie to go to hell. You tell me how you love me. I tell you how I do not love you. I do not love your selfish dis-honestness with you and me. Leave me for always?" Barring his pleading with her parasol. "I solve your nuisance, M'sieu Carradine. I am out when you call, forever. Find yourself a French girl who does not worry your work or your heart. Make yourself a little puppet that hangs in the cupboard when you grow tired of her. I wish you much happiness, much emptiness. Bring me a cab!"

"Look, Claire," he said, oblivious of

passing smiles and comments, "I'm past bargaining with you — "

"You bargain well, but not successful. Bring me a cab!"

He flung up his arms and sat again, clasped his hands between his knees, stalled.

"How would you know," he said, more to himself than to her, "what it is to be so aware of another human being that she becomes more real than yourself?"

"And how do you know," she cried, striking his legs with her rolled parasol, "what it is to see a man, and to know a man, and he will not be that? How do you know what it is always to hope and not to find? Now I find, and you talk of love and say it is simple, and explain it is nothing. You do not like to be discomfortable, M'sieu Carradine. With me, with love, you are discomfortable, but you are not empty. Not because I am me, but because you begin to feel for some-body except your selfish self." She nodded emphatically. "With me — you risk."

She glimpsed a cab, which appeared

to be taking risks of a different sort, and halted it.

"Don't leave me," he asked humbly. "We can go somewhere else. We can dance in Bougival. I promise not to talk. I promise not to say another word." He held out his hand.

She struck it down. "You touch me and I scream for the gendarmes. I go home alone."

He saw she meant it and helped her into the cab. The two vacated chairs seemed sadder than any autumn could render them.

★ ★ ★

Natalie, thoroughly enjoying herself, played one against the other for a few days and reconciled them the following weekend. Subdued, they danced in Bougival: he attentive, looking at her face; she abstracted, looking into some sorry dream of her own.

"Come to London as my guest," he suggested. "Bring Natalie if you wish. I have been thinking about this. You could be established in a respectable hotel, we could introduce you as a widow. I should watch my visiting hours. You could be no more than a friend to me. That will give us both time, time to learn whether love is enough, whether we have more in common than simple attraction. Is that honest enough for you?"

"You make no demand?"

"Lord, no, not the least in the world." He found his submission exhilarating and chastening.

After a few silent turns she said, "I come with you to London, as you say. I come without Natalie. She does not understand, and I cannot fight her too. Then we shall see."

"And you'll sit for me again?"

"Yes, but not in my chemise."

"Even in such a serious situation as this," Carradine said, smiling, "I find your insistence on the proprieties amusing. You have heard me give my word. What on earth makes you think I should retract it at the sight of your posing in a perfectly respectable chemise?"

"We are changed, Nicholas. As your good friend I sit in my chemise. As your lover I do not."

He laughed in spite of her frowning protest. "But your clothes are so unsuitable, Claire. Very sweet, very *jeune fille*, but not you. Suppose I buy you some new ones?"

"No. I shall not be bought."

"I must paint you, then, as an oddity in a bad temper, at total variance with her clothes and her inclinations."

"Do that," she flashed. "It shall be very interesting."

"Are you always going to argue with me, Claire?"

"Perhaps. We shall see if we are together always."

Carradine said, "I wonder why I bother?" But seemed to have no choice.

★ ★ ★

They found words clumsy. Carradine's river of comment had dried, his analyses ceased. Bereft of a combatant, Claire no longer defended or attacked. Their voices became softer, non-insistent. She sat for hours, patient and tranquil, in the gowns that were a charade of girlish innocence.

And Carradine, since he could not have her, observed her faithfully and so possessed her in a different way. He painted now in order to discover her, rather than to discover a new aspect of himself in relation to her. He began to accept things that irked him, such as her occasional cigarette.

"I can tolerate Natalie's smoking," he said, chagrined, "but not you, Claire. What on earth do you smoke, anyway?"

"Russian cigarettes. What do you smoke, Nicholas?"

"Oh, never mind."

When she next came he had bought her a box of fat, black, gold-tipped Russian cigarettes.

"I shall not smoke if you wish — not here. But I shall smoke at home." With a flicker of independence.

"I'm growing used to it," said Carradine.

She found Bessie Lintott's packet of Brooke Bond tea in his cupboard and asked if she might try it.

"It does not taste like French tea," she said uncertainly, sipping.

"The French have no proper respect for tea, my dear girl. Throw it away if you don't care for it."

"I care for it," she replied, "I think."

He felt so sharply for them both, each finding a way to the other, that he kissed her cupped hands in token. She leaned forward and kissed him — as gently and as compassionately on the mouth. The tea, steaming between them in homely contentment, made them smile and then laugh.

"That is enough," said Carradine definitely. "Now we shall work again."

When she had gone he picked up his wrappered copy of *The Times*, which Mrs. Tilling sent daily, faithfully, to remind him of England. He put it down again unopened. Hands on hips, he stared at the studio, searching for occupation. He dusted and tidied everything except his tableful of materials and washed the teacups. He was too weary to concentrate, too full of Claire to think of anything else, too alive to sleep. So he walked, taking Paris in mental camera flashes.

The city was almost deserted at this sacred hour of the evening, as French bellies celebrated the great meal of the day with the absorption of priests celebrating Communion.

Beyond this tangible devotion flared the tangible intangible passion for French soil, for *la patrie*. Carradine had often pondered on what the reaction would be to a cry of *"Aux armes!"* in a crowded restaurant. With delicious pleasure he pictured the heroic response, while the women collected and hoarded all the food they could lay their hands on. *Encore un peu, l'ennemi ne l'aura pas!* A little more, the enemy shall not have it!

Then he saw the vagrants sitting at a table near the pavement, and sat down a little way from them, and ordered cognac.

They had reached a climax of age and poverty, and it was of no account. Faded photographs, they regarded only each other. Between them stood two half-filled glasses of milky Pernod, and Carradine judged that the evening must have been begun and must end with these two drinks, which were all they could afford. One would eventually close the other's eyes, and thank God for a small mercy. They had nothing but each other. They had all that truly mattered.

"Is this what she wants?" he asked himself, and was appalled by their consummate courage, by his lack of that same courage, by the knowledge that Claire possibly possessed it.

He left them still sitting, still exchanging an occasional word or smile, being careful of their Pernod, which must last them until the café closed for the night. He went back to the studio and sketched until dawn broke.

When he woke, Claire had let herself in and was examining the drawings.

"Les clochards," she said, smiling.

"You like that, do you, my love?"

"I like *him*," she replied.

She did not mean the tattered knight beneath the café awning.

15

HE had waited in that hotel room off the Rue Jacob for two hours, six and a half minutes. Years afterward he would be able to draw it in detail. Sunlight slats on faded carpet, dusty crimson draperies hung by brass rings from a wooden pole, their mended lace companions fringed at the hem. The marble washstand, tiled with pictures of the apostles, bearing its china burden of flowered jug and basin. Balloon-backed chairs, scrolled commodes, gas brackets on the wall surmounted by glass shades the shape of upturned lilies. Busy-patterned paper. And dominating the whole, a huge mahogany bed, inlaid, ornamented, bow-legged.

He counted the tiles on the washstand. St. Paul was cracked. He inserted a fingernail into the crack to test its durability. The saint would last some time yet. He pondered the worn patch on the carpet before the long window and wondered how many people had stood there and looked into the well of the courtyard and waited. Perhaps this was a well-known room for assignations. Perhaps the *patronne*, who seemed to favor pink satin tea gowns, only rented it to lovers who would never meet. Perhaps a thousand men had mounted three flights of stairs in delicious hope and stumbled down them desolated.

Claire would not come, even though this hotel's shabby gentility was what she said she preferred. Her final decision had disrupted a serene three days. He found it difficult to believe how much living they had crowded into a little space of time. Those three days had been idyllic years, marriage at its mellowest and best, riding at anchor in mild harbor. Then she had made a theater to end all theaters: accusing him of emotional blackmail, exposing his vile nature, and capitulating without his ever asking her to do so. It was as though, like the White Queen in *Alice*, she must suffer before the event. The whole mood, the entire argument, had been self-induced. Then she set out her conditions. Natalie must never know,

306

never guess. The studio must not be despoiled. Claire would not stay the night. She would not meet him, anywhere this side of the Seine, as if the river were a guardian of secrets and would keep theirs safe.

On the other side of the thin wall, two lovers had been happy. He reflected that there was no lonelier experience on earth than being solitary and forced to share the muffled pleasures of two people crowning a rendezvous. Down in the courtyard, shaded by a plane tree, an old man remembered his youth. Around the house, windows open in mild May, other lives lifted voice.

Carradine had said, head in hands, as one who has sat out a hailstorm with no shelter, "Do I now understand that if I book a room in a respectable hotel on the Left Bank, in the afternoon, you will give up your long-preserved virginity?"

"Yes. But I shall not be pregnated. And I shall not do what Natalie says to do not to be pregnated."

"Certainly not. You may leave the matter to me."

They would have caught humor from

the situation had her mood remained that of Bernhardt hogging a scene, but she turned sad again.

At the studio door she had said, "Now we shall not be friends."

"Lovers *and* friends."

She had shaken her head. "No. You shall not like me when you love me."

He now ordered coffee and *gâteaux* for two, again. He smoked and waited. The afternoon waned, the room sobered to shabbiness. The hours of *cinq à sept* approached. Natalie would be in her boudoir, entertaining either the Minister or his son. Claire would sit at her window, having changed her mind for the hundredth time, raising aloft God only knew what personal standard, following some unfathomable personal crusade.

He was so shocked when she appeared behind the maid who brought the tray that he did not even greet her. She had dressed for battle. A black silk mantle. A close-fitting plum velvet hat with a plum satin band, set straight on. A plum silk dress overlaid by plum georgette, transparent sleeves, her hips swarthed with a black satin sash that looped to her knees in a casually careful knot. Her parasol was domed and fringed.

He realized that she must have borrowed clothes from Natalie to avoid his usual ironies, and they suited her no better. She looked, in fact, the way she saw herself in fancy: a mistress meeting her gallant. She unpinned her hat, removed her gloves and mantle, and sat down near the washstand. Her dignity was ridiculous, was heart-breaking. Her resolution was that of a child about to take bad medicine. So must the great aristocrats have ridden to the guillotine. And this was her idea, he thought, infuriated.

Suddenly she caught sight of the bottle of champagne on the mantelpiece and eyed it with asperity. "I do not have to be drunk," she remarked bitterly, coming down to earth.

"I think perhaps *I* do," said Carradine, resigned.

"You make me feel a dirt!"

He said reasonably, "I am returning to England, Claire, in the next few days. I shall go alone, and you are free to leave now."

Her eyes narrowed, widened, were hurt, were angry.

"No!" she cried. "I give you my word. I keep my word. Please to unbutton by back dress."

"I have never understood monks before," he remarked, "but their wisdom now confounds me."

"You wish to seduce? Then seduce! Be over with it. I do not like this room."

She was endeavoring, by a series of arm contortions, to unfasten her dress. Three satin buttons totally eluded her. She yanked them from their moorings. One flew across the room and hit a cavernous wardrobe. Undeterred, she stepped out of her gown, removed her petticoat, and began on her suspenders. Her stockings and stays were black. Her concentration and lack of enjoyment, her haste, were dampening: an erotic cartoon gone wrong.

"I cannot, by the wildest feat of imagination, find any allurement in your offer," said Carradine objectively, though he would have liked to laugh.

"Oh, you will, m'sieu, you will. I know men. They are animals. They allure very quick. My stays, I cannot. You must."

"I don't wish to appear insulting, mam'selle, but I have seldom felt less amorous."

"Where is there a knife?"

"You wish to kill me — or yourself?"

She unclipped her *pochette*, found a small pair of nail scissors, twisted with the agility of an acrobat, and snipped the stay lace free.

"You stupid girl!" said Carradine, thoroughly annoyed. "How in the world are you going to get dressed again?"

"I do not care. I warn you, and you will not listen. Now I insist you take your pleasure."

A little breathless, defiant, triumphant at her magnanimity and decisiveness, she stood naked in a caldron of lawn and lace. She folded her arms.

"Commencez!"

Carradine could no longer control his hilarity. He laughed until his ribs pained him, until his eyes ran tears, until he could not draw breath. She, railing and weeping, flailed him with her velvet *pochette*. At last he picked up the faded quilt and wrapped it carefully round her, stroked her disheveled hair. Occasionally he caught up a little spurt of laughter before it mounted. Huddled in the quilt, in humiliation, she did not speak. He sat by her on the floor and poured out a cup of hot coffee.

"For God's sake, Claire, forgive yourself and me. I most humbly apologize. Drink this, and let us, as you so often beg me, be good friends again."

"But look what I have done," she whispered, indicating the torn placket, the missing buttons, the severed stay lace.

"Have I not warned you a thousand times to count ten before you lose your temper?"

"I do not learn. I never learn." She wept and sneezed, dried her eyes on her petticoat. "I shall suffer *la grippe*, this room is full of drafts. I hope you suffer too, very much, even more than me."

"I shall share your cold with pleasure and account it an honor. Here, Claire, I've found the prettiest and most delectable cake on the plate for you. Eat it up, like a good girl."

He had his father to thank for that

quiet good humor which now enveloped them, though he never stopped to think about it. His father was present, too, in the acceptance without reproach of feminine caprice. But he possessed, as his father had not, some insight into their origins.

"Have you been tormenting yourself about this all afternoon, Claire?"

She nodded, restored to their old comradeship, and bit at the cream cake. Apart from pink splotches on either side of her eyes she was almost herself again.

"Because you found Natalie and her soldiers disgusting?"

She shook her head and sniffed.

"Because you had committed yourself — and truly, Claire, you made a bogeyman out of the whole business to something you knew but had not experienced?"

She shook her head again and answered him. "Because you will not like me when you love me."

"There seemed to be nothing amiss in what I saw of you," observed Carradine, entertained. "I had begun to think you were in some way deformed." He recollected that amusement was out of place. "Why should I not like you?"

She shrugged. "I know, Nicholas. That is all."

"But I know that we shall find each other everything we could hope for," he said quietly, persuasively.

"It is a terrible risk."

"Who shrieked at me in public and hit me with her parasol because I never took risks?"

She held up the remains of the cake in awful warning.

"Claire, if you throw that at me I shall leave," said Carradine firmly. "You have a most astonishing view of men as being quite invincible. They are not. With my hand on my heart, I assure you that you were in no danger of seduction when you treated me to that little theater of striptease. I never wanted you less. I can feel as humiliated and as defiled as you can, and just as easily. If you are going to fight me I don't want to come within a mile of you. And I don't want to fight you if you want to make love. You must be as honest as you always say I should

314

be, and tell me. Do you, or do you not, wish to spend the evening in this appallingly vulgar bed?"

She finished the cake, wiped the cream from her face and fingers on the coverlet, and began to take down her hair.

"I wish the vulgar bed," she said. Then, extending one arm through the curtain of her hair, she added, "On one condition."

"I thought there might possibly be a condition or two."

"You must never laugh at me."

"What an extraordinary condition," said Carradine, removing his tie.

Nothing was as he had anticipated. He began with restraint, registered her first responses with some relief, responded in turn as she joined him, and remained inside her for several minutes afterwards because she clasped him so closely. They were new to each other, and yet completely familiar, as though they had known and made love for a year. Her sudden reversal from prudery to frank enjoyment astounded him. His vanity was not so great as to obscure his judgment. He moved away and looked at her, lying lazy and replete as a cat. She opened her eyes, stroked his face, kissed his lips, a goddess who had just received just tribute.

"It is sad," she said, "that there is only one first time together, Nicholas. Nicholas?"

He said deliberately, "This was not the first time for either of us."

Enclosed in their kingdom all sound had ceased; now it became clamorous. Children in the courtyard, a married couple screaming at each other, the jarred song of birds, the clash of dishes.

She stopped in mid-stretch, staring at him, tumbling down again.

Oh, be your age, sir, he recalled Lintott chiding him, in chilling retrospect. *That girl's been on the French merry-go-round, as God's my judge. You ain't the first. I'm surprised at you. I really am.*

"And you speak of honesty," he cried, cheated.

She was sitting up, placing both hands on his mouth, beseeching. "You must not say so. You must not spoil us."

"Oh, spare me the pathos!" He swung his legs over the side of the bed and reached for his clothes.

"Before God, this is the first time I make love with loving, Nicholas. Other times never," she cried, terrified by their separation.

"How many men have you had?"

"Just one man. I live with him two years."

"I suppose Natalie fished him out of the slime for you. Was he very rich? Married and unfaithful? Widowed, with money to leave? Single and peculiar, with money to leave?"

She pulled the quilt round her again as though it gave protection, as though it stood between her and violation. She sought to defend herself but had no defenses.

"He was old and he was rich, yes. I do not like him. He was — I am — like King David with the girl. I warm his bed so that he does not die alone."

"You warmed it to some purpose!" he shouted. "Were you a virgin when he adopted you?"

Her eyes lit. She had only herself to fight for now, but she had fought for that one a long time.

"I say, *yes*! and *yes*! And *yes* a thousand times!"

"When did you leave him? When he died? Did he have a little gift for you in his will?"

They were free of each other now. Free to scorn, to cease loving, to explain, to be lonely. She answered him rapidly in a fusillade of French, finding her English inadequate for the occasion.

"I left him because he made me sick. Do you know what it is to rouse an old man who is losing his potency? It becomes one long, weary game that ends in nothing. I know every whore's trick in the book, and I am sick to the stomach with him. Now get out! To hell with you and your stupid purity, the purity that men like you expect of women without having a purity of their own! You make me sick too. Oh, I know you, M'sieu Carradine. Love is not blind, it sees too clearly. You make love to phantoms. You make love to your maman in every woman — but not with me. This afternoon you made love to Claire Picard, and it was like no other woman. Don't lie to yourself! Did you think of your Gabrielle even once? I know you did not. I know that because I am a clever whore, and because I love you. Well, that will be my problem, and I shall survive it. I shall survive as you will not, because you have no faith, no love, not even hope. But sometime I shall find a man who is not a spoiled little boy, and then we shall make love together so that I snap my fingers and say 'Pouf to you, M'sieu Carradine'!"

She too began dressing, back turned. The stays she rolled up. The dress placket would not meet, let alone fasten. She hid her discrepancies beneath the silk mantle.

"You are as old as Eve," said Carradine in fascinated abhorrence.

"I am older than you will ever be. I face the truth — all but that little truth you could not accept. I hoped — oh, I was a fool — that you would be too *bouleversé* to notice. I should have known that your mind never sleeps. That mind! Tick-tock-tick-tock. If you had let your mind follow your body we could have been happy."

"On a rotten foundation? On a lie?"

"How easily you become the good man! Shall I tell you something? We are not perfect, we French, and we accept imperfections. Often a man and a woman are held together by a little secret. He makes love well because another woman has taught him. He does not speak of that. In time his wife understands, she accepts, she does not speak either. You make a parade of your love for the French. You admire us, you mock at us, you prize us and laugh at us. But you are not one of us. You cannot feel, you cannot share, you cannot forgive. You cling to your rags of goodness and reason. You are amused by Natalie, you are amused by M'sieu Roche, because he is faithless to his rich wife and his own son cuckolds him. But he grows old, and Natalie is the last of his youth and needs more lovemaking than he can give. He accepts that his son keeps the balance."

She looked round the room as Carradine had looked, to imprint it on her remembrance. With an irony that matched his own, she said, "I have never made love in a hotel before. What a terrible admission for a woman of my vast experience!"

"Inspector Lintott knew you were like this," said Carradine, incredulous, "but you portrayed yourself differently — admit *that*."

"I portrayed what I was, what I felt. You talk of virginity as though you were an expert. Let me tell you something that will be of no use to you, because you will not accept it. If I had been raped by twenty men in the marketplace I should still have been a virgin, here and here." She touched her heart and her forehead. "Only with you, this afternoon, I am no longer a virgin." Her anger mounted. "And you had better loving than you would have had with a virgin."

She became cynical, hand on hip, screwing up her mouth in derision. "But if your taste is for innocent little girls, M'sieu Carradine, and you do not want their papas confronting you, then I advise you to frequent the brothels. Paris — and, I am sure, London — supply such commodities. Only don't be misled in your eagerness to despoil them. We have prostitutes who are set aside, because of their modest air and appearance, to play the virgin. We have peepholes too so that other men may observe the fun. It is very good business, I believe, and the English are noted for enjoying the roles of both rapist and peeper."

He was speechless as she fired first one salvo and then the next with abominable precision. He could have hit her.

"You may find a cab for me," she said, pale and composed, "to show me you have not forgotten your English good manners. Your manners, M'sieu Carradine, are all that are left to you."

She had penetrated from observation, from dedicated listening, to his utmost weakness and utmost ambition.

"But forget, M'sieu Carradine, the desire to be a Degas, a Renoir, a Toulouse-Lautrec. Please do not interrupt me. I know that each of them is quite different, and you resemble none of them. But they have one great virtue." Prodding his chest with her parasol to emphasize each word. "They live. They are participants, not spectators. They do not lay down rules for everybody but themselves. When you learn what they

322

knew from the beginning, then you may call yourself an artist."

She motioned him to open the door for her. She ruined her exit.

"And *merde* to you!" she cried.

She was gone, in a flurry of plum and black, taking care to have the last word. She had, after all, lost everything else.

Carradine surfaced very slowly, sitting on the edge of the bed. Then he took the bottle of champagne from the mantelpiece, resolving to give it to the *patronne*, who was listening on the staircase. It had not been needed, either as an aphrodisiac or a celebration.

16

ACH might have expected to spend a sleepless night, but the explosion had exhausted them both. In the apartment near the Etoile, Claire rose refreshed and drank chocolate with Natalie in unusual comradeship. Carradine in Montmartre confided in the communal cat over black coffee. Rationally, the affair was impossible. Emotionally, it was fraught. In terms of trust, it was shattered. Yet neither of them could wait to pick up the fragments of the previous afternoon and begin justifications all over again. Their notes, delivered by hand for greater speed, arrived at their different doors around the same time and were written in the same vein. They did not address each other by name but plunged immediately into the good fight.

Carradine wrote deliberately. *I did not object to your past but to the deception you practiced on me. I am not in the habit of seducing virgins, nor have I ever seduced a virgin, incidentally. So you seemed rather a special person, and I acted accordingly. No man enjoys being a fool, and I feel my reactions were fully justified at the time — though I now regret the manner in which my reproaches were delivered. Your inflated sense of your own importance will probably prevent your admitting some responsibility for our present situation. In order to show you that I, at least, was sincerely offering friendship — which admits to faults — I shall be lunching at the Café Procope at one o'clock today. I shall be delighted to welcome you as my guest, and somewhat disappointed by your lack of integrity if you choose not to accept this invitation.* He signed himself simply *Carradine.*

Claire scrawled. *Do not imagine I regret anything I said yesterday. I did not speak to the man who had been my friend but to that stupid, pious Englishman who is my worst enemy — and yours. Still, you have done me a great service in opening my eyes to your hypocrisy, and for that I thank you. You have also shown me myself, and I like her very much. True, she has some small faults, but then we French admit to our faults freely and generously. It will not surprise me to hear that you have run away home to England, but I wish you happiness just the same. A Frenchman would be polite and say good-by, but perhaps you prefer to hide and to pretend you never make mistakes.* She signed herself in full, *Mlle. Claire Picard.*

"Pompous swine!" cried Claire and flung his letter across the room.

"Impudent bitch!" shouted Carradine and startled the cat.

They were at the Café Procope fifteen minutes early: immaculately dressed, hungry, furious, and utterly relieved to see each other. How Claire had found time, money, and taste to select and buy her costume he could not imagine. Perhaps it was the first occasion on which she had felt sufficiently herself to discover herself. Natalie's seductive drapes and loops were absent; so were the *jeune fille* effects she had previously chosen for her younger sister. Claire saw herself as

326

a woman unhampered, unattached, with a penchant for brilliant color and simple elegance.

The jacket was extremely dashing, with wide revers, slanting pockets, and a nipped waist. The high white collar of a Byronic shirt perked round her throat. Black-and-white glacé kid boots peered beneath her narrow skirt. The ensemble was of viridian green finely checked with white. A broad-brimmed black velvet hat reared, cavalier-fashion, from her right jaw and ended several inches in the air above her left ear. It was flamboyantly crowned by an emerald ostrich feather. Carradine felt quite soothed by her old pearl eardrops. They were the only familiar thing about her.

Damaged by her references to his artistic and personal inadequacy, he had decided on fashionable tailoring. A suit of brown so rich that it appeared almost black the cuffs, lapels, and waistcoat pockets piped with coffee-colored velvet. He had bought a new cravat to keep up his courage. It gleamed dully, its bronze folds starting from a diamond pin.

Neither of them apparently noticed

327

the other's appearance. One does not compliment the enemy on his uniform.

Carradine's opening remark was delivered in an offhand drawl best done by the English at their most offensive.

"What an extremely appropriate place to meet, mam'selle. Your countrymen, Marat, Robespierre, and Danton used to dine here."

She replied, "I have always admired the courage of Charlotte Corday, m'sieu. She wasted no time on words."

They ordered *escargots* and sopped up the garlic-and-parsley-butter sauce with fragments of bread. They argued as to fair shares of a Chateaubriand steak. She insisted on dressing the salad herself. They drank a bottle of Château Margaux between them. They ate lemon sherbet with Pompadour wafers. They could not decide on the cheese, and the waiter wheeled up a terrifying array, named every one of them, and extolled their separate properties and origins. He persuaded them to try just a sliver of four different kinds. Carradine said that nothing beat Bath Oliver biscuits for crispness and flavor. She disagreed at once, never having tried them. They drank Benedictine with their coffee, and she poured cream up to the brim of her cup. She smoked a Russian cigarette and blew rings into the air to annoy him.

Replete, they sauntered into the sunshine.

"Are your shoes too tight or your skirt too narrow for walking, mam'selle?"

"Of course not!" Her feet, unable to voice protest, would punish her later.

They whiled the afternoon away, peering into the cages of small birds who cheeped singly and in pairs, tier upon tier. They examined books and pictures on the stalls. He bought her a spray of lilies-of-the-valley from a child who sold flowers on the pavement. A horse-driven omnibus rolled past them, full of girl communicants. The driver seemed a drab charioteer for his cargo of maidens, miniature brides of Christ, in their veils and white dresses. The flowers in their hands spelled purity, their faces registered nothing but the little hour of importance.

Claire stopped and watched, remembering, perhaps regretting. But Carradine, seeing an analogy between these truly innocent ones and the donned innocence of Claire, smiled involuntarily. She caught the smile, was momentarily shocked, connected it with the humor of yesterday's farce, and started to laugh. They both laughed.

She said, "I can walk no farther. My shoes pinch."

He said, "I knew damned well they did, and I was extremely delighted."

She raised an admonishing *pochette*. He held out his arm. She shrugged, smiled, accepted it.

"I have a mind to be extraordinarily foolish," said Carradine, though the arm beneath her fingers shook slightly.

She reassured him with a slight pressure. "After all," he said, "I can always run away. I am adept at that, as you remarked."

He twirled his cane thoughtfully. "Shall we be married and damn ourselves for good, Claire?"

Only her elegance gave her the strength not to weep, to cling, to thank God. She summoned up *sang-froid* to match the outfit.

"Yes," she replied. "I think so. Better to marry than to burn. But I shall not be a respectable English wife, if that is what you wish."

"Good God," said Carradine, "it is only your total lack of respectability that makes me offer."

Afterwards they went back to the studio, and she complained that the bed was too narrow.

"Oh, do shut up," said Carradine, "unless you prefer the floor."

Part Four

'Tomorrow the gipsy wagon will roll again, to be stuck at the next turning.'

Georges Rouault

17

THE journey from Orange to Paris was long, warm, and weary. By the time Lintott set foot on familiar pavement he was so far gone as to cry, "Home at last!" though it was not home in the least. Some weeks had lapsed since he and Le Jallu had set out on the last lap of the case, traveling and waiting, traveling and tracking.

"And all for an hour's interview," Lintott mourned, trying to find his quarter of Brooke Bond tea in Carradine's studio cupboard. "It must have cost our friend a small fortune in expenses. Bless me, if he hasn't used my tea. Well, I'll be blowed! He didn't ought to have done that."

A spoonful in the crumpled packet. Lintott shook out every grain into a mug and poured boiling water on it. No milk, of course. Three damp lumps of sugar.

"No milk, puss. Pardohn," he said to the mewing cat, who recognized him and hoped for substantial proof of friendship. "I shall have to eat out tonight and shop tomorrow. How ever shall I go about that? Oh, well, it'll be something of an adventure. I wonder what the French is for mutton chops? Now where are we with these here blessed letters?"

Two pushed under the door from himself to Carradine. So the man must have left for England some time ago. Another addressed to Lintott in a feminine hand, postmarked in Paris. A fourth was propped where he could find it, against a jug of dead flowers on the table. He recognized Carradine's strident script and opened this one first.

My dear Lintott, I am forced to return to London, and for this I apologize, since I should have preferred to greet and thank you on your return. Yet, by now I have no fear that you will find your way home, seasoned traveler as you are.

Oh, never mind the twaddle! Let's get on with it, sir.

I trust that the money I sent was more than sufficient to bring you and your poetic guide safely back to Paris, but I have left some with Madame Picard to cover further expenses.

More fool you, you'll never see a franc of change, sir.

I enclose Mme. Picard's address, and instructions how to contact her, and I should be obliged if you would call on her at your own convenience and hers. May I suggest that you speak simply and slowly, since her command of English, though good, is not perfect?

Oh, my Gawd!

I hope that you will find it in your heart to enjoy a few days' holiday in Paris, and to allow me to provide the means for doing so.

Not on your dear life, sir. I'm off to England, home, and Bessie.

Whatever the results of your exhaustive and skilled inquiries, I thank you for your efforts. My circumstances have changed, but we shall speak of this when we meet in London. I look forward to remunerating you for these past months of hard work, and to shaking you by the hand. Nicholas Carradine.

Well, that's handsome. Very open, very gentlemanly.

The second letter was written on pale

337

pink paper with a spray of painted carnations starting coyly from the top lefthand corner. Lintott sniffed for perfume and sniffed again in contempt as he discovered it.

"One guess as to who wrote this," he commented aloud and was correct in his assumption.

Dear Inspecteur, M. Carradine has tell me that you are sometime in Paris by yourself. He leaves me much money for you.

She's crossed out the *much* but I can read it through the ink. Well done, madame. Don't get greedy, Lintott.

Please to call on me when you are arrive and we shall see how much you get.

That wasn't exactly what the lady intended to say, but it is what she means.

Please to carry your accompte with you and I look at it. M. Carradine tells you the road to my house. I give you good wishes. Mme. Natalie Picard.

She wouldn't give me a farthing in a tin plate if I was blind and legless. My *accompte*, eh? I can guess what that

338

means. Where's that notebook of mine? It's Greek to me. I shan't have to let on that I can't make head nor tail of it. How many centimes to the franc?

Where's my phrase book?

For he had dutifully entered every expense, under the instructions of Le Jallu. He spent half an hour totting-up the two columns and penciled the outcome in good round figures.

"And now for supper," he said with satisfaction.

After considerable use of eyes, ears, and nose, he hunted out a humble café in Montmartre and found a small table in a dark corner. Heart hammering, palms sweating, he reached for the menu, which was written by hand. He hoped he had enough money on him. The girl smacked down a carafe of red wine without being asked and demanded his order. Panic-stricken, he scanned the oblong of cardboard.

"What's pottage?" he asked himself.

His desperation and the two words of English conveyed their own message. The girl bent over him, grinning, curious, maternal. Man was in difficulties. She spoke slowly, loudly. He could not comprehend. She summoned the *patronne*, who swept up to the table, scarlet from her exertions, wiping fat hands on a greasy white apron. She smelled of sweat, garlic, and bitter coffee.

"You don't understand a word we say, do you, m'sieu?" she condoled, taking the menu from him. "You are English or American, I can tell. We'll find something you like. If you can't read the menu, then I'll read out the names of the dishes, one by one. It's no trouble, my friend. They are all very good. I cook them myself."

He sat, head bent under this hail of warmth, and reached surreptitiously for his hat. Better to go hungry. She stayed him with an emphatic gesture and, hand on hip, began to read very clearly, enunciating each syllable. The diners applauded her and nodded reassurance at Lintott.

"She knows!" they cried. "Madame Jeanne knows!"

"Pot-au-feu!"

"Pot-o-fer, madame. I like that. Pot-o-fer, if you please."

Light broke. The café was full of friends.

"*Pot-au-fer* for m'sieu!" she bawled. "First the broth, with a *baguette* — my brother bakes our bread. He is the best baker in Paris. Then the dish. I shall choose the richest pieces for you, m'sieu. Have no fear. The fowls were killed only this morning in my sister's yard. I chose the different cuts of meat from the butcher myself. He is my cousin — the best butcher in Paris. Oh, you have come to the right place to eat. You show discernment, m'sieu. You are a gourmet!"

Her audience agreed, their mouths' full. They thumped their fists on the tables in appreciation, toasted her in the rough wine. Several shouted, *"Bon appetit!"* to Lintott.

He understood that, lifted his bowler hat in acknowledgment, and said, "Bon swah!" several times. Some of them laughed.

"Silence!" yelled Madame Jeanne.

They winked and subsided. One fellow waylaid her amorously as she swayed back to her kitchen. Hardly pausing, she knocked him down with one casual swing of her round arm. His friends picked him up, none the worse, bearing no malice.

Lintott shook his head in admiration and addressed himself to the meal, napkin tucked into his collar like all the rest. From time to time the *patronne* sailed in to inquire tenderly as to his appetite, to press second helpings, to urge him to try her specialties. He was amazed, taking the watch from his waistcoat pocket, to see its plain dial record eleven o'clock.

"I must have been sitting here above two hours. Getting into a regular Frenchman over my food. No, no, madame. Lord love you, I couldn't eat nor drink another morsel or drop. Now what's the damage?" Taking out a handful of notes.

Several pairs of eyes gleamed. The big woman stared them down dreadfully. Then, loud and cheerful, she subtracted her bill and counted out his change.

"Have you taken your tip?" he asked. "Tip?" He recollected Le Jallu's explanation — *for to drink*. For to drink? His museum of a memory did not fail him now, relaxed and replete. "Poor bwah," said Lintott, beaming.

"Pourboire," she said, demanding her customers' congratulations. "He is a good Frenchman, this m'sieu."

Lintott smiled and nodded as they toasted him. He pushed a note toward her at random. "Poor bwah," he repeated.

She patted his shoulder, counted out more change.

Her meticulousness touched Lintott. "You're an honest lass," he said.

He would have liked to thank her as Carradine thanked people, fluently, generously, with polish and perception. But that could never be his way. So he raised his bowler in acknowledgement, slapped his stomach humorously to indicate utter contentment, and bowed. He left in an uproar of good fellowship, feeling particularly proud of himself.

Suddenly, as he trod the cobbled streets he realized that he would never go there again. Night after night Madame Jeanne would pour out her cornucopia of simple, excellent food. Night after night her clientele would gobble, swill, and be noisy. And he would not join them. That little space of time had fled him, leaving a companionable imprint and sadness.

Sturdily he began to whistle 'God Save the King' to lift up his spirits, though to him it was still. 'God Save the Queen', for she had died only the previous year, and he had been born in her reign and had grown used to her.

★ ★ ★

His interview with Natalie Picard was arduous. She donned her role of financier seriously, using a lorgnette to peer at the figures, checking items one by one, exclaiming over costs, giving advice that was now useless. A stranger to interrogation, usually being on the other side of the inquiry, Lintott showed signs of impatience. She raised one plump, ringed hand.

"I do not ask for myself, m'sieu, but for my friend M'sieu Carradine."

"Well, you're making a spanking good job of it, madame, I'll say that. You should have been in the Force, you should. You'd have been a star turn, without a word of a lie."

Natalie caught the gist of his remarks. "You are very genteel, m'sieu." And

344

returned to the fray. "When M. Jallu pays this bill in Orange, does he not say rude to the *patronne*?"

"He had a bit of an argy-bargy with her, yes. But he paid."

"What is this *argy-bargy*?"

"He shouted at her, in a manner of speaking."

"He does not shout much. I shall speak with him. When you pay this carriage to M'sieu Cluny's house, do you also give a . . . a . . . "

"Poor bwah? Yes, we did."

"Monstrous! When you are in . . . " and so on, until he wrung the brim of his hat and prayed to be let out.

Finally she was satisfied as to his honesty, if not to the amount that had been spent, and handed over an envelope full of francs.

"M'sieu Carradine does not know when you arrive so he does not buy tickets. You know how to buy them? Where to buy them?"

"No, madame, but I'll find out somehow."

"When do you wish to leave, m'sieu?"

"As soon as possible, if you please."

"I shall buy them for you. No, no, it does not trouble in the smallest, m'sieu." She retrieved the envelope, extracted a sizable sum. "Where do you eat while you stay in Paris?"

"I took myself off to dinner in Montmartre last night, madame," said Lintott with quiet pride.

"So? You will eat there tonight also?"

"I hadn't thought of that," said Lintott. "I can eat there tonight, so I can. Bless my boots!"

She cut across his exultancy. "You eat all times in restaurants?"

"No, no, madame. I'm going to do a bit of shopping on my way back."

"You speak French well now, m'sieu?" — with amusement.

"No, madame, but we seem to understand one another" — with dignity.

"I shall send Valentine with you, yes?"

"No, thankee," said Lintott family. "I'd sooner manage on my own."

"Then that is all, m'sieu."

She held out her hand. He shook it. She sighed for his bad manners.

"My best regards to you and Miss Pickered, madame."

Natalie laughed. "Does M'sieu Carradine not say? Ah, he is a sly one. My sister is in London with him. He wishes to marry with her."

Not a muscle of Lintott's face moved. He would not have given her the satisfaction of his surprise. "In that case," he said steadily, "I look forward to the honor of meeting Miss Pickered in London, when I see Mr. Carradine."

Natalie weighed him shrewdly. "You think much of M'sieu Carradine and little of my sister, m'sieu. But you need not fear for him — as I fear for her."

"It's not my business," said Lintott, unmoved. "I expect they both know what they're about by this time. When shall I have the tickets, if you please, madame?"

"You cannot leave before Friday, m'sieu, but I send Valentine with them tomorrow."

"Wouldn't it be simpler to pop them in the post?" asked Lintott, fearing the girl might lose them and herself on the way to Montmatre.

"As you wish, m'sieu. But if she post them, then you must go Sa-tur-day."

"Why, I'll be here four days at that rate."

She shrugged. "M'sieu Carradine is generous. He wishes you a little holiday. You shall see Paris — the *Folies Bergère*, perhaps?" — with a twinkle.

"No follying for me. I'm a married man, madame. No. But I'd like to go to the top of the Eiffel Tower, I would. And I'll walk my blessed boots off, I will. If I'm here I may as well make the best of it."

It won't cost him a ha'penny more than my keep, he reflected. I'll write to Bessie this afternoon and tell her to expect me for Saturday suppertime — else Sunday breakfast. My old girl! I'll go to Madame Jeanne's again tonight and look up the lingo so's as I can thank her properly. Pot-o-fer and van rouge. What a regular lark!

Natalie watched him stow away the envelope in the breast of his coat.

"Take care, m'sieu, that they do not pick your pocket."

"You can't tell *me*, madame," said Lintott, on home ground here. "Pickpockets are the same all the world over. I'd like to see any of 'em, French or English, as'd pull a fast one on me."

★ ★ ★

"So that's that," he remarked to himself, mellowed by the evening and two cognacs shared with Madame Jeanne.

He managed to light the oil lamp without setting fire to the studio. The cat was winding round his legs.

"Folks might not speak the same language, puss," Lintott ruminated, philosophical in his cups, "or be the same sort, or live in the same way, but get down to rock bottom and you touch human nature. And human nature's always the same, good, bad, and indifferent. Yes. Bless my boots!"

He began to unlace them, then paused, staring dreamily into the shadows. "I think I've had a drop too much of something," and he wagged his left boot at the winking cat. "Well, you don't get more than one goose-chase offered at my age, and lucky to get that. It ain't that I don't want to go home, for I do. Yes. Only, looking back, it's been an eye-opener. If I'd been younger, puss, like my lad John, I might have seen a bit more of the world than I have done. It's a big place. A big place."

He found the milk and poured out a libation for his companion without spilling very much. He laughed and shook his head. "And I said he talked wild! I've got a wilder tale to tell him, and I'm sorry for it and glad of it both at once. Sorry for the hurt, and glad I found out. John Joseph Lintott, the Nose. Oh, yes, puss, we all have our weakness, our vanity, you might say. And I like to see clear through a mystery as is black as pitch to other folk. Talking of black — I'd best brew myself some black coffee. This here room keeps giving a lurch."

He tutted over Carradine and Claire, padding round in his stockinged feet.

"L'amoor is all very well, but what happens when you get old? She's ladylike enough, mind you, in a French sort of way. Not like that madame of a sister. He fair jumped down my throat when I said what I did, but I meant it for his own good — and I was right. Might as well have saved my breath to cool my porridge for all the notice he took of me. When you come to think, I've done nothing for him. He's done a lot for me. I'll have a few memories to mull over of an evening by the fire. A few tales to tell."

He set the oil lamp and coffee on the model's dais, unlocked his Gladstone bag with some fumbling, dusted a space with tremendous care and fastidiousness, and spread out his papers in orderly fashion. He filled his pipe and lit it. He turned over a page here, read a personal note there.

Mr. Roach — kidnapper? He had forgotten to tick that one off.

Out of habit he picked up the list of passengers to make doubly sure of the late Lucien Fauvel. There he is, in company with the dead.

M. Lucien Fauvel (37).

Mlle. Odette Carradine (6). Poor little wench! That was l'amoor for you! She'd have probably been alive and well now if they'd kept their heads and minded their morals.

A married couple: *M. Joseph Maxime*

351

(52), *Mme. Irène Maxime (46)*. In their prime, in a manner of speaking.

Soeur Bernadette (31). That's be the nun.

Guy Fulbert (25). A young man, dear, dear!

A maiden lady, *Mlle. Valerie Damien (60)*.

Seven people who might as well have stepped into their open graves as into that carriage.

He sorted and stacked the notes, enclosed them in their buff cardboard folder, tied string round the lot. A crayon had rolled up against the platform at some time and been forgotten. He wiped a thread of dust from its blunt point, tried it on a scrap of paper. Then he printed, tongue between teeth, large and black and very neat, from side to side of the folder, THE CASE OF ODETTE CARRADINE. It was finished.

The first night's sleep at the end of a long task was sweeter than any other he knew. Lintott let it come to him through the night sounds of Montmartre.

★ ★ ★

The railway carriage was almost full. Eight seats, seven passengers. Lintott scanned them closely. He knew their destinations better than they. Their tickets need never be rendered up. M. and Mme. Maxime, well fed, well upholstered, had wasted time and money stocking their capacious picnic basket. Guy Fulbert was turning over ambitious plans for a future that would not materialize. Soeur Bernadette, telling her beads, was within sight of the heaven she had surely earned. The withered Mlle. Damien approached divine love, having been denied my other. Lucien Fauvel faced divine judgment. Odette Carradine, in life or death, drew her mother always after her.

Lintott slammed the carriage door, blew his whistle, swung down his green flag. First stop, eternity.

Seven French coffins in a forest of rotting wreaths and marble chapels. A flying wooden hearse seared by flame. Nuns chanting, sweet and steadfast, their faces wiped clean of worldly experience. No mourning there for Sister Bernadette, wise virgin, bride of Christ. An epithalamium,

a rejoicing for her soul, at the Orphelinat
Barnabas.

★ ★ ★

He was wide awake, throwing aside the
covers, shivering with more than the night
cool as he hunted through Carradine's
dictionary . . . *Orphée, orphelin, orphelinat*
— orphanage.

"What's got into me?" he asked,
bewildered. The match burned his fingers.
He started. "Best get a bit of light on
the matter," he mumbled and found the
oil lamp. He sat hunched in its glow, a
quilt round his shoulders, filling his pipe.
"Something Berthe said about those who
should have died and were saved."

*Of a child nobody wanted, whose
reason had been impaired, taken to an
orphanage. And the other child, burned
to death, with a bracelet on her right
wrist.*

"There must be thousands of orphans
and hundreds of orphanages in this
country. It don't have to be this one.
I took it that the child lost its reason in
the crash and was sent to an orphanage

354

because nobody wanted it. It needn't have done, of course. It could have been an orphan in the first place. *A child nobody wanted.* It could have been on its way to this orphanage, with the nun, in the carriage. Don't talk so soft — it could have been a boy. But it could have been a girl, couldn't it? *Whose reason had been impaired.* In the accident? The eighth passenger, thrown clear perhaps at first impact. Badly shocked, hit on the head, something of that sort. You're running mad with speculation, John Joseph."

But the image nagged him. And he remembered the painting of Gabrielle and Odette. The girl in white with the bracelet on her left wrist. Did she always wear it on that wrist?

"Suppose," he hazarded, pointing his pipe stem at the sleeping cat, "suppose this nun was taking a normal girl to the orphanage? Suppose she was the same age or size as Odette, in the same carriage? Two little girls, however different, jammed up for a long journey with six adults, get to talking. This here orphan admires the other's bracelet, say. 'Here', says Odette, being a nice sort of child, 'try it on for a minute'. You have to amuse children on a journey, don't I know it! You let them have the window seat so they can look out and that. They're near the door, perhaps one of them's leaning against it. They do, you know. Particularly when you've told them not to. The brakes go on hard. One of them's flung against the door and the impact's made it loose or thrown it open. Odette gets chucked clear, lands some yards from the crash, in a bonny mess. Knocked on the head so she can't remember who she is, or anything else. *Reason impaired.* They pull what's left of the bodies from the gutted carriage and find a little girl about the same build with a bracelet on her right wrist. Odette's found in the bushes and can't tell them who she is. They cut off what's remaining of her clothes — and they'd be in a right state if she'd gone down a slope, say, and landed in bushes or water or mud. They cut off her hair because of a bad scalp wound, and clap her in a hospital with all the other casualties. Only seven bodies in that carriage, and the nun's dead. *They identified the nun by her cross.* Mrs. Carradine recognizes the bracelet and don't look further, nor ask which wrist it was on. The nuns go round the hospital, searching for this here orphan of theirs, and see a child as won't look up to much after all she's been through. And nobody else is claiming her naturally. God be praised, they say, the child's been saved. When she's well enough to be moved they take her back with them. A pretty girl but a bit soft in the head. Oh, my God!"

He paced the studio, smoking and pondering.

"Too many *ifs*," he decided. He knocked out his pipe.

He paused. "And if I don't check it out I'll have it on my conscience to the end of my days."

He conjured up Valentine as he had seen her yesterday. Clean-cut features, black curly hair, small-boned and refined. He imagined her face lit by willfulness, by intelligence, by feminine power. He groaned. Then his jaw dropped.

"If she didn't come from that orphanage," he said, appalled, "then I shall have to track the place down and find out who it was. I'll be here forever, following up one blooming clue after another. And all because I got a hunch."

He could do nothing before morning. His plain watch figured — four o'clock, the hour of physical ebbing. He crept back to bed.

★ ★ ★

Clumsy with pregnancy, Valentine rolled over, in her cupboard of a room at the apartment near the Etoile. She was reliving Carradine in her sleep, telling him that this was his child. She had shut out Claire, destroyer of dreams, usurper, like Natalie, like M. Emile Roche, like M. Paul, like the men whose names she had never known and would not have remembered. Even though Carradine had deserted her he could still help. Her portrait hung in a gallery that was all long corridors, lit by chandeliers. One room opened into another, and at the far end of the last she saw her father, white-haired and tall and handsome. A kind man of wealth and position. He stopped at the picture, he looked, he knew her. The small hands and fine features. The image of her beloved maman who was his beloved also.

I've waited ever so long for somebody to know who I really am.

★ ★ ★

Lintott's opaque brown eyes opened again, pained for life's derelicts: the harmless, the innocent, the uncomplaining, the from-birth-defeated.

"If it's you, my dear," he addressed the wistful phantom, great with child, "he don't need you anymore."

18

SHE descended levels of sleep, passed doors open, doors closed. Dream shutters clicked and flashed fragments of days recorded and forgotten. People familiar and strange materialized from the shadows and whispered, but whether among themselves or to her she did not know, and it was not important. She opened the cupboards of her imagination and folded clothes away. Fantasy, outmatched, Uncurled from her hands and drifted. Past and present were one, and the future an inevitable conclusion. Freed from the prison of time and space she floated, rapt and all-comprehending. The cloud over her mind dissolved, dispersed.

She could hardly see the pavement through the fog, and her nurse covered her nose and lips with a thick scarf against the pollutions known as 'a London particular'. Yet she was excited by lamp posts transformed into a dark blur and an aureole, by footsteps and cab wheels muffled and invisible, by the taste of metallic moisture drops on the soft wool. The mirror in the hall was cold and misty. All the energetic rubbing of muff and mitten could not reveal her image.

The luminous globe of the Christmas tree in the parlor window reflected a distorted room in minature. A white world outside, a white world inside, and herself all in white. Her slippered feet found hold on a chair's rung. She climbed and climbed, to melt into the looking-glass as Alice had done, and found an adult face staring into hers from the other side. She tumbled slowly down, mouth open, and changed into a doll on the carpet.

The sun glittered on silks, gleamed on satins, glowed on velvets. Three vast trunks, their lids yawning to display interiors lined in striped cotton, stood in the middle of maman's bedroom. A black knob of hair bobbed over them, a black figure moved silently to and from the cavernous wardrobe. Within the cage of the boy's arms she wriggled for freedom. His Norfolk jacket felt hot and prickly. He smelled of warm cloth, of ink, of boy. On maman's dressing table the scent bottle of shimmering crystal held magic. It's silver top, unstoppered, released femininity. She gazed earnestly into the big mirror. The dark woman, stern and unsmiling, walking to and fro. Maman, hand on hip, turning to watch them. The boy's arms encircling nothing.

Summer in the long, narrow strip of walled garden. Maman switched from French to English, drawing their visitors into conversation. A forest of rearing legs, a crush of crinolines, an Olympus of nodding heads, which sometimes loomed down to speak to her. She understood both languages and did not find this curious. The little fish in the pond her father had made for her flickered under the lily leaves. Her reflection was as pale and blank as an egg, no features. She flailed the water with both hands. It crashed into the air and splintered on the lawn.

Winter. Muffin men with bells, an organ grinder with a shivering monkey in uniform, a child no older than herself holding out a bunch of drooping violets. Pictures in the flames behind the brass-railed fireguard. Her wax-faced doll was splendidly and fashionably dressed, its cloth body ending in china limbs. She sang a French lullaby, pushed her against the wire bars to see the people going to church. Flecks of soot momentarily caught by fire. The features ran, molten, indistinguishable. Tears of separation, of protest, of abandonment. A cloth and china nothing, clad in scorched finery.

Walls closed and receded. Mirrors clouded. Furniture was menace. Mother and daughter, imprisoned in paint, smiled head to head and did not notice her. She crept, unwanted ghost, from room to room of their lives: hearing scales fumbled by small fingers, watching stitches appear one by tedious one on a linen sampler, remembering a jungle of letters turn, by some mysterious alchemy, into words. She hung round doorways and envied this other self, reveling in a power made possible only by love. No answers there, only eternal questions. Footprints inexplicably ended in a white landscape:

Softly she ascended, entering the frame of day, turning to the day's images, the day's knowledge.

Beyond her lay a long road scattered with bureaus, with cabinets, with roll-topped and flat-topped desks, with escritoires, with any and every receptacle that might hold information. Two men approached, growing larger as they drew nearer, capes flapping. They were searching each drawer for documents. A trail of discarded papers behind them was carried away by the wind. She held out the envelope of herself, but it was irrevocably sealed.

★ ★ ★

Carradine has painted the deep cream flesh, whose delicate shadows of olive and umber and modulated purple are cast by a richer ground. The broad square brush strokes move across the portrait, nullifying outlines.

She is reflected in glass and so becomes four women: two in the picture, two posing for it. None of them is herself. And though he captures her in a hundred moods, using all the cunning of his craft and the infinity of his palette, she still eludes him. More strange than his twilit interiors, more emotive than the harmonies and clashes of his color, more precise than his impeccable draftsmanship, is her secret identity.

This lost child, this stranger, will be a responsibility he cannot shed. He cast a net into the sea, and she has been harvested. He opened a locked door that may not be closed on her again. He must reckon with her in mind and heart. And whatever he discovers her to be, and however difficult the truth, he must receive her. For he asked a question of the emptiness, seeking an answer for himself, and the void has posed him yet another riddle.

19

MORNING brought further counsel, and a nostalgia Lintott could not place.

His paucity of French, and the French lack of Wiltshire bacon, had curtailed his breakfast to fried eggs. These he consumed in the window seat, looking out on Montmartre. He had mixed the suds vigorously in his shaving mug, drawn the razor skillfully round his whiskers, trimmed his gray mustache with a pair of nail scissors, and turned his head from side to side to admire the effect. Spruced and fed, his mission lay heavily upon him. His usual sense of controlled power had deserted him, and in its place sat apprehension — and nostalgia.

"Now when did I last feel like this?" he wondered, setting himself a conundrum. "God bless my soul! It must have been forty years since."

His young man's fancy, meant for a richer catch than a struggling young policeman, swayed past in her open carriage beneath a silk parasol. Though she occupied his thoughts and dreams for the whole of one summer, she had never noticed him. He had wakened each day, looking forward to the few minutes when she would ride past.

Sunshine made him whistle. Rain silenced him. Then his beat was changed, love lost its cruelty, he met Bessie. Until now, staring out at the white confection of Sacre Coeur on a June morning, he had forgotten that girl. Here, in the untidy beauty of an artist's studio, in the transient aura of Paris, she lived again for him.

"I'm catching a bit of the old l'amoor, like the rest of them," said Lintott humorously. "Back to business."

He washed up his breakfast things, made his bed, let out the cat. In broad, clear print he copied Natalie Picard's address, to show the cab driver.

★ ★ ★

Since he could not understand Valentine's explanations he stood stolidly in the hallway until she pointed to a chair. Then he sat stolidly, hat in hand, with such an air of permanence that the maid shrugged and disappeared. He heard her agitated remarks, Natalie's amused replies, and was at last rewarded by a full-voiced summons from a room to his left.

"If you insist, m'sieu, I will see you."

Valentine appeared, motioned him to enter, closed the door softly behind her. Nonplused, he stared round Natalie's boudoir. The parquet floor reflected his thick boots with brutal frankness. A full-length mirror reflected his plain face and figure. Chairs and footstools, upholstered in petit point, formed barriers between himself and his quarry. Cream rugs, patterned in carmine, amber, and apple green, threatened his footing. At the far end of the room Natalie sat up in the center of a vast, draped four-poster, enjoying her breakfast.

Lintott summoned his vocabulary. "Pardohn, madame," he said, and wished himself well away.

"Aha, *M'sieu l'Inspecteur*! What shall they say in Scotch Yard, that you speak to a lady in her chamber?"

368

She registered his acute embarrassment and with consummate tact overlooked it. "Please to sit down. No, no, not there" — as he sidled toward a sofa near the door. "I do not wish to speak loud. Here, if you please." He trod gingerly over the little rugs and settled himself on the edge of an armchair. "That is good. Valentine! Coffee for m'sieu, and please to take his hat. Croissants? No? You have eaten? You are the early bird? You admire my room? Do not fear to look round you."

"Very pretty," said Lintott lamely.

Natalie buttered a croissant with a generous hand, more cream into her coffee. In the soft light, filtered through pale amber flounces and hangings, she was the picture of opulent youth. He was relieved to see her fully, though seductively, clad in an embroidered satin bedjacket. The length and richness of her unbound hair worried him slightly, but her perfect composure enabled him to concentrate on the job in hand.

"I wouldn't have bothered you, madame," he began slowly, "but this is a matter of considerable importance."

"Here is your coffee. Please to enjoy

it, and then tell of the importance. You wish Valentine to stay so that we are res-pectable?"

"No, that's all right," said Lintott, surveying the girl with compassion.

Even the most masterly dreamer is hampered by pregnancy. Valentine's distorted shape, the hopelessness of her bearing, saddened him. Again he imagined her as she might have been, in happier circumstances, in full possession of mind and body, and the resemblance was there.

"She couldn't help me anyway," Lintott continued as the door closed. He cleared his throat. "Mr. Carradine told me that you found her in an orphanage. Would you mind telling me the name of it, madame?" And as she frowned slightly, he guessed she feared some revelation perhaps unknown to him and would evade the point. "Was it the Orphelinat Barnabas?"

"But how clever. I have forgot."

"In a matter of six years, madame? How did you come to hear of this orphanage, and why choose Miss Valentine in particular?"

"Somebody tells me. I forget. I go there, and I see her. I am sad for her. I give her a good home."

"Very charitable. What can you tell me about Miss Valentine? Who were her parents and so forth?"

"You wish to know only of Valentine?"

For the moment, Lintott thought, alerted by the word *only*, and nodded.

"The nuns take her in. They are kind but dull. It is very dull at the *orphelinat*."

"Well, it's a far cry from here and no mistake. Still, she didn't get in the family way there — didn't have a baby — did she? No babies, madame?" — as Natalie wrinkled her forehead in puzzlement.

"Of course no baby, m'sieu. There are no men there."

"How old is Valentine, madame?"

Natalie calculated and exclaimed. "But I think of her as a child always. She is twenty-six years."

His throat was thick. "How old was she when the nuns took her in, do you know?"

"I am not cer-tain. Quite young. You do not ask how old *I* am — I shall not tell

371

you, m'sieu" — roguish and yet wary.

He changed the subject, resolving to return to it another way. He saw a long trek ahead of him to the orphanage, otherwise.

"You seem to be the sort of lady that takes care of everybody, madame. Mr. Carradine said your own parents had died early and you took care of your sister — "

She was on him, framing her suspicions that were not his.

"M'sieu Carradine has ask you to say this to me, yes? I tell Claire a thousand times. He will not marry with her. He wishes an excuse not to marry."

Confounded, Lintott said soothingly, "Now why shouldn't he, madame? He knows your situation, and that didn't put him off." He decided this was hardly tactful, but she did not heed him, pursuing her own course.

"Of course he must know, but not yet. I tell Claire not to say yet, to wait. But he is clever, our M'sieu Carradine. He smells the mouse, and you, m'sieu, are the cat."

Lost but dogged, Lintott said, "We

may as well straighten matters out, madame. He had to know anyway, as you say. Better now than later. When did your parents die? And how did you manage to look after yourselves?"

I said that girl had been on the French merry-go-round. I said!

"I wish Valentine to take my tray and brush my hair."

"Half a minute, my dear. Never mind the hairdressing. No cwoifewer!" — as she glared at him. She pouted, but complied. "Just you tell me about your parents. Where did you live?"

"They die when we are very young. I forget."

"You've got a bad memory, haven't you, my dear?" said Lintott, enjoying himself. "You must have lived somewhere. You couldn't have sprung up full-grown in Paris six years ago."

"Who tell you six years? Please to give me my brush, m'sieu. I brush my hair myself . . . "

Obdurate, he padded over to the dressing table and back, watched her draw the bristles through that rich fall of black hair, expressionless. He knew a liar and a prevaricator when he met one, and had she been Helen of Troy he would have wrung the truth from her.

"Please to pass me a ribbon, m'sieu. It is by the mirror."

He switched a lilac ribbon from the crystal tray full of scent bottles and pots of cosmetics, handed it to her. Sat back in the armchair, planted a square hand on each knee. Coquetry never moved him an inch.

"Now, lookee here, Mrs. Pickered. Let's not play games. There might be money for somebody, somewhere in this, if I get the truth. Nothing but the truth will fetch you a brass farthing — franc. Understand?"

Instantly she was ten years older, shrewder, wiser. The ribbon taut in her fingers. Then she smiled and adopted an air of guileless intimacy.

"We are *bâtardes*, m'sieu. You comprehend me?"

"I see. That's a bit of a facer, isn't it? It will surprise Mr. Carradine, I mean. So where were you brought up?"

"In the Orphelinat Barnabas, with Valentine, m'sieu."

Damn me, thought Lintott. I'll be forgetting my head next. Valentine.

"About Miss Valentine, madame. You say she's twenty-six years old. You're sure of that? It's important, mind. Now how old was she when she came to the orphanage? Or did she come later than you, and you can't remember? I must have the truth. Don't tell me a story as you think might please me, because it won't."

Natalie's dignity was immense. "I remember perfect, m'sieu. She is already there. She is found on the door stair when she is a little baby. The nuns take her in from pity. Yes, yes, yes, I swear it." Nodding emphatically. "I fetch her birth paper, if you please?"

Such relief, and such a terrible question mark. For he must now pursue the hunch to its source, and God knew what half-witted creature he might find at the end of it.

"I tell you another truth," said Natalie, heady with honesty. "Claire is the sister of my heart but not of my blood. We do not meet until I am at the *orphelinat* during four years. But we are *bâtardes*."

375

"Well, never mind," said Lintott heartily. "I don't expect Mr. Carradine'll take much notice. He's a bohemian sort of gentleman. Now can you help me out with another matter, madame? Where's this here orphanage situated?"

"Ah, how well I remember! I am a woman of passion, m'sieu. I was a child of passion also. I am a mad when they bring me to this place. I am ill. My head hangs, so. I cannot weep, but my heart weeps. I lie many, many days and do not speak. I have no one. I, who have every-thing until they carry me here. M'sieu, you have a nature of tenderness" — appealing to the embarrassed Inspector — "you will know how a child of six years is griefed."

His face changed.

"You were six years old when you entered the orphanage, madame? And ill? When was this? Who were your parents? Can you remember them?"

Oh, by God, This is worse than Miss Valentine. She'd milk him dry and penniless.

Natalie was far away, recollecting a time when she had no need to claw for

376

a living. "My papa is a good man, rich and kind. My maman is beautiful. We live in a grand house, a château. I have a *bonne d'enfant*, a nurse. We are parted. I do not know how or why. They bring me to the *orphelinat*. I am desolated."

Lintott leaned forward, "How old are you, madame?"

She recovered immediately. "I do not tell you, m'sieu. Never."

Lintott's heart hammered, but he controlled himself, managed a little jocularity.

"Shall I tell you how old you look?" he asked, persuasive. "Not a day over twenty!"

She smiled, suddenly young again.

"But you're a few years older than that, aren't you, my dear? Not that anyone would guess, of course. How old might that be? Twenty-five? Twenty-six?"

No answer, eyelashes lowered.

"Here," said Lintott, troubled but fatherly, "write down the year you were born on this piece of paper, and I'll crumple it up the minute I've read it, and we'll forget all about it."

Her fingers touched his deliberately as

she took the paper, but without effect. She passed it back, sighing.

His heart thundered, faltered, leaped. "I'd never have believed it," he said.

Thirty. Thank God. Well, I'm not at all surprised, come to think.

"Never would have believed it — and I call myself a detective."

The figure 1872 disappeared into a small white ball and was deposited in her lap. She touched it tentatively, as though the scrap of paper were time itself.

"How come you and Miss Claire are both called *Pickered* then?" he asked.

"It is the name of the people who look after me, when the count, my father, cannot admission to me. They are good people but they died when I am six. I go to the orphanage. I am *désolée*."

"The count wasn't Miss Claire's father, of course," said Lintott, amused, "but I daresay she was related to the aristocracy too, wasn't she?"

Never. A couple of by-blows if ever I saw a pair!

"Oh, no, m'sieu. Claire is not of good family. She has no name. My name is Picard, because of the good family who a-dopt me. The nuns give her a name — Marie-Claire. I am sorry for her. I ask them that they call her *Picard*. We must have some name, m'sieu, to face the world. But you do not tell this to M'sieu Roche? I say we are unlegitimated daughters of the count. If he knows she is not my sister he is enraged. He have kept her for six years.

"Now, now, now," Lintott soothed. "I've never met the gentleman, and I'm not likely to, and it's not my business. I shan't breathe a word, madame."

He set down his coffee cup and relieved her of the tray. "Now, if you can tell me where this orphanage is, madame — because I'll have to go there — I'll be obliged."

"But why do you go?" Fearing further revelations. "Have M'sieu Carradine ask you?"

"It ain't very nice to play tricks," said Lintott honestly, "and I'm sorry it was the only way I could find out about Miss Valentine. Mr. Carradine never said anything about Miss Claire, and I don't think he'll give a rap anyway — probably just give me a dirty look. So I don't care four-pence about you and your sister, I'm on the track of a blooming ghost . . . a . . . a . . . phantom."

"*Fantôme*? Pff! You are a mad."

"Very likely. I'm looking for a little girl as might not exist. If she does exist, then she was probably traveling with Sister Bernadette on her way to your orphanage in 1882. You remember Sister Bernadette, I expect?"

"But yes." Slowly. "She is a good woman. Kind, even to me that they call the bad one. She dies. We have a *service commémoratif*. I weep, m'sieu. Before, with the others, I do not weep." Suspicious again. "Why?"

"Did they tell you how she died, madame?"

"No. Just she dies. She is good, she goes to . . . to . . . "

Natalie pointed heavenward. "But there is a child, m'sieu" — warily — "and she is no *fantôme*. Sister Bernadette goes to bring her but does not return. Much more late they bring the child, and she is ill — "

Lintott cried, in his excitement and

380

apprehension, "Is she an orphan a bit soft in the head, mad, deranged? About six years old? Lost her memory? Doesn't know her name?"

Natalie stared at him long and coolly. "She is not mad, m'sieu. She is shock. She have been treated bad. She does not lose her memory. She have no memory to lose. No name. She is call *l'Inconnue* — the one who it not known."

"Will she still be there, do you think?" said Lintott. "Will they be able to tell me where she is, if not?"

He was half out of his chair, ready to leave at once.

Natalie watched him bitterly. When she answered him her tone was hard and dry. She looked every day of her age.

"I save you a long journey, m'sieu. The child is my Claire."

Lintott sat suddenly down again, cold.

"I tell you, m'sieu, that she is *une bâtarde*, of no good family. I now save you and M'sieu Carradine much time, much money. Do not trouble to ask of her maman, her papa. No person have heard of them. In the village they shout

381

rude, they throw stones. She live with the priest until they say she is his child. Then he ask the *orphelinat* to have her, to make her happy. Do *you* suffer like this?" she cried fiercely.

She mistook his silence for shame and attacked him with words. "And Claire is not six years when she come, she is eight years. Addition *that* for your curious M'sieu Carradine, *Inspecteur!* I say she is twenty-two years? Well, I lie. She is twenty-eight years. Ah, but how clever you are to discover these things of her, to pretend to talk of Valentine, of me. And so? Let M'sieu Carradine discard her like a rubbish person. I take her back, m'sieu." Her eyes filled with tears that were both angry and honest. "*I* love her if he does not love her. She have her sister of the heart for always. She find a man more better than your rubbish M'sieu Carradine — "

"Here, half a minute, madame. Let me get a word in, will you, please? Shut up, will you?" Lintott commanded.

She was instantly quiet. She smoothed the coverlet, resigned.

"Will you please listen to me just for a bit, madame?" he asked gently. "You've got hold of the wrong end of the stick." And the right end's a damn sight worse, he thought to himself. "Nobody cares about Miss Claire being an orphan or anything else. What worries me is that she might be Mr. Carradine's sister. Now are you with me?"

"*Continuez*, m'sieu." Immediately calm, intent.

"Sister Bernadette was killed in the train accident that killed Mr. Carradine's sister. She was in the same carriage, and so was this orphan. You say Miss Claire was eight? Well, an undernourished child of eight would be about the same size as a well-nourished child of six. Am I speaking plain enough? You understand what I'm driving at? Now the only means of identification was by a gold bracelet, on the right wrist . . . on the right wrist," he said in a lower tone. "Now there's just a chance that these two little girls got talking and trying things on. The orphan was flung clear — anyway, she was saved. Now suppose it wasn't the orphan but Miss Odette — along of the orphan having her bracelet on?"

Natalie considered. "Have you seen how an orphan is dress, m'sieu? Like to poverty. Your Miss Odette has fine clothes."

"Have you ever seen a bad railway accident, madame, and how folks look when they're fetched out of it? There's not tuppence to put between any of 'em."

"But you do not know, m'sieu? You guess clever, but you do not *know*?"

Lintott spread his arms and subsided. "No, I don't know, madame. But my nose don't half twitch."

"How shall you discover this?"

Lintott said, "She might remember something as'd tie up with being Miss Odette."

Natalie laughed, but without her usual robustness, and shrugged.

"We orphans can all remember a rich papa, a beautiful maman, a grand house, m'sieu. What else have we? We are nothing if we do not dream. I, too," she admitted. "I am honest with you, m'sieu. The Count is not my father. I am not *une bâtarde* of good originations.

384

I am the daughter of M. and Madame Picard. My father sells the fish. But I am rather the *bâtarde noble* than the fish-daughter!"

Human nature, Lintott mused.

"This is strictly between *us*, madame," he remarked with gallantry "It won't go any further, you may be sure."

"What shall you do, m'sieu? You shall break her heart?"

"I'll just have to find out what I can, as best I can. I don't expect Mr. Carradine will be exackly joyful, neither," he replied slowly. "He seemed to think quite a bit of Miss Pickered. I'll not be troubling you any further, madame. Thank you kindly." He drew a deep breath that was more a sigh. "I don't always like what I have to do, but it's my job, you see. It's my job."

She surveyed him with understanding and some pity, but her real concern was for Claire.

"And if she is his sister, m'sieu," and she crossed herself, for though she was an erring Catholic she was still a Catholic, and this was mortal sin, "what shall she do?"

"Mr. Carradine will see her right for money, of course," he offered. "She won't go short of money."

"Oh m'sieu, m'sieu, m'sieu! Say such things of me — but not of her."

20

LINTOTT had telegraphed simply, I THINK MISS ODETTE MAY BE ALIVE, and with Natalie's help reached London on the Friday evening. He took a cab straight to Carradine's house. The peace of the London square made him feel doubly an intruder. He guessed that each of the two people he came to shatter thought they had reached the end of a long road. It was his duty to inform them of another turning.

Carradine himself, hearing the engine throbbing as Lintott fumbled for change, flung open the door. Close behind him came Claire, anxious to miss nothing, and behind her hovered Mrs. Tilling, intrigued and curious.

"Welcome home, Inspector," said Carradine heartily, running down the steps. His eyes searched Lintott's keenly, his eyebrows registered a question.

"I'd like a word privately, if you please, sir," said the Inspector, nodding at the

387

ladies, and followed Carradine into the study. He stood at the window, hands clasped behind his back. "I'm afraid that what I've got to say will come as a shock to you, sir, and I'm sorry for it."

Carradine sat in his father's swivel chair and surveyed the instrument of his destruction.

"What's wrong?" he asked, colorless.

As Lintott spoke, briefly and steadily, Carradine felt the walls of the room closing fast upon him. He had stepped into a picture of which he was afraid, and squarely at its center was fate, in the homely guise of a retired detective. Above the desk that had been his father's, Gabrielle smiled, untouched by time, her arms round the little world of her daughter.

Lintott said apologetically, "That's how it is, sir. We don't know for sure, but there's reasonable doubt. And while there's doubt, sir, if you see what I mean . . . ?"

Fragments of dreams, forming nightmare. Gabrielle's painted smile. Carradine put both hands over his face and was silent for fully three minutes.

Then he said, "What shall we do?"

Lintott said, "Does Mrs. Tilling, for instance, know of any identifying mark that Miss Odette and Miss Claire might have in common? Wait a bit, sir" — as Carradine began slowly to rise from his chair. "Excuse me. Just let me ask her by myself. I don't want this case prejudiced by blurting everything out. I think I can put it better than you, sir, at the moment. Sit yourself down and take it easy."

He was back in a few minutes, grave and quiet and no wiser. Silently Carradine poured two glasses of brandy.

"What now, Inspector?"

"Has Miss Claire told you about her childhood, sir? Mrs. Pickered coughed up to me, after a lot of gassing about nothing. So I know."

"Oh God, yes. The damned orphanage, the fact that Natalie isn't her sister, that she herself is illegitimate. Yes, Inspector. The lot. And quite frankly I don't care in the least."

"Just so, sir. And that's the childhood the young lady believes — or what she knows. We ain't jumping to conclusions. I think it best, sir, if you've no objections, that I have a chat with her by myself. Oh, you needn't worry, sir. I'm not going to be unpleasant or anything of that sort."

"I should prefer to stay." He meant that he intended to stay.

"Very well, sir, on two conditions. You don't speak yourself, and you sit where she can't see your face. You've got what might be called an expressive face, sir, and I don't want it suggesting anything to her — good or bad. Right?"

Carradine nodded.

"One more thing, sir. Is Miss Claire the fanciful sort, like Miss Pickered?"

"She is one of the most honest women I have ever met."

"Thank you, sir. Now I know where I stand. If you'll kindly ask the lady to step in here, sir, I'd be obliged."

She came in, clutching Carradine's arm, exclaiming, questioning, afraid.

"Now just you sit over here, my dear," said Lintott, strengthened by a neat brandy. "Nice and calm. There's nothing to fret about. You don't see me fretting, do you? Not a bit of it. I'm lighting my pipe, I am, if you'll allow me?"

She made a little flurried gesture of permission.

"Don't you take any notice of anyone but me, Miss Claire. Mr. Carradine's had a bit of a shock, not expecting his sister to be alive, that's all. Well, we don't know she is, yet. She might not be. That's right, make yourself comfortable. Now you and your sister — sister by adoption, as you might say — happened to come across Miss Odette, if it *was* Miss Odette, while you were at the orphanage. I've had a long chat with Mrs. Pickered, and she helped me all she can — and very open and frank she was too. But I think you might remember more than she did."

He had talked easily, relaxing in the swivel chair, filling and lighting his pipe, watching her as he prepared to smoke, giving her time. Carradine sat by the window, back turned.

"On the other hand," Lintott continued, as though it were of no account, "you might not. I don't want you to tell me anything you aren't sure of or don't rightly know. I don't know *you* very well, come to that, my dear. And I'd like to, I should indeed. Would you call yourself a dreamer now, like Miss Valentine, for instance?"

Claire was puzzled still but no longer frightened, Lintott had seemed dour and formidable when she first met him. Then he had amused them by drinking too much wine and saying he was in queer company and no mistake. Now he radiated kindliness and strength and a genuine interest in her welfare. Only Carradine's stillness troubled her, and she glanced toward him again and again.

"He's all right, Lord bless you," said Lintott. "You pay attention to me, my dear. You're a regular worrier, aren't you? I saw a picture of you, fretting, in Carradine's studio. Ah, I said to myself, this is one of the serious sort. Did you fret in the orphange, my dear?"

"I am not happy there, no m'sieu. They are kind, but I am not at home."

"Not at home? What was home like, then?" Drawing away at his pipe, watching and listening.

"I do not remember, m'sieu. They tell me it is bad, but I am ill when I go to the orphanage, and when I am better I do not remember."

"What was wrong with you, Miss Claire, do you know?"

"I think I have a fever. They cut off my hair."

"I see. Well, in my experience, when people don't have what they want, or what they need, or what they ought to have — come to that — they make up something nice to look forward to or look back on. Miss Valentine now — "

"I am not like *her*!" Claire cried suddenly. "I am not like *her*!"

She was half out of her chair, hands clenched, thumbs tucked into palms.

"Inspector!" Carradine began angrily.

Lintott whipped round on him. "I did warn you, sir," he said levelly. "Now, please, will you keep quiet?"

Carradine returned to the shadows, suffering.

"No, Miss Claire," said Lintott firmly, "you're not like her. She makes things up, don't she? Mr. Carradine here says you're an honest person, so you don't make anything up, do you? Do you?"

He saw her struggle: anxious for his

393

approbation, anxious for her self-esteem, treasuring Carradine's opinion of her, fearful of losing it.

"I think I make things up," she replied slowly and spread out her fingers and looked at them. Carradine's ruby glowed in the soft light. "Yes, I too," she said. "I make up myself a family. But I do not speak of them, as Valentine does. I keep them for myself. Now I have . . . him" — she nodded at Carradine's bowed shoulders — "I do not need them."

"It's natural enough," said Lintott. "Mrs. Pickered said as all orphans had a dream or else they had nothing. I understand that. Has Mr. Carradine shown you round the house?"

She nodded.

"Has he shown you the attic?"

She shook her head.

"I have put all that behind me," Carradine said.

Lintott did not even turn his head. "If I have one more word from you, sir!"

"I beg your pardon, Inspector."

"No offense meant," said Lintott serenely. "Shall you and I take a look at the attic, my dear?"

"Why? Why should we? Why is this to do with your questions?"

"You're a bit on the excitable side, aren't you, my dear?" Lintott said, smiling. "It's got nothing to do with my questions. It's because — to speak plain — I spent above an hour with your sister, Mrs. Pickered, trying to find out two or three facts as I could have got in five minutes, if I'd understood the lady. Now I don't want to spend that length of time asking questions of you, do I? And Mr. Carradine here is like a dog with a bone, if he'll excuse me saying so. So let's you and me have a quiet look round and a chat, and then I'll know what to ask you. I want you to trust me, Miss Claire. Do you trust me?"

She looked at him intently, frowning with concentration. Then she smiled, was pretty again.

"Yes, m'sieu. I trust you *absolument.*"

"I beg to come with you," said Carradine, tormented.

Claire turned from one man to the other, bewildered, doubtful.

Lintott shook his head. "You're making this twice as difficult for me and for her, sir. Oh, very well. Hold the lamp, and leave her to me" — in an emphatic undertone.

The slight comedy, during which Mrs. Tilling insisted on arranging them in overalls, lightened the atmosphere considerably. The attic restored tension.

"But she is here, still," Claire whispered as Lintott opened trunks, and set the dappled-gray rocking horse in motion, took out a bundle and some papers.

She put both hands to her cheeks, staring around her as Carradine held high the oil lamp.

"I'm not much of the imaginative sort," said Lintott cheerfully, "and I saw this place in broad daylight, as much as you can get daylight through that top window. But I felt that too. Nice little lass," he said gently. "A bit of a madame, eh? Look at this, my dear."

Dear Papa, I am clever. Love from your Odette.

"Would you say you were the imaginative sort, Miss Claire?"

She started. "I? No, m'sieu. Not like Nicholas. But I feel things. I walk into a room and I know things that I do not know. You understand?"

"I do that," said Lintott, fatherly, watching her hold up the white dresses, fondle the dolls. "I'll often get more from an empty room than from a mort of questions. Funny, ain't it? What was she like, do you think, this little girl? And that is a question. You might turn up something as I'm looking for."

He turned on Carradine, anticipating his reaction. "And if you aren't up to this, sir, I want you to hand over the lamp and take yourself off."

"No," said Carradine, sitting on his old box of wooden blocks, "we'll see it through together, one way or the other."

"I had a doll," said Claire, "much like to these, but I melt her face."

"How did you do that, my dear?"

"Oh, I hold her to the . . . *garde-feu?*"

"Fireguard," said Carradine tonelessly.

"Yes. I think to warm her. Outside there in the *brouillard.*"

"Fog. She means fog, Inspector."

"So I warm myself and her, and suddenly she have no face." She clutched

397

one of the dolls to her breast and doubled over. "She have no face. She have no face."

She rocked to and fro, head bent, sitting in the dust by the trunk.

"They bought you another one, I expect, my love?" said Lintott quietly.

"Ah, yes. But not my Antoinette, not my Antoinette."

"I daresay she was just as fine. Who made her clothes, I wonder? Did you, my dear?"

"Oh, no. Maman made them, always."

"When she had time. Mothers haven't a lot of time. My Bessie used to dress our girls' dolls, bless you," said Lintott in the same quiet conversational tone. "But it had to be of an evening when her work was done."

"Sometime Maman sews, sometime she sings, sometime she teach me. Always she have time for me, always."

"Who else did you have in this imaginary family, Miss Claire? A sister, perhaps?"

Claire rocked the doll. "You see how I dream, m'sieu? I only dream."

"What's wrong with dreams of that

sort?" he asked kindly. "You'd got nothing else, had you?"

"I have a brother," she continued in a light tone, to conceal what he had meant to her. "He is very kind also."

"You must forgive me, m'sieu. Orphans dream grand. Oh, yes, very grand."

"A baby brother to make fuss of, like enough."

"Oh, no, m'sieu. *I* am the fuss! He makes up stories for me about myself. We pretend that we are many people. But he is more clever than me. He pretends he is twenty people. I am only myself, with him, in these different . . . theaters."

"Does he write them down for you, my love?"

"But of course," she cried, eyes brilliant with tears.

"Of course, m'sieu. Nothing except the best for me. Oh, I beat Valentine to the cocked hats? Her dreams are not so real. Me, I shade them well. They seem very real, very true."

"And what was your papa like, my dear?"

399

She was silent over this question, head bent.

"That I am not sure. He changes. Sometimes I like him old, sometimes younger. Sometimes with hair almost white, sometime dark, with mustache. Of him," she said with desperate gaiety, "I am not sure. I have not make up my mind, m'sieu."

"And Miss Odette now — because we're wandering off the point, aren't we?" said Lintott, who held the thread in a vise. "What kind of a little girl do you feel? I think you said you felt things, didn't you, my dear? How does your feeling coincide with mine, I wonder?"

"Oh, this one. I know her well. She is the *bien aimée*, the well beloved. She holds — ah, how she holds. To everyone. She have everything, and she knows this. She expect everything. She pay with a kiss, with a smile. *Charmante!* All is before her, and then she die."

She crossed herself. "For a little time, God forgets her."

She sat motionless, clasping the doll.

"Well, that's much the impression I formed of her, my dear. But then Mr.

Carradine will have given you a pretty good idea of her, won't he?"

"No, he does not talk of Odette. Of Gabrielle, yes, he talks much."

"So you figured this out by yourself, my dear? Very good. Now you're all settled in life, so's to speak, with Mr. Carradine. What if I fish up his sister?"

"She come to live with us, m'sieu. Does she not, Nicholas?"

He could barely nod.

"It might be a bit difficult for you, Miss Claire, mightn't it? If it's the young lady I'm thinking of. She's had a rough passage, you see, my dear. No money, no proper home, no husband to take care of her. Folks in that sort of position are inclined to be greedy. She might think you had nicer clothes and trinkets and so forth and want the same."

Claire drew her brows together, not at this prospect but in an effort to divine his meaning. Then she laughed.

"But I give her everything! You like this?" Miming to an invisible audience of one. "Take it! What else you like?" Eyebrows raised. "Take this also." She opened her arms, the doll fell into her lap and lay spread-eagled, smiling blandly. "You are worry about *me*, m'sieu?" Pointing to herself in astonishment. "I am not change with my good fortune. When I have much I give, I give always. Once, I am dress very fine, and there is a poor one. I say to her, 'For a little while you shall be me. Here is my hat, my mantle'. She has wood shoes, I give her my slippers. She smiles, she is happy. Everyone say, 'Bravo'! They clap, they laugh."

"Who is *they*?" said Lintott.

"I cannot remember, m'sieu."

"You made it up? Did you make it up?"

She hesitated.

"Where did it happen? At your sister's home, in Paris somewhere?"

She was lost, but her silence was bewildered rather than embarrassed. "I must have make it up," she said finally.

"What makes you think that?"

"Because she is a child, and I am a child."

"And when you were a child you had nothing to give away, did you? You were a poor one too, weren't you? Did another little girl visit the orphanage and let you dress up? Was that what really happened?"

She shook her head from side to side, compressed her lips, shrugged. "No, m'sieu. I must have make it up. Please to excuse me. I am bad like Valentine."

Lintott reached for a bundle he had laid aside. "Did you make this up too?"

She unfolded the tissue, afraid.

It was a doll dressed in scorched finery with a melted face.

The attic yawned, opened, swallowed her into unconsciousness.

"Here, give me that lamp, sir, you'll set us all afire," cried Lintott. "Yes, that's right. Give her a bit of comfort. We're not quite through yet. I want her to remember a bit more." He bent over Claire, obdurate, ignoring high words and Carradine's furious face. "That child was an orphan. She was in the railway carriage with you. You gave her your bracelet. What else do you remember? Come on now, *anything*. What do you remember? Forget about making anything up. You've made nothing up. It's the truth. Here" — and he riffled through the paper books he had also set aside — "who were the Night-Walkers?"

She stopped sobbing and stared at him. Carradine stroked her hair.

"Do you remember the Night-Walkers, Claire?" Carradine asked gently.

She wiped her cheeks with a corner of her dusty skirt, sad and resolute.

"I do not like them one little bit. They give me bad dreams. They are tall and thin and black. They have no face. Papa beat you for making up the Night-Walkers, and he is right."

They were back in their childhood, as though they shut out the adult world which was beyond endurance.

"*And* the man with long fingers who grows soldiers from the ground."

"The War-Gardener!" said Carradine, in terrible satisfaction. "But there were the nice ones, too. Mother Riddle, who asked very easy riddles and always gave you a sweet when you guessed . . . "

"And the Pavement Children, who lived under the pavement and liked me better than anyone, and I give them tea parties . . . "

" . . . because they only had dry bread

404

and broken biscuits."

"And the Twelve Singers who sing me to sleep, only I never hear them and I listen always. You say you hear them. I do not!"

"And dozens of others," said Carradine. "I had forgotten them, too."

They were in the Inspector's blunt, sensible hands: fragments of imagination, written and pictured, to delight, to mock, to tease, sometimes perversely to frighten. All there.

Lintott laid them down, and rewrapped the spoiled doll.

"I'd best be going, sir," he said quietly. "It's all right, bless you, I can find my own way. I'll leave you the lamp."

Because it seemed merciful, while memory obliterated reality, not to disturb them.

21

CARRADINE and Claire sat opposite each other in the darkening room. They did not address each other by name, nor use the loving forms of address. Only their eyes fixed on one another, as though they strove to record an image for the empty time ahead of them. They had known her identity twenty-four hours.

"I shall provide for you, so that you have complete independence," said Carradine. "Money is a form of liberty. You will be able to make your own life — here, in England, if you wish."

"No, not here. I shall go to Paris."

"As you please. Just as you please."

"I shall not live with Natalie. I shall not live like her. But I shall see her, if you permit, because I love her."

"There's no need to ask my permission."

"But I wish it."

"Then, of course, you have my permission. Even my good will."

Mrs. Tilling knocked, softly, and entered.

"Would you be wanting me to light the gas sir?"

He, who had been contemplating the luxury of electricity, now said, "Oh, candlelight will be sufficient, Tilley."

"And won't you be dining nor wanting anything, sir?"

He raised his eyebrows at Claire, though he could not have eaten, but she shook her head.

"Will you bring us a bottle of my father's claret, Tilley? Any bottle. They are all good. Thank you." He added tightly enough, as the housekeeper left them, "I can tell that our excellent friend is not herself, or she would certainly have informed me that wine turned to acid on an empty stomach."

But Claire, bereft of humor, said, "I shall be desolated without her, without her too. It is too cruel, too hard."

He was silent, striving to keep up some appearance of composure.

"Ah, how you are English!"

He could bear nothing more. He withdrew to safe ground, to stoicism.

"We shall be wretched for some considerable time, I know that. But we must remember that humankind is adept, above all else, at personal survival. So we shall survive. Perhaps, eventually, we shall accept the situation and grow used to it. We must hope so."

"Never!" she cried. "Never!"

She saw him already retreating, already drawing on the old armor she had removed, piece by inexorable piece.

He would become as remote, as ironic, as he had been when they first met.

She stretched out her hands. "Do not die to me again. Do not die to yourself. Better to suffer than to be dead."

"Oh, my dear girl," he said, exhausted. "I'm sick of suffering. I've had enough. Let's not clutch the knife to our hearts. There's no future for us. Better to accept, to make things as easy as we can for ourselves. Best of all, if it were possible, simply to forget."

"I accept nothing. I never accept. I rather suffer and die than accept."

Mrs. Tilling moved her tray of wine and glasses rapidly to one side as Claire ran past her, then set it on the table beside Carradine.

"I used to think it was because Miss Claire was French that she flew up so," she remarked tentatively, "but I think now it's because she's like her maman. Mrs. Carradine never give up without a fight, poor lady."

Carradine sighed and half-smiled.

"How did my father react to bursts of temperament, Tilley?"

"He just used to sit until she came back, sir, quietly. And she always did."

"Well, well, Tilley. I'll sit too. As sorry as he must have been, and with the added misfortune of having no remedy to offer."

"If she could look to her God," said the housekeeper shyly, "and offer up her sorrows. Nothing's wasted, sir, however hard it seems. You might both of you, in a year or two, be ready to take second best. That seems a poor way of putting it, you could settle down yet. I'm not saying it would be all you wished, but then I think folk ask too much of life. Steady and comfortable has always been my motto. If you can't have what you like, then like what you have, sir. Not speaking out of turn, I hope."

"Inspector Lintott once gave much the same advice, Tilley."

"Then you know what I mean, sir."

"I do indeed," he replied. "I do indeed. A safe and sensible policy."

He sat with his wine until he heard Claire come softly into the room. He held out his hand without looking at her. He knew, without seeing, that she had made herself pretty again. Penitent, she hovered by the door, hoping for reconciliation, for attention.

"I have been given some excellent advice, Claire. A slice of honest wisdom with which no one could find fault. Come here, while I tell you."

He turned.

She shook her head tremulously.

"As you please, Claire. All my life this advice has followed me, and I have openly repudiated it and in secret fashion adhered to it. I was told never to question the ways of Providence. As a child I was informed that boiled mutton and rice pudding were good for me, even if they made me sick. That God, though He rules a wicked and incomprehensible world, knows best and is omnipotent. That I should be grateful for something shabbier and meaner than I desired, envisioned, or needed. Do you understand me?"

She nodded, but only from understanding, never from compliance.

"I now most recklessly, possibly stupidly, but finally, set it at naught. I know there is no help for me. I know that if I do not thank life for its confounded crust I shall go without bread. I accept that, but I accept nothing else. And if there is a heaven — which some vigorous minds seem to doubt — then I shall shake the gates until something hears me. And I shall say, "'You owe me what I lived for. And until I get it, there I shall stay, a perpetual reproach'." Smiling now, in utter conviction, he said humorously, "I shall make a thorough nuisance of myself for a few thousand years, my love. What do you think of that for an idea?"

She was by his side in an instant, placing his hand on her cheek.

"I like it. I too shall chain myself. I shall say to them, 'You owe me'!"

"Oh, you will be even more tenacious

than I. The French have such an impassioned dislike of bad debts."

"You mock me," she said, looking at the flames, eyes bright.

"This decision of ours alters nothing, you know, Claire," he reminded her as she sat on the floor and kissed his hand and smiled into his face.

"I can bear it now you do not die to us. I can bear everything."

"Very well. Then no hysterical dashings off to the Continent without your luggage. Take your time. Write to Natalie. Ask her to find you an apartment. Stay here until you are absolutely ready in your mind to leave. Try to be sensible, won't you?"

"I am very English with the upper lip. But you will visit me sometimes?"

"Whenever you wish. That is for you to decide."

"Not always for me. I wish to be surprised."

"Then I shall most happily surprise you."

"I am now very hungry," she announced.

"And it is nine o'clock at night, and Tilley can hardly be expected to produce a dinner out of nowhere. Shall we go to

412

Rule's? Jugged hare — and you can mop up the sauce with a slice of bread. Do you know how very impolite that is in good English circles? Only our working classes clean their plates with bread."

"Pff! They are the common sense. I leave nothing on my plate. Never. The enemy shall not have it."

But, coming home afterward, she cried, "I hurt here. I am damaged *here*," and struck her breast lightly but emphatically with her clenched fist.

"I know," said Carradine. "We're both damaged, and both alive."

★ ★ ★

My dear one, Claire wrote to Natalie, *My name is Odette Carradine. All has changed for Nicholas and me, except in our hearts. I am writing to ask you to find me a small apartment near you, and yet I am not. Oh, yes, find me somewhere. Not very grand, not very large. You know me, you are clever, you understand what I want. I leave this in your hands. But I am writing to ask you for what is not possible, for my happiness.*

You are my sister. It does not matter that your name is Picard and mine Carradine. We have shared so much, and been so much to each other, that we are sisters as few real sisters are. I do not have to explain. When we were children you said I could ask you for anything, and though many things were beyond you, still, you tried. So, though you cannot help me in this matter, it gives me comfort to ask. Forgive me for my foolishness.

Here all is very English. I stay, as I have stayed from the beginning, at a good hotel. Very respectable, very dull. I spend each day with Nicholas. The English are not like us. They like to pretend that all is proper. So, for the sake of the servants, we are still engaged. Mrs. Tilling said it would be difficult for her if we said I was Nicholas's sister. Soon I shall return to Paris, and then they will say the engagement is broken. It is easier that way. I do not understand why, but I do as Mrs. Tilling says. She is a good woman, and kind, and she loves us both.

I wait to hear from you. I love you. Help me. Claire.

"You'll excuse me interrupting you, sir, but there's a *lady* wanting to see you," Mrs. Tilling said, with such slighting emphasis that Carradine first stared, and then came over to question her privately.

"*That* sort of lady, Tilley?"

"Never set eyes on her before, sir. But she looks like one of those madams as you used to paint."

"Where have you put her, Tilley?"

"In the study, sir, while I asked you if it was right."

"Very commendable. I'll come at once. Excuse me, Claire."

He was back in moments, head round the door, crying, "A surprise for us!"

"*Bijou!*" Natalie said, weeping a little from sentiment, disheveled a little from the Channel crossing. She clasped each of them in turn. They all spoke at once in French. The housekeeper's disapproval washed coldly on this emotional shore.

"Have you dined, Natalie?" Carradine asked amused and embarrassed.

"I can't eat a mouthful. I want nothing — perhaps a small glass of wine to settle my stomach. A morsel of bread, a piece

415

of fruit, some pâté — nothing at all."

"The lady will be joining us for dinner, Tilley," said Carradine. He explained. "Madam Picard is an old and dear friend of ours."

"But what excellent taste!" Natalie cried, mentally pricing the furniture. "Quite exquisite! I thought the English only bought ugly, heavy things."

"This was all chosen by my stepmother."

"That makes sense. Ah, yes!"

She longed to finger the velvet curtains, and would do so when dinner was over.

"Your housekeeper dislikes me, Nicholas. But I don't care. Perhaps she thinks I am a former mistress?"

"Very probably."

Natalie threw back her head and laughed. She had gained a little weight, which added to her exuberance.

"Come with me, Natalie, and I'll show you to maman's room," said Claire. "Where shall we stay tonight, Nicholas? At my hotel?"

"Are you short of rooms here?" Natalie inquired ironically, drawing off her gloves. "My respectability is of no consequence, Nicholas."

"I hardly think . . . under the circumstances . . . how was the crossing?"

"Ah! Your Channel is a monster. I am almost dead."

"I suppose the Channel changes nationality with the weather," he remarked, "and will find itself suddenly French; when fine."

"To be French is to be reasonable. It wasn't reasonable."

"But why are you here?" Claire asked, though she had formed her own conclusions. "You've found me an apartment? You know I'm unhappy? So you come to take me that I might not journey alone?" She reacted to her own notion. "I'm desolate. With or without you I'm desolate." She attacked those presumably responsible for her desolation. "You wrote to Nicholas and he advised you to come. That isn't kind, isn't loyal. If you are my friends, why do you treat me like a child?"

"Claire, Claire, Claire," he said patiently. "Don't make a theater."

"What you say is stupid, ridiculous," said Natalie firmly, "and I shan't tell you

417

until we have eaten."

Claire put out one hand for help, looked from face to face for reassurance, resigned herself.

"No theaters," she promised, without life.

* * *

"And how is my dear Inspector Limcock?" asked Natalie, accepting a second helping of apricot pudding.

"Did he tell you I entertained him in my boudoir?"

"No, he certainly did not."

"He is very shy. He didn't know what to do with his hands, his eyes, or his boots."

"He'll probably spend the rest of his days trying to forget the incident."

Natalie pointed a solemn finger at Carradine. "Oh, no, he won't, my friend. He'll spend the rest of his days trying to remember every detail." She pronounced the dessert excellent. "A little too sweet. But I'll speak to your housekeeper and advise her to use less sugar and a squeeze of lemon."

418

"I would far rather you did not, my dear."

"Why? Doesn't she want to learn? How very English. We French always want to learn."

"You must try to forgive us, Natalie. We prefer to cling to our own barbaric recipes."

She shrugged, uncomprehending, unperturbed. She offered to try the Stilton out of kindness.

Claire had given up even the pretense of eating. Now sat silent, watching Natalie.

Carradine glanced at her frequently and tried to draw her into conversation. Her attempts to respond were more painful than her stillness.

"And now do you wish to sit by yourself, Nicholas, over the port and walnuts?" Natalie asked, appetite sated, "and tell yourself dirty stories?"

"I'm prepared to forgo that pleasure for one evening, under the circumstances."

"Good. Yes, I'll take cognac with my coffee. It settles the stomach." As they retired to the drawing-room she said graciously to Mrs. Tilling, "Your food

419

is very good, madame. Too much, but very good."

"I'm glad you enjoyed it, madame," said the housekeeper, tight-lipped at the amount Natalie had consumed.

"You will pour the coffee, Miss Claire, of course?" Fearing that the stranger would carry even this small custom before her.

Natalie paced the room and narrowed her eyes at the silver. Then she settled herself, arranged her gown becomingly, stretched one round arm across the sofa back.

"Now I'll tell you why I came." But she could not, without first describing her feelings. "Oh, I thought you were doomed when the Inspector told me of his suspicions. So impractical, so romantic, my friends. You beg life to wound you. I wept for you both when I received Claire's letter. And then I asked myself — why do I weep? Why don't I use my head? So I stayed in bed all day to think for you. My baby knocked at my door — I sent him away. The young must learn to be patient. It is a salutary lesson."

And what conclusion did you reach, Natalie?" asked Carradine, entertained in spite of their trouble. "Claire, my love, may we have our coffee?"

She was sitting listlessly, hands in lap, watching Natalie's face.

"I reached a further conclusion than your Inspector Limcock. Oh, yes, he is clever, but he is English. What can an English detective know of the French heart? Nothing! So I went to see Berthe Lecoq. Le Jallu told me where to go, where to stay, where to hire a carriage. And I paid much less money than he did. I bargained, my friends."

Carradine could not help himself. He laughed aloud. Claire's head lifted quickly. She caught his mood and smiled. But Natalie, tremendously dignified, ignored it.

22

THE village was empty in the sun, the silence meant siesta.

Thick white walls shielded sleepers from the fierceness of heat. Slumber removed dumb lives from the treadmill of the daily round. Their world was contained within a few miles. The dark wineshop served as their social center. The church carried fear of hell and hope of heaven.

Natalie rang again, louder and more impatiently. Sweat started under the crown of her hat. Patches of wet stained her tight sleeves, her tight bodice. Her stays were damp, her flesh protested.

The silence was so absolute that Berthe's clogs sounded like a regiment on cobbles.

"I shan't open, whoever you are. We know nobody. We want nobody. Go away!" From behind the locked door.

"We want no money. We want nothing."

Natalie concluded that Berthe asked little of life. Her brows drew together. She lowered and furled her parasol though the sun was pitiless. She decided on a direct attack.

"Madame Lecoq? They have found Odette Carradine. She is alive and well. I wish to speak of her."

Another short silence. Then the bolts scraped top and bottom. The door opened two inches, revealing a stout iron chain.

"Who are you, madame?" Berthe demanded.

"One who had known Odette Carradine for twenty years and was a sister to her. She asks your help, through me, madame."

Berthe jerked the chain from its slot, pulled Natalie into the dim hall, secured the fortress once more, and surveyed her from head to foot. Contempt struggled with curiosity. "She sends a strange messenger." Reading the signs.

Natalie shrugged, good-humored. "Nevertheless, madame, I am all you have in the way of news."

A wailing tone from the back of the

house alerted Berthe. She motioned Natalie to follow. The old man crawling on all fours, chuckling at his new freedom, whimpering at the terror of it, needing his nurse to tell whether this was a good or bad idea on his part. Berthe picked him up like a child, thumped him down in his chair, retied his linen bond. While she settled him she scolded reassurance. He listened, fretful but comforted, gaping at Natalie's Parisian splendor.

"This hard for you, madame," Natalie observed with some sympathy.

"He is all I have. Tell me of Odette."

"I can't speak without water, madame," said Natalie firmly, seeing that neither a seat nor refreshment was to be offered. She removed her hat and sat down unasked.

"I have been traveling too long in the heat."

Berthe filled a mug from the bucket beneath the sink, handed it to her guest, folded her arms.

"Odette Carradine was mistaken in the train accident — for an orphan, madame. She and I were brought up together in the orphanage. I knew her as Claire Picard, and so did M'sieu Carradine. As Claire Picard she fell love with him, and he with her. They wish to be happy together. As brother and sister that is impossible."

Berthe weighed and measured this information, under lip pursed.

Then she said dryly, "What had she become in all those years, so close to you? For I know what you are, madame." She jerked her head in the direction of her interested charge. "Even this old child in his dotage knows what you are. Though he would have driven you from the door with his whip ten years ago."

"You insult me to no purpose, madame. I deal with life on my own terms. I am as I am. As for m'sieu here, with his whip and his morality, he now sees too clearly — and too late. Too late, old man," she chided, laughing, and shook her finger at him. "You should have enjoyed yourself while you could."

"What do you want of me?"

Natalie hazarded a guess. "I know all that you told the Inspector. I wish to know what you did not tell him, madame. Their happiness depends upon it."

"Happiness? To live with him as his mistress? To be discarded when he is tired of her? She is his sister. He must provide for her."

"You're still ordering the lives of those you love, madame. Why not let them decide for themselves?"

"I have harmed the child enough," said Berthe slowly. "So she loves him more than she should? Time will heal her. She will forget him. With his money, his connections, she can marry well, if *you* have not spoiled her."

Natalie reached for her hat, drew on her damp gloves. The clock on the wall ticked time over. The old man had fallen alseep suddenly, as the very young and the very old do. He sucked in breath, blew it out again. Berthe sank into a rocking chair and creaked to and fro, to and fro. Her face was a mask of sorrow, of perplexity.

"I can do nothing for her without you," said Natalie decisively. "But remember this. Once you made a decision that destroyed two lives and spoiled three others — and your own. That is a high price to pay. Take care that your silence does not spoil two more."

The silence was prolonged. The struggle hard.

Then Berthe said with difficulty, "Odette was not M'sieu Carradine's child."

She lifted both hands in a gesture of renunciation, then let them drift into her lap. "I can do no more for mother or child," she said. "Odette must live as she — pleases. Tell her I pray for her, madame."

Natalie sat down again and waited.

"The Englishman was her husband in every way. Oh, yes," said Berthe, as though the fact were disputed, "madame went to him as a virgin. That is true. But in the first six months of the marriage she did not conceive by him. She was young and passionate. She turned to M'sieu Fauvel, and this time she was not afraid of becoming his mistress. We stayed six weeks in Paris that spring. When we returned home to the husband she already suspected herself to be with child, and she was right. The child was Odette the father M'sieu Fauvel."

"And M'sieu Carradine did not question a daughter who was born a little late?"

"Madame, with a first infant the birth is often a little late. By madame's reckoning Odette arrived a little early. Between the two suppositions her coming seemed correct. And M'sieu Carradine — had neither cause nor desire to — doubt the child's parentage."

"Why did you not tell the English Inspector this? It would have saved time and trouble, madame."

Berthe raised an obdurate face. "He would not have known *this much* from me, madame," and she snapped her fingers, "except that — he knew much already. My lady is dead, madame. I shall not let them spit on her grave."

Her face changed, was troubled. "If this will harm Odette — you say you have been a sister to her — I daresay you have been good to her in your fashion — I beg you not to tell her or him. Be wise in this, madame."

Natalie patted her arm, smiling. "M'sieu Carradine wishes to marry Odette, madame. Yes, yes," she said as Berthe shook her head, bewildered.

"I swear it. I swear it on the sacred memory of my mother."

The memory of her mother was both faint and faulty but brought tears to her eyes and conviction to her voice.

She was weary with victory, with triumph.

"And you did not tell me?" Berthe asked slowly. "You let me suffer and doubt for nothing, madame? Why use me like this?"

Natalie replied kindly, "I know something of your devotion, madame. Certainly, I may be wrong, but I thought that if I told you they wished to be man and wife, you might think of a way of making them so. Come, madame, don't stare at me. I've seen how you cast down morality when it serves those you love. Well then, I ask your pardon, but I had to be sure."

Berthe rose majestically. The suggestion had taken her breath and then returned her strength. She answered proudly, "I am a good Catholic, madame."

"I too," Natalie replied, "and I could not risk being party to so great a sin."

"But what do you English know of true passion?"

Natalie mused over her third cognac. "Look how you strangle it in marriage. There are sensible marriages, of course, but no passionate ones. Beware of contentment, my friends. Passion, passion, and again passion, should be your watchword."

Claire was kissing one plump, ringed hand. Carradine raised the other to his lips.

"My dearest Natalie," he said, "we cannot possibly pay what we owe to you. Allow me, at least, to defray your expenses in this matter."

"Not a franc. How can you speak of money at such a moment. Oh, you English, how mercenary you can be!"

Nevertheless she dried her eyes and scolded Claire for weeping restored.

"Don't let your lover see you looking ugly. Always the smile, the charm, the poise." She mimicked each mood. "Tears are for private moments only. And do not argue with him. Listen, agree, then do as you please. You have much to learn."

"Stay with us for a holiday, chérie," Claire begged.

"One night only. In your hotel. Then I'll attempt the English Channel again." She adjusted the shoulders of her gown. "Emile will be impatient for me. I wonder whether marriage is wise. A man tires of what he possesses absolutely. No, no, no, I will not!" — as Carradine opened her jet-fringed *pochette* and slipped a banker's order inside it. Smiling, she murmured, "I shall never forgive you!"

The amount would soothe her to sleep that night, calm the Channel crossing, and assume the high tone of a reward for virtue.

23

"MY heart's treasure," said Emile Roche, adjusting the set of his tie in Natalie's mirror, "I believe I have found a husband for Valentine."

Natalie played with the white cat, now allowed back on the bed, and raised her eyebrows. "There's a young man in the provinces, training to be a steward of my wife's estate. Personable." He studied his reflection. "A cut above his station in life." Smoothing his mustache. "Quite the gentleman, in fact." Looking ironically down his fine nose.

"Why should this paragon wish to marry Valentine, my dear?" she asked lazily, watching him.

He shrugged. "Oh, he was reared by foster parents and believes himself to be of gentle birth — the usual thing."

"How old is this love-child, did you say?"

"A little older than Paul, I believe."

Natalie smiled and half-closed her eyes. "But why should he wish to marry so young, and to a girl some years his senior, my dear?"

"I have influence over him. I have been in the nature of a patron. He is worth attention and knows I have his welfare at heart." He buttoned his waistcoat. "And Valentine is foolish, pretty, and affectionate. She has her small dowry. He should find her most amenable."

"And their dreams of gentility will coincide?"

"Precisely."

Natalie considered the cat's composure and yawned.

"How will you arrange this, my dear?"

"When her unfortunate affair is concluded I can bring him to Paris on pretext of business. There is one little point" — he laughed and frowned, reaching for his coat — "he believes me to be his father."

"Imagine!" Astonished. "What a scandal that would have been, my dear, at an important point of your career, and with the prospect of a rich wife."

"Exactly. As difficult to believe as that

you, my dearest, were the daughter of, say, a country baker."

"Quite ridiculous." Her smile and gaze did not falter. "So that is settled. I must find myself another maid."

"And I must regretfully take my leave of you, Natalie." Satisfied. "My wife is giving a dinner party this evening."

"But I shall be alone." She pouted as he bowed and kissed her fingers.

"Oh, I think not. You have so many friends. Our dinner parties bore Paul," he added inconsequently. "How much the young have to learn! A certain amount of boredom is necessary in public life, but for the moment he puts pleasure before duty."

"He must try to combine both, as you do, Emile."

They smiled. Her face changed.

"Did you consult your doctor, my dear, as you promised me?" she asked.

Roche replied casually, "He told me nothing new. I must apparently choose between length of time and quality of living. Well, that is the way of it. One moment a man is alive, the next moment he fails." The subject was closed. "Until we meet again, my heart?"

She rustled forward and kissed him gently on either cheek.

"My friend," she said with some emotion, "I hope to hear you mounting the stairs to my apartment many years from now. The climb will make your pulse quicken when I cannot?'

"There will be no time when your beauty does not rule me, madame," he answered. Much had been understood without words. He said idly at the door, "Is this love, perhaps?"

She recollected that seriousness is unflattering to a woman and smiled. "Who is to say what love might be, Emile? We understand each other. We accept each other for what we are. We give pleasure and are content. Why trouble God with questions?"

★ ★ ★

"John! John! Bless me if you aren't miles away! That fire needs a shovel of coal if it isn't to go out this minute." Lintott roused himself, laid his pipe carefully on the tiled hearth.

435

"And it's raining fit to burst outside, John," Bessie called after him. "Put my shawl over your head and shoulders. You'll find it on a nail by the back door."

"I'm not a baby yet," he called. "When a drop of wet hurts me you can lay me underground?"

He came back, treading coal dust onto her parlor carpet.

"And now you've got your coat and slippers damp. It's worse than minding a child. Look at the mess!"

"Leave me, Bessie, leave be, my lass. I'll soon sweep this little lot up, you needn't fret."

He retired to his pipe and contemplation. "What a year that was, eh, Bess?"

"Ah, King Teddy crowned," she said, nodding and knitting, "and the war well over in Africa?"

"Mr. Carradine and Miss Pickered married."

"Two hundred pound for the work you did, John!"

"He wanted to give me five hundred. I wouldn't take it. Nobody needs *that* much."

"My picture!" Her eyes loved *Windy Day*, hanging resplendent on the parlor wall. "He don't paint proper pictures anymore," she observed, critical of this new departure. "I didn't think much of those we saw at that exhibition, though it was nice to be asked. I'm glad he thought to give me a good one. That little chap flying the kite is the image of our Joey." She noticed the hour. "Shall we have a bite of toasted cheese for supper, John?"

Lintott stirred, nodded, dreamed again as he watched the flames licking up the chimney front.

"You have a set and a think while I get the supper things," Bessie advised maternally.

His itinerary was once more transformed by fire. There was the lanky, gesticulating figure of Le Jallu, who had sent him a letter at Christmas, which Lizzie translated as being a poem about the friendship of passing strangers. Very nice, that. A nice thought. Bessie had chosen a jolly card, depicting a coaching inn heavy with snow and guests. Lizzie had printed *Bon Noël* underneath *Merry Christmas*.

437

Lintott had signed it and gone to no end of trouble getting it addressed and properly stamped.

Here was Madame Jeanne, ordering and feeding her customers. When he was leaving she embraced him, the cognac on her breath mingled with garlic. Nothing of l'amoor in this, just honest friendship. He did not mention her to Bessie, nevertheless. He drank coffee again, in the boudoir of a Parisian courtesan. He gazed from the Eiffel Tower. He turned the corner of a street, and the city caught his breath. He watched the animated brown landscape of the Old One's face. He sat in the exotic solitude of Carradine's dusty studio He felt the thin cat wind round his legs. These would be with him until someone closed his eyes.

"I'm not wasting a penny for your thoughts," said Bessie tartly, spearing a slice of bread as though it were France itself.

"My lass, my lass," Lintott chided, shaking his head. "There's nothing to fear from an old bobby dozing at his hearth. I'm home with you, ain't I? What do you want me to say as'll please you?

An Englishman's home is his castle, and his wife's his queen. How about that, Bess? I wouldn't be anywhere else in the wide world, nor want anybody but you, now would I?"

She tossed her head and compressed her mouth. He gave her a clumsy hug.

"Be off with your nonsense, John. I've got this bread to toast."

"Then let me set with you while you toast it. Here, give me the other fork. Then it'll be twice as quick."

"Fiddlesticks," said Bessie, mollified, flushed by the heat and his attention. "You'll be kissing my hand next — and I'll fetch you a slap if you do, John Lintott."

★ ★ ★

"You'll excuse me, sir," said Mrs. Tilling, agitated, "but the cabman's come back specially to say that Mrs. Carradine is in a bit of trouble and he'll take you there."

He had been weltering in vermilion, in cadmium, in viridian, and Antwerp blue, forgetful of her. He threw his brush, pulled off his smock.

"She would be, blast her! What sort of trouble?"

"She's at Buckingham Palace, sir, chained to the railings.

"Almighty God!" Carradine implored. "I thought she was shopping."

Mrs. Tilling helped him on with his coat, saying, "She was, sir, but she saw these suffrage women and got out. The cabman says they'll send for the police."

He wiped the paint from his fingers, exasperated. "Damn, damn, damn, damn, damn! Sorry, Tilley, I was right in the middle of this." His face brightened, softened. "What do you think of it?"

"Very cheerful, sir," said the housekeeper firmly. "Oh, do hurry, sir!"

There were only a dozen women, after all, and their protest was patient rather than obtrusive. Three or four were from the upper classes: articulate, intelligent, confident in their cause and themselves. The rest were humbly respectable, a little dowdy, but as determined as their more fortunate sisters. A crowd had gathered, jeering, sympathetic, or merely curious. The two sentries, bewildered but mindful of their duty, stood motionless, staring ahead of them as though nothing existed. As Carradine jumped from the cab he saw a group of policemen, accompanied by a locksmith in a leather apron, clearing the way.

"Move along now, if you please. Move along there."

The women braced themselves, apprehensive but obstinate.

"Come along now, ladies," said the sergeant soothingly, arms akimbo, genial. "We don't want no trouble, do we?"

"Give us the Vote!" cried one handsome girl and held her placard high.

"Give us the Vote!" another repeated, and then in unison, "The Vote! The Vote! The Vote!"

Carradine saw Claire side by side with a tall, plain woman of the lower middle class whose bearing was as resolute as her own.

"Just get these here padlocks unfastened, will you, Mr. Lynes?" begged the sergeant.

"Hold on to the railings!" their leader commanded. "Don't let them take us away!"

Awkward, puzzled, struggling against old mores of chivalry and class distinction, the bobbies hesitated.

"I have to warn you ladies," said the sergeant, harassed, "that if you obstruct the police in the course of their duties you'll be committing a breach of the peace."

"The Vote! The Vote! The Vote!"

"If you won't come peaceable," he pleaded, "we shall have to use force, and we don't want that, do we?"

"Call yourselves women!" shouted an outraged matron in a feathered hat. "You're a disgrace to our sex. Go home to your husbands — if you've got any!"

"The Vote! The Vote! The Vote!"

"Give 'em a taste of the stick!" bellowed a retired colonel, shaking his own. "That's what they need to bring them to heel."

"Be reasonable, madam," the sergeant begged their leader.

"If you wish us to leave here you will have to take us by force," she replied calmly. And to her cohorts she called, "Hold on to the railings!"

"All right, lads," said the sergeant,

resigned. "No rough stuff. Just firm and comfortable. Mr. Lynes!"

Carradine, elbowing people aside in his effort to reach Claire, felt their excitement rise like heat. The suffragettes, in pursuit of other rights, had forfeited the right of womanly dignity.

One cockney woman darted forward and snatched at leader's hat, clapped it on her own head.

"Oooh! I'm a lidy! I'm a lidy!" she shrieked.

The onlookers cheered and clapped as she flourished her skirts, the expensive piece of millinery pulled over one eye.

"Resist them!" cried the handsome girl and brought her placard down smartly on the sergeant's helmet.

He blinked and gasped, grabbed her arms and pinioned them to her sides. She kicked his ankles furiously.

"Forward, lads!" he shouted in rage and pain.

Red-faced, the police dared to grasp members of the sacred sex in a manner hitherto regarded as unthinkable.

Scratching, biting, threshing, the women fought as best they could. The crowd whooped at the spectacle of flashing drawers and petticoats.

Carradine reached the front. "No! Claire!" he yelled, thinking just a fraction of a second ahead of her.

Heedless, she lifted her umbrella and flailed her opponent about the shoulders.

"Aux armes!" she cried, jubilant. *"Couarge, mes soeurs!"*

"Oh, my God! Claire! You'll be up for assault."

Her thighs embraced by a pair of stout arms, her umbrella wrested from her hands, she screamed, "Nicholas, do not let him! Do not let him!"

She was hoisted high. "My wrist!" she shrieked. The plain woman was handcuffed to her.

The two policemen, sweating and shouting, moved quickly together, their prisoners aloft.

"These two are handcuffed, Mr. Lynes," they bawled. "Can you come?"

Carradine grappled with Claire's policeman. "Put her down, damn you! How dare you! This is my wife!"

"You didn't ought to let her out then," the man argued. "Get off of me, will you, sir? What am *I* supposed to do?"

A sturdy figure shoved its way through the crowd.

"Bob? Charlie? It's me. Mr. Lintott. That's my Lizzie. Don't hurt her."

"Hurt her, sir?" said Charlie, outraged. "She hasn't almost scratched my eyes out, has she? Oh, no, not half!" Sarcastic.

"Lintott!" cried Carradine. "Thank God. Get my wife out of this, will you?"

The Inspector was perturbed and helpless. Carradine had never seen him like this before.

"They've put themselves outside the Law, sir. Here, Lizzie, Mrs. Carradine, will you come quietly if they set you down? No nonsense, mind."

Hatless, breathless, the two women nodded, Lintott looked reproachfully from the handcuffs to his daughter's face. He selected a key from his key ring, freed them. They rubbed their wrists, subdued.

"They'll have to come to the station, Mr. Lintott," said the sergeant, embarrassed.

"I know that," he replied, damaged. "That's your duty, Fred."

445

"They won't be imprisoned surely?" Carradine asked, horrified.

Claire was sobbing.

"Give 'em a fine and a caution, more like, sir. But I won't answer for them next time. Lizzie, do you hear me? What do you think you're about, my girl? Bessie'll have to mind the children, and Eddie won't know where to turn."

"How did you know I was here, Father?"

"Your mother told me. Meeting and marching and chaining yourselves up!"

"I'm sorry, Father."

"For what?" he cried, wounded. "For what?"

"For upsetting you all."

"Ah, I thought it might be that. Not for what you've done and the trouble you've caused."

"I'm doing what I think's right," she answered, and her jaw lengthened.

Their relationship was apparent.

"Then God help us all," said Lintott sadly. "What do you know of prison? This here's a picnic compared to what it will be. When you throw away your privilege as a member of the weaker

446

sex you leave security behind you. You were safe as houses with Fred and his lads. Wait until they fetch the mounted police in, and the rough ones. Get on the wrong side of the Law and you'll find no friends, outside or in. Give up the rights you've got and you face an ugly world. I've walked St. Giles. I know. I've seen society without its rules and manners, and it's a cruel face to look upon, my girl. A cruel face."

They did not say any more, separate and silent. She possessed little and was risking all she had. He saw no peace ahead for her, or himself through her.

"As for you, Claire," said Carradine, infuriated, "I'll wager you don't even know what this is all about, do you? *Do* you?"

"It is the Mrs. Pankhurst."

"Damn Mrs. Pankhurst!"

"I fight for women's rights."

"You've got all the damned rights any woman could have!"

"I know. I fight for my sisters who have not."

The crowd was dispersing, satiated. The fun was over for today.

"Oh, well," Carradine observed lightly, humor coming uppermost, "I can't recollect appearing in court before. That should be quite an experience."

Claire dusted her hat, concerned to set it at a fashionable angle.

"Your theater is not quite over," said Carradine, wryly. "You must face another — not organized by yourself, madame." He handed her her broken umbrella. "Claire, for heaven's sake, my dear girl, why look for a new fight?"

She replied, part gaily, part earnestly, "Why not?"

THE END

NURSE ALICE IN LOVE
Theresa Charles

Accepting the post of nurse to little Fernie Sherrod, Alice Everton could not guess at the romance, suspense and danger which lay ahead at the Sherrod's isolated estate.

POIROT INVESTIGATES
Agatha Christie

Two things bind these eleven stories together — the brilliance and uncanny skill of the diminutive Belgian detective, and the stupidity of his Watson-like partner, Captain Hastings.

LET LOOSE THE TIGERS
Josephine Cox

Queenie promised to find the long-lost son of the frail, elderly murderess, Hannah Jason. But her enquiries threatened to unlock the cage where crucial secrets had long been held captive.

THE WILDERNESS WALK
Sheila Bishop

Stifling unpleasant memories of a misbegotten romance in Cleave with Lord Francis Aubrey, Lavinia goes on holiday there with her sister. The two women are thrust into a romantic intrigue involving none other than Lord Francis.

THE RELUCTANT GUEST
Rosalind Brett

Ann Calvert went to spend a month on a South African farm with Theo Borland and his sister. They both proved to be different from her first idea of them, and there was Storr Peterson — the most disturbing man she had ever met.

ONE ENCHANTED SUMMER
Anne Tedlock Brooks

A tale of mystery and romance and a girl who found both during one enchanted summer.

CLOUD OVER MALVERTON
Nancy Buckingham

Dulcie soon realises that something is seriously wrong at Malverton, and when violence strikes she is horrified to find herself under suspicion of murder.

AFTER THOUGHTS
Max Bygraves

The Cockney entertainer tells stories of his East End childhood, of his RAF days, and his post-war showbusiness successes and friendships with fellow comedians.

MOONLIGHT
AND MARCH ROSES
D. Y. Cameron

Lynn's search to trace a missing girl takes her to Spain, where she meets Clive Hendon. While untangling the situation, she untangles her emotions and decides on her own future.